"I honestly th[...] I didn't have to [...]

"Why do you hav[...]
"Do you have another job lined up?"

Rebecca tilted her head so her cheek touched his shoulder and she didn't have to look at him when she avoided telling him the whole truth. Not that looking away made it feel better.

"I do have another job," she said, though she left out details. "I have a commitment, and I can't back out."

"As a lady's companion?" he asked. He leaned back so he could see her face. "You seem overqualified somehow."

"I'm qualified," she said. "I make sure Flora's comfortable, entertained and happy. Just like any good companion or friend would do. Plus, I can drive a stick shift and play the piano." She smiled at Griffin. "You know, maybe you're right. I am overqualified."

He leaned in and touched his cheek to hers. "I think you're just right."

Dear Reader,

What is the allure of islands? The very word conjures up images of vacation, solitude, peace and an escape from the everyday. *I'll Be Home for Christmas* is the first book in the Return to Christmas Island series, and it checks all my feel-good boxes. I love Christmas, romance and islands!

Christmas Island is in the Great Lakes region of the United States. Just off the Michigan shoreline, it has warm summers and snowy winters. It's a beautiful area with clear water, trees and rocky shores. Several hundred people live on the island all year, but Christmas Island really comes alive for the summer tourist crowd. Day visitors travel aboard the ferry owned by Griffin May and his brother, Maddox. On the island, tourists bike, zip around in golf carts, shop in downtown boutiques, enjoy the scenery and buy souvenirs of their excursion.

In *I'll Be Home for Christmas*, Rebecca Browne hops on the ferry for a ride to the island, where she'll work as a lady's companion for the summer. She has a secret goal, but she has no idea that she'll fall in love with the island and its residents—especially Griffin May, the handsome ferry captain.

I hope you'll love your visit to Christmas Island and come back for the rest of the series!

Happy reading,

Amie Denman

HEARTWARMING

I'll Be Home for Christmas

—

Amie Denman

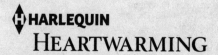

HARLEQUIN
HEARTWARMING

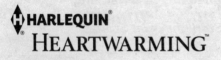

HARLEQUIN®
HEARTWARMING™

ISBN-13: 978-1-335-42645-1

Recycling programs for this product may not exist in your area.

I'll Be Home for Christmas

Copyright © 2021 by Amie Denman

This edition published by arrangement with Harlequin Books S.A.

For questions and comments about the quality of this book, please contact us at CustomerService@Harlequin.com.

Harlequin Enterprises ULC
22 Adelaide St. West, 40th Floor
Toronto, Ontario M5H 4E3, Canada
www.Harlequin.com

Printed in U.S.A.

Amie Denman is the author of forty contemporary romances full of humor and heart. A devoted traveler whose parents always kept a suitcase packed, she loves reading and writing books you could take on vacation. Amie believes everything is fun, especially wedding cake, roller coasters and falling in love.

Books by Amie Denman

Harlequin Heartwarming

Starlight Point Stories

Under the Boardwalk
Carousel Nights
Meet Me on the Midway
Until the Ride Stops
Back to the Lake Breeze Hotel

Cape Pursuit Firefighters

In Love with the Firefighter
The Firefighter's Vow
A Home for the Firefighter

Carina Press

Her Lucky Catch

Visit the Author Profile page
at Harlequin.com for more titles.

CHAPTER XIV

CHAPTER ONE

THE CHRISTMAS ISLAND ferry sounded a deep, throaty blast. Rebecca Browne had the sinking feeling the long blasts of the horn meant the boat was about to leave as she ran through the parking lot and approached the sloping dock. Her enormous wheeled suitcase nipped her heels, and the heavy bag on her shoulder slipped, its handle murdering her elbow as she kept running.

She couldn't miss the last ferry. For one thing, she had no place to stay on the mainland. For another thing, she was not the kind of girl who missed ferries, planes, or the correct answers on exams of any kind. Rebecca paid her bills on time, fertilized her office plants according to a schedule and replaced the baking soda box in her refrigerator precisely every three months as recommended. Exceeding expectations and depending on herself had been saving her life since she was old enough to tell time and pack her own bags.

Rebecca ran faster and the plastic wheels on her suitcase whirred like an overtaxed engine. Even from fifty paces away, she saw a small strip of lake appear between the ferry and the dock. The ferry was pulling away. The gap grew wider with every one of her strides, but there was no slowing down now. She reached the edge of the dock, ignored the teenager who waved both hands over his head in a universal *don't do it* gesture and leaped onto the moving ferry.

She would have been all right if it wasn't for the laws of physics. The heavy suitcase behind her did not leap. It didn't soar. And it didn't make it onto the boat. She heard the splash and felt the terrific tug of the suitcase as the lake water clutched it and pulled it in. Rebecca braced her feet and pulled with all her might, but the ferry continued to back away from the dock and the weight of the suitcase was daunting.

From long experience moving from place to place, Rebecca had learned to fit anything she really valued into one suitcase. She never took things for granted, and she couldn't let the suitcase go. It had all her clothes and books for the entire summer. Her favorite hair dryer. Her laptop. Everything she would need for a season on an island.

"Man overboard," a voice called over the boat's loudspeaker.

In the brief moment before the suitcase pulled her in, Rebecca felt unjustly treated by the announcement. She wasn't entirely over-board…yet. Her outrage didn't last, though. Cold water took her breath and loosened her grip on the suitcase as she went under. It was early in the summer season, and the water felt like ice. She struggled to swim, fought her way to the surface and heard angels singing when a hand gripped hers and pulled her onto the boat. Someone dragged her away from the edge, and she felt the gentle humming of the ferry engine beneath her.

Rebecca, the girl who could usually solve any problem and who'd been trusted by her company with an important summer mission, lay soaking wet on the hard deck. It was almost dark, and she hoped that either the ferry was empty or all the passengers suffered from poor night vision. Perhaps no one had seen her disgrace.

She opened her eyes and saw dark trouser legs and black uniform shoes. She rolled to her knees and shot up, but the man put both hands firmly on her upper arms as she swayed.

"Slow down," he said. "Are you okay?"

Just her luck, her rescuer was brown-haired, blue-eyed and muscular. He also had a voice resonant with concern and authority. If she was lucky, she would never see his handsome face and crisp white shirt again.

She squared her shoulders as she sought the correct answer. "I'm fine, but my suitcase..."

"It might float up. We'll watch for it."

"Are you kidding? Isn't there a way we can dive down and get it before it's ruined?"

The man looked at the sky as if he was considering how much daylight he had left, and Rebecca hoped he might be crafting a plan to rescue her suitcase.

"What are we doing, Captain?" a teenage crew member asked. He had a dock line looped over his arm, obviously ready to fulfill whatever orders he got.

Rebecca took a closer look at her rescuer. *He was the captain.* This could work in her favor! On a boat, the captain's word was final, and he could choose to take mercy on her earthly belongings marinating in the lake.

"We're going to Christmas Island," the captain said. "If a suitcase floats up in the next few days, grab it."

With one long look at Rebecca's face, the captain strode to the pilot's house and the ferry lurched into movement. Rebecca numbly picked up her shoulder bag. At least she had a granola bar, her wallet and phone, keys to a car she wouldn't need for months and her favorite big book of piano classics. Not that she needed the book. All the music was in her head, where it had always been.

She sighed, wondering if this was an indication of how her summer was going to go. At least she might flap her clothes dry in the warm summer evening and be presentable before the boat docked and she had to face the indomitable woman she'd been assigned to babysit for the summer.

It had been two weeks since the CFO of Winter Industries had closed Rebecca's office door and sunk into the chair across from her desk. Jim Churchill had begun by pointing out the one picture on her desk—Rebecca and her college friend Camille in front of the Welcome to Christmas Island sign that had stood in the island's waterfront park. He'd then asked her to return to the island for an assignment requiring the loyalty and professionalism he'd come to expect from her.

Rebecca fluffed out her wet hair, put a hand on the steel railing and got a good look at her fellow passengers. Only a dozen or so people sat on the open-air benches, most of them staring at her to see what the reckless lady with the submerged suitcase would do next. Thanks to her unexpected swim, her clothes clung to her and left her without her professional armor.

The Christmas Island ferry was both a passenger and car service, so there were several vehicles on board. A spectacular silver vehicle sat between a family minivan and a pickup truck. She squinted in the evening light. Was that a Bentley? It had to be from the nineteen fifties judging from its massive fenders and curves.

Who would be taking an incredibly expensive vintage car to the island?

A white-haired lady with a cane made her way toward Rebecca, taking careful steps on the moving ferry. In a flash, Rebecca knew who she had to be and began walking toward her, trying to convey responsibility and employability with her confident strides.

"I saw the whole thing," the older lady said.

Rebecca tried to smile and stand up straight, but she knew her days on Christmas Island were over before they had even started. No way was the titular head of Winter Industries going to want a hapless and soaked summer companion. Rebecca would fail in her assignment and disappoint the CFO at a company that had given her everything.

"That was a plucky performance," the old lady said. "And I'd have gone in the drink to save my suitcase, too."

Really? Rebecca calmed her breathing and tried to hope.

"I'm Flora Winter, and you must be Rebecca Browne," the woman said. "Your friend told me you'd be arriving on the last ferry today, and you're the only single female on board. Aside from me, of course."

"I don't always look like this. I'm usually much more...put together."

"I'm sure you are," Flora said.

Rebecca didn't think Flora believed her.

A tiny dog poked his nose out of the bag over Flora's shoulder, and Rebecca reached out a hand for him to sniff. The dog lapped at her hand and perked up its ears, and Rebecca hoped it was a nod in her favor.

"This is Cornelius," Flora said. "We'll wait in the car with my luggage while you…dry out."

When Rebecca had imagined herself posing as a lady's companion, she had pictured herself behaving with a lot more dignity. She would serve scones and select shawls to make Flora's outfits. Instead, she swiped a hand through her wet hair as Flora and her brown Yorkshire terrier got into the backseat of the Bentley. In the darkness she couldn't see if there was someone in the driver's seat. Surely, a car like that came with a driver?

Rebecca avoided the spectators on the bench seat and went to the rail, where she could get a clear view of Christmas Island. A large hotel perched on a bluff, and the downtown area was twinkling with hundreds of lights. Her college friend Camille had told Rebecca stories of growing up on the island and enjoying five-course dinners at the Great Island Hotel, with orchestras and ball gowns.

Rebecca had visited once with Camille for a weekend, and she remembered the hotels, bars, souvenir and boutique shops, ice cream and fudge parlors, bicycle and golf cart rentals and the island scenery. A cheerful Christmas theme dominated the downtown with wreaths on the lampposts, a giant

Santa statue near the harbor, welcoming day tourists, and perpetual holiday music playing. Christmas Island came alive during the summer and again in December, but it was also a year-round home to several hundred people including her friend Camille. According to her, the Christmas in July celebration was a luscious ode to the holiday and the biggest event of the summer.

"I hope I'll still be here July twenty-fifth," she said aloud as she watched the island lights grow closer. As soon as she said it, she looked around, hoping no one had heard her over the ferry's engine and the waves churning in their wake.

The ferry coasted smoothly alongside a downtown dock on Christmas Island just as the last light disappeared from the sky. The app on Rebecca's phone told her when the sunset officially ended, but seeing it from the deck of a boat, she was surprised at how much leeway there was between the official sunset and the moment the delicate balance between daylight and darkness tipped over into night.

The captain and the deckhand worked together to secure the boat, and then a shore hand rolled out the gangplank. The minivan and the pickup truck drove off the boat first, and Rebecca waited, wondering what she should do.

"You're next," the captain said. "Pedestrians usually get to go first, but there aren't too many of those tonight, so you can get in and take your passenger home."

"You want me to drive the Bentley off the boat?" she asked. She shivered in the night air with a wave of trepidation washing over her.

"I wouldn't have pegged you as a lucky woman when you flopped onto my boat, but getting to glide through the gears on that car ups your good fortune a lot."

"Gears?" she asked.

"Sure. You can drive a standard, right?"

Rebecca hesitated. "I know how to drive one," she said. "In theory."

"There's a theory on driving standard?"

"Well…there's academic knowledge and then there's practical application, just like everything else."

A grin spread slowly across his face and Rebecca counted to five before his smile had reached its full proportions. The captain had a beautiful smile, and she wished she had the leisure to enjoy it. Instead, she had an important job to do and there was already an unexpected obstacle.

"You're having a tough first day at work," he said. "We heard a friend of Camille's was coming for the summer to match wits with Flora Winter, but I guess I somehow pictured someone more—" he spread his hands as if trying to describe something, and Rebecca was quite glad he chose not to finish his sentence "—competent," he said.

"I'm competent," she protested.

His grin faltered and then widened and Rebecca was tempted to elbow him in the gut. But then he did something she would never have expected. The captain without a name took off his jacket and draped it over her shoulders.

"This was our last run of the night, and I wouldn't mind a chance to drive that car. If you think you can operate a golf cart, you can follow me to the Winter Palace up on the bluff."

Rebecca was speechless. He was offering her a way out, a chance to save face and survive until the first full day of being a companion—and possibly chauffeur—to Flora Winter.

"You…you know where she lives?"

"Everyone knows everyone on Christmas Island. If you want, I'll tell your new boss that you didn't want to get her car seat wet and I couldn't resist an opportunity to talk to an old friend on the drive."

"Thank you," Rebecca whispered as the window on the classic car rolled down.

The captain leaned in close to Rebecca and he smelled like fresh air and lake water. Or was she the one who smelled like the lake? "You'll have to figure out how to survive tomorrow on your own," he said quietly.

"Griffin May, come over here and give me a kiss now that you've docked this old battleship of yours," Flora said.

Rebecca smiled as her employer held up a cheek for the captain to kiss as if she was his grandmother. Flora didn't have any children or grandchildren, so her relationship with the captain must be one of the many things about Christmas Island Rebecca was about to discover.

GRIFFIN MAY LOVED driving almost anything. Well, not golf carts, with their lack of heart-pounding horsepower. Boats were a pretty tasty bread and butter for him, and the occasional run around the island in someone else's powerful car was chocolate cake and cold beer.

The dark-haired woman in the golf cart following him was attractive, impulsive and would probably last three days on Christmas Island. Maybe four, depending on the status of her sunken suitcase. In his twenty-seven years on the island, he'd seen plenty of things, but remembering her spectacular leap onto the moving ferry made him smile.

"I can see you in the rearview mirror," Flora said. "Even in the dark, I see that grin."

"It's the company."

"Hmmph. More likely it's the way you're careening around this island toward my summer house."

"I'm doing thirty-five."

"Feels like a hundred. Too bad my usual driver refuses to step foot on an island, or more specifically, a boat. He's going to have a lonely summer, but there was no talking him into coming with me."

"Who's going to drive you around every day?" Griffin asked. "I could give up my job on the ferry, but I think my brother would get tired of doing all the work himself."

Maddox was the other captain, and the two of them were knocking themselves out after taking over from their parents, who started the ferry line. His father's death the previous year had laid a whole lot of things bare, especially the fact that the main burden was on Griffin's shoulders.

"How is your mother?" Flora asked. "I got a Christmas card from her and was surprised to learn she was moving in with her sister in Texas."

"She's enjoying retirement, I guess," Griffin said.

"Hmm. She hardly seems old enough to retire."

Griffin smiled. His mother probably did seem young to Flora, who had to be in her mideighties because she had grown up with his Grandpa May on the island. He'd seen pictures of them with groups of young people at skating parties and summer dances.

"You'll have to get caught up with everyone on the island this summer, although not much has changed," Griffin said. That was both the beauty and the curse of the island, in Griffin's opinion.

"Most of the people I used to know are gone now, which is why I hired a companion and helper. Although…"

Griffin could imagine why Flora might be

regretting her choice. He considered jumping in and defending Rebecca, but her wild fall from his boat could have turned into a disaster for herself and for his family's company. The lawsuit and liability insurance would triple if someone had an accident, no matter whose fault it was. Griffin was grateful Rebecca was okay, but he didn't need any more surprises.

"Although she's much more interesting than I had pictured," Flora continued. "I thought she would be smart but dull and would show up with a notebook, an umbrella and a book of manners under one arm."

"Maybe those things are in the suitcase at the bottom of the lake."

Flora sighed in the backseat. "Tired?" he asked.

"No."

Griffin hoped she was okay. What was behind her decision to spend the summer on the island? Memories, maybe. The Winter family was the wealthiest family with the longest history on the island. As long as Griffin could remember, he'd found the elderly lady a bit intimidating even though she had always insisted that he and his brother call her Aunt Flora.

"This will be so much fun," Flora said. "Don't you think so, Cornelius?"

The dog snuffled in reply.

"I hope you'll teach Rebecca how to drive this car," Flora said.

"Maybe she knows," Griffin replied, not wanting to blow Rebecca's cover.

"Ha," Flora snorted. "If she knew, she'd be driving me now instead of following a mile behind us on a dark road in a golf cart. I think you lost her before we even left downtown."

Griffin slowed as he neared the entrance of the road that wound up a hill to Flora's impressive Victorian mansion. "I'll give her a chance to catch up. She can't get lost on the one road that loops around the outside of the island."

"Such a gentleman."

Cornelius sneezed right behind Griffin's head and Griffin laughed. "Are you sure your dog is going to like island life?"

"Cornelius has been here before. He spent the summer here four years ago, the last time I spent the entire one hundred wonderful days of summer on Christmas Island. My doctors talked me into short visits since then and told me I should stay on the mainland and close to medical care. I say phooey on them. I'm sick of hanging around waiting to die."

Griffin felt a familiar cold squeeze in his chest as he thought about his father's death last fall, which had seemed sudden despite several years of decline. Coming home halfway through college five years earlier—when he first realized his father was sick—hadn't been in his plans, but someone needed to save the May Ferry Line, and it had to be him. It was still all on his shoulders, even though his brother was a lot more helpful lately.

As he glanced out the window of the rare and expensive car, he caught the sight of dim headlights on the road behind him. Rebecca might have been driving the golf cart at top speed, but its lawn mower–size engine was no match for the elegant horses under the hood of the Bentley. He would have to remember to thank Rebecca for the chance to drive the incredible car. It was likely to be the most fun and carefree night of his summer.

"I'm ready for my nice, soft bed," Flora said from the backseat.

Knowing Rebecca was close enough to see where he turned, Griffin put the car in low gear and wound up the long driveway to the home perched high on the cliff.

"The lights are on," he said.

"I hired a housekeeper from the village—the same one who takes care of the place while I'm gone. She said she'd have everything ready for me."

Griffin got out and held the door for the elderly lady and her dog.

"Want me to come in and make sure no one is hiding in the closets or under the beds?"

Flora laughed. "On Christmas Island? No one would have the nerve to mess with me."

The golf cart bounced along the driveway and stopped right behind the Bentley. Griffin watched Rebecca climb out of the cart and hoped for her sake she didn't mind facing unusual circumstances. Would it be a lonely summer bumping around in that massive home on the cliff with an eccentric but interesting old lady? What would compel a person to take such a job?

Life on Christmas Island, no matter how scenic and quaint the day tourists found it, could be lonely. Luckily for him, he didn't have time to be lonely.

"Good luck," he said as he exchanged sets of keys with Rebecca. She pulled off his jacket and handed it to him, but he was close enough to see her shiver as she was outlined by the headlights of the golf cart.

"Thank you," she said.

"Keep the jacket for the night." He put it back over her shoulders, and his fingers brushed long, soft hair that still felt damp. "It's all you've got."

He got in the golf cart and made his way carefully down the hill in the darkness, hoping there would be a soft bed and a warm bath waiting in the Winter Palace for Rebecca Browne, and that daylight might help him find whatever was left of her suitcase.

CHAPTER TWO

GRIFFIN HANDED A crate of mail to the island postmaster, Bertie King. Bertie, with his long history of taking his position seriously, handed Griffin an invoice to sign and then cosigned below him.

The Christmas Island Post Office was just up the street from the dock, nestled between a T-shirt shop and a fudge-and-candy store. The entire downtown was built on the day-tourism industry—entertaining people who hopped on a ferry for a Christmas-themed escape—and Griffin loved the boat horns and bicycle bells that made up the music of summer.

"Packages are on the cart," Griffin said, pointing to a flatbed contraption with wheels and a tall handle. One of his dockhands waited patiently to transport the packages. The May family's ferry service had participated in mail delivery for decades, and Griffin had noticed a subtle change in the past fifteen years. It seemed that the crate of letters got lighter with each year, but the cart of packages got heavier. He smiled at Bertie. "Everyone orders online these days."

"Thank goodness. There was a time about ten years ago when the federal government considered shutting down the island post office because everybody went to that blasted email. Package delivery from online shopping is going to get me to my golden retirement at thirty-five years of service."

"What will you do with yourself if you ever retire?" Griffin asked.

"I'll cruise around the island on my bicycle, even if it takes me all day."

Griffin laughed. "If I find the time, I might join you."

He glanced up and saw an old-fashioned bicycle wobbling down the hill toward the ferry dock. Even from a distance, he knew it was Rebecca Browne. The bike was probably left over from a time when her employer was nimble enough to ride one. The silver frame flashed in the sunshine and Rebecca waved at the men as she bore down on them.

"Think she has any brakes?" Bertie asked.

Griffin smiled, wondering if anything was capable of stopping the newest island resident. She seemed like a very determined, if reckless, woman. "The better question is if she knows how they work on ancient bikes like that."

Bertie shrugged. "If she made it down the hill from the Winter Palace, she must know something."

Rebecca put both feet down and dragged them on the concrete entrance to the ferry docks. She hopped off the bike and kicked down the stand with a flourish.

"I'm here for Flora Winter's packages," she announced, gesturing at the cart covered in brown parcels. "I'm Rebecca Browne, her helper for the summer."

"Bertie King, postmaster." He cocked his head and studied her. "Have you been to the island before?"

"Just once with my friend Camille Peterson."

"Ah," the older man said.

"She recommended me for the job."

Griffin nodded. At least that part of Rebecca's arrival made sense now. If she was friends with Camille, he might be able to find out something about her. Not that he was interested beyond a pure concern about Flora's well-being as a friend of the family's.

"Flora is hoping her favorite foot cream arrived in the mail along with some specialty treats for Cornelius."

Bertie smiled. "Good to hear that old dog is still alive. I don't know what's in the packages, but you'll have to come along to the post office so I can scan them in before I hand them over," Bertie said. "Rules are rules."

Griffin gestured to his dock worker, who followed Bertie with the cart, and then he turned to Rebecca.

"The post office is right next to Island Fudge. You'll see the dark blue awning tucked between red and yellow ones. Bertie's been the postmaster since I was born and he's a nice guy but he takes his work seriously."

"So do I," she said.

"Have you always been a babysitter to rich old ladies?"

"I'm not her babysitter. I'm her companion, and it's just for the summer."

"Okay."

Griffin wanted to ask what she would do then, but Rebecca didn't volunteer the information and he had no right or reason to ask. She was only here for June, July and August. He'd managed to get her to the island alive and then deposit her at the castle on the hill.

What happened after that was her problem and her business.

"Your suitcase washed up," he said.

Rebecca's face lit with joy and she clasped her hands in front of her chest in anticipation. "You found it!"

"It floated up not long after we left the dock last night. One of my workers fished it out and called me. We picked it up on the first run this morning." He pointed at her suitcase, which lay on another cart similar to the one loaded with postal packages. "You'll need help getting it to the Winter Palace."

Rebecca ignored him and approached the suitcase as if it were the body of a beloved relative. She gingerly tugged at the zipper, coaxed it open and laid back the lid, exposing her summer's worth of possessions to the sun and the view of any onlookers. Griffin winced as she picked up a laptop computer and water dripped from it. She flipped up the screen and pushed a button, but nothing happened.

Her shoulders sank and Griffin couldn't help but pity her. Next, she pulled out a purple sweatshirt. It sagged soggily in her hands and she shoved it back into the suitcase and closed the lid.

"I'll have it delivered," Griffin said, coming up behind her and scraping his feet so he wouldn't scare her. He noticed she was wearing the same clothes she'd worn the previous night on the ferry. They appeared clean and dry, but clearly, she needed a more permanent solution. "While you're at the post office, you might grab a new sweatshirt at the store next to it. It'll say Christmas Island, but you'll have a choice of colors."

Rebecca smiled sadly. "Think they have purple?"

"They have everything."

"That sounds like the perfect place for a girl who has—" she paused and swallowed, and Griffin wanted to give her a hug and tell her things would get better "—nothing," she concluded with an attempt at a smile that totally failed. Without another word, Rebecca turned and crossed the street, narrowly missing a family of tourists on bicycles. She apparently wasn't worried that someone would steal her old bike, which she left parked at the dock.

Griffin watched her as she peered in the window of the souvenir clothing shop next to the post office and then disappeared under the blue awning to retrieve the packages for her employer.

There were tough days running the ferry, days when the winds and weather didn't co-operate and he wondered if plundering the same waters back and forth was really what he wanted, but at least he had his own apartment downtown with a view of the harbor, a closet full of dry clothes and a laptop that didn't drip.

REBECCA STRAIGHTENED HER spine and counted her blessings. It was a beautiful day right at the beginning of June, and she was on a resort island for the entire summer, working for a woman whom she found quixotic but fascinating. So far. Also, her clothes and shoes had taken a spin in the washer and dryer at the Winter Palace, and she hoped she could salvage the rest of her clothes from the soggy suitcase at the dock.

Being assigned to this job by Winter Industries' CFO had seemed surreal, and she was still uncertain what she was supposed to be watching for. Would people show up on the grand porch of the Winter Palace asking for Flora's stock portfolio? Or approach her with investment schemes? As a financial analyst, Rebecca knew all about portfolios and schemes, but she wasn't sure how much of Flora's personal business she would learn about. It hadn't come up during the morning's tour of the house or over breakfast on the veranda. So far Flora had been polite but reserved—qualities Rebecca could understand because she didn't jump into relationships quickly, either. Her childhood had taught her about the importance of protective layers.

She juggled three packages and several letters from the post office, being careful not to let the lake breeze flap away with the mail, as she passed by one of the waterfront hotels. A menu was posted in the window under a tantalizing picture of the "steak and cake" special, which was exactly what it sounded like—a generous slab of beef and a piece of chocolate cake five layers high.

Beneath the picture was a help-wanted sign.

Cocktail piano player.
Three nights a week.
Inquire within.

Flora had already told Rebecca that she'd have evenings off. After dinner, which would be acquired with help from Rebecca—by driving downtown, ordering in, or making an arrangement with the housekeeper, who would cook if asked—Flora enjoyed reading or watching the sunset from her upper windows in her private quarters. As long as Rebecca had a cell phone in case of an emergency, the older woman had said she saw no reason to impose on Rebecca's every moment.

Pushing through the door, Rebecca let her eyes adjust to the dim light of the hotel bar area. The lobby was visible through an open archway and appeared bright and cheerful with yellow walls, painted white trim and floral cushions on wicker furniture. A Christmas tree with flashing green-and-red lights stood in the corner, and a holiday song played over invisible speakers. Was the Christmas theme everywhere on the island?

To her surprise, the bar and lounge area was different than the bright decor of the lobby. With dark hardwood floors, tables and a long bar, it was elegant and quiet. Her gaze fell on the baby grand sitting in the corner. It was black and shiny, the lid propped halfway, gleaming white keys inviting her. There was no one at the bar, so Rebecca crossed quietly in her sneakers and touched a few keys.

Tuned. It was a nice surprise.

"Can I help you?" The woman behind the bar set down a tray of clean glasses and began arranging them in an overhead rack. She wore a name tag with the hotel logo over HADLEY in all capital letters.

"Hello," Rebecca said. "I saw the sign in the window about a job playing cocktail piano, and I thought I would ask if you were still looking."

"Still looking," Hadley said. "Not a lot of piano players in the usual crowd of teenagers signing up to work for the summer on Christmas Island."

"I'm a piano player." *But definitely not a teenager.*

Hadley smiled. "Good. You'll have to talk to the boss about it when he gets off the ferry, but if you want to play something for me while I put these glasses away, I could put in a good word for you." She cocked her head and gave Rebecca a friendly grin. "If I like it."

Rebecca laughed. "I take requests."

"Okay. How about something everyone knows the words to?"

"Something other than 'Happy Birthday'?"

The bartender laughed. "Oh, heavens,

please don't. That song is a dirge in the wrong hands."

"No doubt," Rebecca agreed as she pulled out the bench and sat. She didn't have any sheet music with her and she hadn't played in weeks as she'd been busy making arrangements to leave for the island, but she had never really needed it. The muscles in her fingers remembered the notes. She played the opening bars of "What a Wonderful World" and when she glanced up, she saw the bartender smiling and singing along. When the piece ended, she transitioned right into "Over the Rainbow" and knew she'd struck gold when the bartender continued to nod and sing along.

Unless a local prodigy came along, Rebecca was confident she'd found herself a way to fill her lonely evenings. It would also be a good opportunity to meet people on the island and snoop around in the interests of protecting the elderly head of Winter Industries. Bars and lounges were a notorious gossip exchange, and Rebecca had no doubt that would be true on an island, too.

"When do you think your boss will be available to talk to me about a job?"

"Depends on the weather," Hadley said.

"Just like everything else on an island. Wait a minute and I'll ask."

The bartender disappeared for a moment and Rebecca played a classical piece she'd known for years. She remembered playing it at a piano competition in middle school and seeing her music teacher nodding with approval in the audience. Other performers had parents watching them, but Rebecca had been content with pleasing herself and the teacher who had signed her up. Until Winter Industries had sponsored her college education and changed her life, she had never had to worry about disappointing anyone.

The piece she was playing morphed gracefully into a Rachmaninoff piece filled with sorrow and passion, and she didn't realize there were two people behind the bar until she glanced up.

"It's a bit serious for our usual crowd," the man said. "But it might make them drink more."

"Sorry," Rebecca said. "I didn't know you were standing there, or I would have played something cheerful, like a pirate song."

The man smiled and there was something familiar about him even though Rebecca didn't believe they had ever met.

"I'm happy to say we don't get a lot of pirates around here," he said. Rebecca indulged him with a few bars of the *Pirates of the Caribbean* theme until he laughed. "My brother does the hiring for our hotel, and he'll be around most of the day tomorrow. Why don't you plan to come in during the late afternoon or early evening?"

Flora had already told Rebecca she liked to eat dinner early, around five, so Rebecca agreed to come and meet the elusive brother at six the following evening. As she gathered her packages and mail and left the bar, she felt as if she'd just had dessert after a satisfying meal. Maybe everything was going to be okay and she'd discover that her company's CFO was worrying over nothing and she'd be free to enjoy an island summer in a mansion with a piano gig on the side.

After walking back over to the dock where she had left her bicycle, she tucked everything into the giant wire basket mounted on the front and turned its old front wheel toward the Winter Palace perched up on the bluff. She noticed a tourist with his camera taking a picture of the elaborate home and she wasn't surprised. It was a beautiful ornament above the downtown area, and its elegance made

Christmas Island seem like it was part of another world. The house itself was three stories tall with a turret. A small upstairs balcony hovered above the wide front porch on the main level, and the entire house was painted with a Christmas color scheme. Creamy white with red-and-green accent colors.

When she reached the steep driveway leading up to the Winter Palace, she hopped off her bicycle to walk it up the gravel path. If she continued to bike around all summer and build up the muscles in her legs, she might reach a point where she'd take on the steep incline on her bike, but it was only her first day.

As she reached the garden level just below the main house, a golf cart passed her. On its open back end was her red suitcase, just as Griffin May had promised. Rebecca parked her bike next to the golf cart when it stopped.

"Thank you," she said to the young woman driving the golf cart. "Can I pay you for your time?"

The woman shook her head. "It's part of my job, and coming up here got me out of a roundtrip on the ferry. The waves are bigger than they look today, and I'm not sure I have the stomach for this business."

"Maybe you could get a job downtown?"

Rebecca suggested, thinking about the help-wanted sign that had drawn her into the hotel bar.

"I'll stick it out another week. Captain says I'll get used to it by then or I never will."

Rebecca shrugged. "I guess he would know." Griffin May was only a year or two older than she was, Rebecca guessed, but the wrinkles around his eyes made him seem older. He also carried himself as if the world depended on him. Was being a ferry captain a stressful job?

The woman with the golf cart left, and then Cornelius rushed out of the house and jumped up and down beneath Rebecca's bicycle basket as if he knew one of the packages contained his special treats. Flora followed, leaning on her cane but already looking younger and healthier than she had the previous night. Maybe it was the fresh island air.

"He's a genius," Flora said. "And he knows what comes in brown boxes. If I had half his senses and energy, I wouldn't need a keeper."

Although Flora had been pleasant, Rebecca wondered if she regretted hiring a summer companion. She knew how hard it was to learn to trust people. A stab of guilt pierced her as she carried the packages into the house.

CHAPTER THREE

"I NEED A serious break from candy, fudge and Christmas music, and I just got here last week," Camille said. She flopped down onto a lounge chair next to Rebecca.

"I don't know how you resist all those sweets," Flora said. She balanced a glass of iced tea on her bosom and looked as pleased as her beloved canine to be outside in the sunshine, her chair in a prime location on the front porch that overlooked the water. Cornelius snoozed next to her feet on a footstool.

"Believe me, if you'd grown up pulling taffy and boiling fudge every minute of your life, you'd be able to resist it." Camille accepted a glass of tea from Rebecca. "It is definitely possible to have too much of a good thing."

"I thought you were working in the office, not making and selling candy," Rebecca said.

"I am." Camille sighed. "But I still go home smelling like chocolate."

Flora tossed a throw pillow at her visitor.

"You'd have more fun if a handsome man was sending you chocolates."

Camille laughed, but Rebecca's thoughts strayed to the intriguing boat captain. What was his story? Aside from the fact that driving things was his superpower and he came through on his word, she didn't know much about him. She'd been close enough to enjoy his lake-blue eyes, but he also seemed distant and busy. She was busy, too, with an important job that only her friend Camille knew about. If she was going to figure out how Flora's fortune and interests could be threatened, she had to keep her suspicions secret.

"And you shouldn't look so serious," Flora told Rebecca. "You only have to hang around with an eighty-five-year-old woman for part of the day, and then you should take advantage of the season and the island. That's what I did when I was growing up here."

"Did you grow up in this house?" Rebecca asked. She'd been looking for subtle ways to learn more about her employer without appearing to be prying.

"I was born in this house, and if I'm very lucky I'll die here."

Rebecca and Camille exchanged quick glances.

"Don't look so frightened," Flora said. "I'm not going to die this summer. I've already decided that."

"Good," Rebecca said, grinning at her boss. "Because I really need this job."

Flora rested her head on the back of her chair and closed her eyes. Rebecca thought she had gone to sleep and was about to suggest that she and Camille tiptoe inside so they could talk without disturbing the older lady. However, Flora opened one eye and trained it on Rebecca. "One of these days, perhaps a rainy day, you can entertain me by telling me how a smart young lady like yourself happens to be available for a summer job."

"I'm between jobs," Rebecca said. "And you have a Steinway. I couldn't pass up a job that came with a summer vacation and a Steinway. I could play you something soothing while you look at the lake." She was happy to have a chance to change the subject before Flora asked any more pointed questions. What if she guessed Rebecca's real reason for taking the job? It was already obvious that Flora was very observant.

"Psh," Flora said. "Soothing is for babies. I'd rather hear show tunes. Something I could dance to if I weren't already so nice and comfortable in this chair."

"Best summer job ever," Rebecca said. "A medley of Gershwin coming right up, and I think I'll mix it with some really weird stuff from nineteen-seventies Broadway."

Rebecca went inside to the grand piano in the living room. Flora would hear every note through the wall of windows that opened onto the front porch. She was happy to accommodate her boss with some music, but she was equally glad for the chance to practice before her job interview. She had no idea who she would have to impress, but Hadley and the interviewer's brother seemed to enjoy her earlier performance. Maybe they'd give her a recommendation.

By the tenth song, Camille came inside and leaned on the piano while Rebecca finished. "Flora says we should go sightseeing for the afternoon since you haven't seen most of the island."

Rebecca closed her book of show tunes. "I'd love that. Can we take your golf cart?"

"Sure."

"Let me just ask Flora if she wants us to pick up dinner later and bring it back here." Rebecca was excited about having a tour of the island from someone who'd grown up here, but she didn't want to neglect her elderly employer. She got Flora's dinner order, promised to bring back a newspaper and patted Cornelius before running upstairs to get her purse and sunglasses.

She had been here for a weekend once, but Rebecca had forgotten how beautiful the island was. Despite its allure as a tourist playground, much of the island was undeveloped, with woods sloping down to the rocky beaches. As Rebecca rode in the passenger seat of Camille's golf cart, she breathed in the fresh pines and lake breeze.

They passed a couple on a tandem bike and another couple walking hand in hand along the quiet island road.

"People on this island have a serious romantic streak," Camille grumbled. "My sister Chloe is getting married this Christmas and it's all I hear about at home. My mother listed off all the eligible locals in case I want to pick out cake toppers, too."

"You grew up here." Rebecca laughed. "You've probably dated them all already."

Camille didn't look at her and didn't respond, but she gripped the wheel with both hands after adjusting her sunglasses.

"Wait. Have you?" Rebecca asked.

"Not seriously."

"But recently?"

"Not recently," Camille said. "And remember that I was a history major in college, which means I'm too smart to repeat any mistakes from the past." She turned down a narrow road that appeared to lead into the center of the island. "The creepy cave is this way. If we're lucky, all the bats will be sleeping."

Rebecca wanted to ask about the not serious and not recent dating of an island resident, but she decided to wait. Camille had dated casually at the University of Chicago until senior year when she started a lengthy relationship that had ended after several years. Rebecca had hardly bothered to look around the dance floors at parties. Keeping her hard-won scholarship and studying economy until her eyes bled was the only way she was going to build a life for herself, and thanks to Winter Industries, she had. All she had to do now was watch over Flora Winter and possibly safeguard the future of the company.

GRIFFIN'S DAY OFF from the ferry was never a real day off. It was a land day, not a sea day, but there was no such thing as downtime during the summer. Griffin and Maddox had purchased an aging hotel and restaurant in downtown Christmas Island two years earlier, and they'd poured their money and free time into the Holiday Hotel. They'd thought the project would be a fun expansion of the family ferry empire, but it was more work than they'd anticipated.

A new roof had been step one, and then Griffin and Maddox had spent the next two winters rehabbing the inside of the Holiday Hotel until it looked old but was completely new. Griffin had decided he never wanted to sand, paint, or refinish anything again, but then they had turned their attention to the bar. They wanted it to feel like an old-fashioned piano bar instead of a local dive—something with some class to match the hotel. They had hardwood floors, classically upholstered furniture, low lighting and a polished bar, but they were missing an important element that had proven difficult to find.

"Piano player coming in early this evening to see you," Hadley told him as he sat at a computer desk in the small room between the bar and the reception area. He used the computer for everything from reservations in the sixteen-room hotel to scotch orders for the bar.

"Anyone we know?"

Like Griffin and Maddox, Hadley had grown up on Christmas Island. She also knew everyone in town and could tell an islander from a visitor from a mile away.

"Never seen her before. Pretty, about your age, dark hair. And she's a heck of a piano player if the little sample she gave me and your brother was any indication."

"And she's here all summer?" Griffin asked. He could think of one person who met the description of pretty with dark hair, but Rebecca Browne already had a job for the summer. He should stop thinking about her. The busy summer season didn't allow time for distractions, especially for him.

"I assume," Hadley said. "Will you go over to the bike rental across the street and see if they've got a missing purse? The lady in room twelve lost hers somewhere. I tried helping her retrace her steps, but she can't remember which bike rental place she was at this morning. I called the one by the dock, but they didn't have it. I tried calling across the street, but no one answered. The lady and her husband are walking through the downtown shops trying to remember which one she bought a Worth Island umbrella in."

"I could watch the bar while you go," Griffin offered.

Hadley shook her head. "They'll ignore me if they're busy. You get more respect in this town than I do."

Griffin sent her a look.

"Plus, I had an awkward kiss with the owner back in high school and we're both still trying to forget it."

"I'll be right back," Griffin said. He grabbed a plastic takeout sack from behind the bar, just in case he found the purse.

"I sort of hope it's too big to fit in there," Hadley said, "but all I know about it is that it's colorful. I hope you find it. That poor lady was in tears and I'd hate to see this wreck her vacation. They're staying two more nights."

Griffin grinned. "I hope I find it and it matches my outfit."

He crossed Holly Street and walked half a block south to the Island Bike Rental, which was owned by his friend Mike. Griffin was relieved to find his guest's purse waiting under the counter, and glad to have an excuse for a short walk to clear his head. Running both a hotel and a ferry line left him little time to enjoy the food and fudge smells of the main street of town and feel the *whoosh* of passing bicyclists.

Back at the hotel he reunited his guest with her bag. After that Griffin spent the rest of the afternoon finishing paperwork and interviewing a part-time housekeeper for the summer. He ate a sandwich at his desk while he waited for his piano player interview to come in. The hotel lobby was quiet this time of day while the guests got ready for dinner and before the bar got busy. He hoped the piano player wouldn't be late because he wanted to go back to his apartment overlooking the harbor, put his feet up and let the DVR surprise him with something good to watch.

At six o'clock Hadley poked her head into the small hotel office. "The piano player is here. I hope you like her because we've had exactly zero other applicants."

He got up and walked into the bar, where Rebecca Browne stood next to the piano, one hand on its lid.

CHAPTER FOUR

As Rebecca waited for Griffin to cross the empty bar, her mind quickly ran an analysis. The man she'd met earlier who seemed familiar had said his brother did the hiring. So Griffin May had a brother and a lot of demands on his time. He was also tall and handsome and moved easily, as if the stationary wood floor was no challenge after spending time on the deck of a boat.

"You pilot the ferry and run a hotel?" Rebecca asked. "How do you handle it all?" Considering his connections on the island, he might be someone who could enlighten her about Flora's affairs. However, he seemed close to the older woman, and Rebecca hadn't figured out who to trust or how she could accomplish the mission the CFO of Winter Industries had tasked her with.

Griffin smiled and shook hands with her. "Time-management skills. Even though I grew up on an island where it's always Christmas, I know how to make the most of every single day."

Rebecca laughed. "I'm prepared to play Christmas music for my audition if that's what you want." Next to show tunes, Christmas music was her favorite. They both represented the spirit of hope that had kept her moving forward all her life.

He shook his head. "It's not what I want."

"Sea shanties?" she asked.

"Wrong again. Do you have any experience playing cocktail piano?"

She nodded. Although she had no qualifications for being a lady's companion, the piano keyboard was something she did know. "Quite a bit."

"Then surprise me," he said. He took a seat at a nearby table. "Play what you think a person enjoying a drink in my bar would like to hear."

"Your bar?"

"My brother and I own this hotel."

So he doesn't just run the Holiday Hotel, Rebecca thought as she sat on the ebony bench and put her fingers on the keys. She glanced over at Griffin and held his eyes as she played the opening bars to the Billy Joel song "She's Always a Woman." She played one verse and the refrain, and then transitioned to a popular song about summer. With a subtle key change, her fingers flowed into "The Most Wonderful Time of the Year."

Griffin stood and came over, leaning one elbow on the top of the baby grand. Rebecca didn't acknowledge him and kept playing, transitioning to "Moon River" and then a love song made popular by a recent movie.

"Do you take requests?" Griffin asked.

She nodded, not missing a beat as she continued to play. "Of course. What would you like?"

He thought for a moment. "Say I'm here with my friends celebrating the island baseball team's big win over the team from the mainland."

"There's an island baseball team?"

Griffin nodded. "And sometimes we actually win."

Rebecca laughed. "That's easy." She played "Take Me Out to the Ball Game" and blended it seamlessly into the theme song from a famous baseball movie.

"And now I've brought my sister here for her birthday," Griffin said.

Rebecca glanced up. "Do you have a sister?"

He shook his head.

"So is this fictitious sister old-fashioned, a free spirit, a fan of musicals?"

"Yes," Griffin said, grinning.

"Boy bands from the nineties," Rebecca said. "Everyone loves them."

"Wait, I changed my mind. Maybe I'm here on a date."

Rebecca's heart fluttered in her chest. Did Griffin date someone on the island? It would seem obvious. He was attractive, well connected, hardworking and her employer seemed to think the moon and stars of him. Unless the women on the island were very distracted by sleigh bells and tinsel, they would certainly have put Griffin May on their Christmas list.

"First date?" Rebecca asked.

"Let's say it's the second. And I'm working hard to get a third."

After playing cocktail piano all through college, Rebecca had seen everything. Birthdays, anniversaries, first dates, last dates, bachelor and bachelorette parties, friend groups, holiday celebrations and sad singles casting their eyes longingly around the bar. She'd seen second dates with their layers of familiarity mixed with fresh uncertainty. And she also knew enough to be wary of attractive men like Griffin. She reminded herself that she was pretending to be someone she was not, and she needed to be careful.

Beginning with the introduction to "Moonlight Sonata," she moved into a minor transition and then into "I Will Always Love You." Griffin rolled a chair over and sat next to her, watching her hands. She let the song softly fade into a gentle ending chord, and then she turned on the bench so she could face her audience of one.

"You're good," he said.

"I cleaned up at talent shows during middle school."

He laughed. "That's where you learned to listen to people but also ignore them while playing exactly what they want to hear?"

"You make it sound like a paradox."

"Are you a paradox, Rebecca Browne? Your timing leaping onto my ferry was a disaster, but you obviously have plenty of rhythm at the piano keyboard."

She shrugged. "It was my first time jumping onto a moving boat. I'll do better next time." She knew a lot about picking herself up and moving on.

Griffin held up both hands in a mock surrender. "Let's not have a next time on that."

"How about another song, then?"

"I've heard enough. I'd buy drinks all night long just to listen to you play, so it's a safe bet you'll be good for business. When can you start?"

"I'm free every evening," she said. Did she sound too eager? The advertisement asked for three nights a week. "Flora says she doesn't need me in the evenings. She's very independent."

"I was surprised she was willing to admit she needed any help this summer," Griffin said.

Rebecca didn't want to go down the dangerous road of talking about why she was here, but it was too good a chance to pass up.

"She didn't have help previous summers?" she asked.

He shook his head. "I've known her my entire life and I don't think she's ever let anyone help her across the street. Something about her seems..." His words trailed off and he sipped his soda.

"So," she said, switching back to the business at hand since it appeared Griffin wasn't going to give up anything interesting about Flora. "Whichever nights you'd like me to come in, I could be here."

"We'll start with three nights and see how

it goes. How about Tuesday, Friday and Saturday from seven to eleven?"

She smiled. "I'll be here."

"Will you stop at the front desk and pick up the paperwork?" Griffin asked.

She nodded. Griffin hesitated, and she wondered if he was going to ask her to stay for a drink. Would she if he asked? "I should get going," she said, choosing a quick and graceful exit. To do her job well, she needed to get close to people on the island who were involved in Flora's life, but not too close... "I'm going to see if any of the shops are still open and pick up a dress or two. I didn't come prepared for a piano gig."

"The Island Boutique is probably still open. My brother went to school with Violet, who owns it. If you don't find anything there, I could give you a free ride to the mainland on my ferry."

"Your ferry?"

"My brother and I own it."

Rebecca cocked her head. "What else do you own on this island?"

He laughed. "Nothing. The ferry line and the hotel are enough. In fact, most of the time they're too much and I feel like they own me instead of the other way around."

Although living on Christmas Island might seem like a permanent vacation, Rebecca recognized how hard the locals must work to keep it that way. She'd never owned anything of much substance herself aside from a decent car, but she respected Griffin's work ethic. Perhaps that was what Flora liked about him.

Rebecca left the hotel and strolled down Holly Street. Most of the day tourists were gone, and the downtown streets were quiet, only populated by island residents and tourists staying in the hotels. The Island Boutique had its doors propped open and lights on, and Rebecca took a moment to admire the clothing on display in the front windows. An ocean-blue sundress with a fun asymmetrical hem paired with sandals and a wide straw hat. Very resort-appropriate, she thought. The other window had something more suited to her new part-time job. A mannequin wore a black A-line dress with a lace overlay.

"It's washable and it has pockets," a woman said from the doorway. "The holy grail of dresses."

"I'll take one in every color you have," Rebecca said.

"You're my kind of shopper," the woman

said, laughing. "But I only have that one in black. Come in and try it on."

Rebecca ducked inside and waited while the clerk sorted through a rack and handed her exactly the size she would have asked for. "I could use two or three cocktail dresses if you have any suggestions," she said.

"Are you staying at the Great Island Hotel?" the woman asked.

Rebecca shook her head. "I'm staying with Flora Winter for the summer as her companion. But I just got a job playing piano three nights a week at the Holiday Hotel."

The woman smiled. "Griffin and Maddox are really classing up the place." She held out her hand. "I'm Violet. I own this boutique and I've known those brothers—and Flora—all my life."

So what Griffin had said to her on the ferry was true. Everyone on the island knew everyone else. In that case, she'd have to be careful. Each person she met might reveal something about Flora's plans for her wealth and her recent change to her will, but they might also blow her cover.

"Rebecca Browne," she said, shaking hands with Violet. "I went to college with Camille Peterson if you know her."

"Of course. I was so glad when she moved back and joined the rest of our generation taking over our parents' businesses. Camille and I should probably join a support group with the May brothers. It's not easy."

"This shop was in your family?"

"My grandparents actually, but my parents had other things going on. So I took it over. Giving up the real world to live on Christmas Island was an easy choice for me because I love clothes and I always thought I'd follow in my grandparents' footsteps, but some of my friends have made some big sacrifices."

As Rebecca went into the fitting room, she thought about Christmas Island and the family ties that seemed to be everywhere. Without parents of her own to inherit anything from, she felt a twinge of longing for the missing pieces of her history. But what about the sacrifices people made to carry on family traditions? Ties could cut or bind both ways.

"Try these." Violet's voice came through the slatted fitting-room door and she draped three dresses over the top.

"Thanks," Rebecca said. One dress was a rich plum color in a midi length. Another was a white sheath dress with a floral pattern, and the third was deep sapphire blue with a set-in waist and elbow-length sleeves. "They're beautiful."

"I can bring you shoes, too," Violet offered. "I don't know what Flora Winter is paying you, so I grabbed these off the sale rack."

Rebecca's salary from her finance job at Winter Industries was plentiful enough that she'd saved quite a bit. She was putting her salary from Flora Winter back into the scholarship fund at the company, an arrangement she had made with her CFO, Jim Churchill, to avoid double-dipping. She bought the black, plum and blue dresses and one pair of low black heels that would go with all three. Back home her closet was filled with work dresses and suits, but she hadn't brought a single one to the island. It was just as well. The plunge into the water would have ruined the dry-clean-only garments.

Walking out of the shop with her purchases, Rebecca turned her face to the beautiful golden sunset for a moment before getting into the golf cart belonging to the Winter Palace. Griffin was just coming out of his hotel as she drove past. He waved to Rebecca, and she waved back and then watched him in her rearview mirror as he crossed the street and disappeared.

CHAPTER FIVE

TWO DAYS LATER Griffin stared at his phone, second-guessing the message he'd typed.

He had found Rebecca's phone number on her job application, but that wasn't really snooping. Not at all.

And if he had been looking for any clues to the mystery of Rebecca Browne, he would have been disappointed. For an address, she used the Winter Palace. Previous work experience listed two bars in the Chicago area where she'd played piano. No references, no personal details.

If he wanted to know anything about her, he was going to have to find out himself. All he really needed to know was that she was a good and versatile piano player. That was why he'd hired her.

But she was also the companion of Flora Winter's, whom he considered family. Nothing about Rebecca seemed at all dangerous. Except perhaps the quiver of interest from his heart every time he saw her. She was definitely attractive, but that wasn't all. There was something at once vulnerable and plucky about her that reminded him of how he'd been before he gave everything up for the family business. He'd been open and hopeful. The past few years had been daunting, but was it time to look beyond the immediate horizon again?

He stared at the phone in his hand and read his message twice before hitting Send.

I have the afternoon free for a driving lesson.

Griffin leaned on the balcony railing of his downtown apartment overlooking the docks. He only had to wait a minute.

Who is this?

The message was accompanied by a smiley face emoji.

He smiled.

The man who knows your secret.

More specific, her response said.

I'd like Aunt Flora to be in good hands on the island roads.

She's not your aunt.

Ask her.

Griffin watched a sailboat negotiate the harbor entrance of Christmas Island. He and Maddox had a small sailboat they'd inherited from their father, but they never took time to go out in it. Maybe this summer. Now that the hotel was renovated and starting to repay their efforts and the ferries were running smoothly.

Rebecca's response came back five minutes later with two smiley face emojis.

She says she's not related to you but she forgives you for that and loves you anyway. She also says I should let you teach me to drive her car.

You told her?

No point in trying to fool her.

Griffin smiled at that. She was right.

Be there at two o'clock.

An hour later Griffin braced a hand against the dashboard of the Bentley as Rebecca negotiated the curve below the Winter Palace. "Okay," he said. "Now that we're on the road, just listen to the engine and watch the tachometer. You'll know when to shift."

"How many RPMs?"

"Just feel it, listen for it."

"I hate this," Rebecca said. "I prefer to have a definite number."

The engine wound up and Rebecca pushed the clutch and shifted into second gear.

"Good," Griffin said.

"There should be a science to this."

"There is. I just thought you might be a fly-by-the-seat-of-your-pants kind of woman."

Rebecca laughed. "I have no idea what makes you think that."

Griffin relaxed a bit as Rebecca shifted into third gear and the car hummed along the road, passing the lake on one side and stands of thick green trees on the island side.

"Then set me straight," he said. "You seem like you can play the piano without having to follow directions."

She shook her head. "I learned by following the directions before I branched out and began to improvise. That's the best way to do it."

"Rules first, style later?"

"How did you get your boat captain's license? I'm guessing there was a book you had to memorize before you even got behind the wheel. You must have learned all the rules and now you make it look easy."

Griffin watched the island scenery instead of answering. Rebecca had to know she was right about that.

"How long have you been a captain?" she asked.

"Officially, five or six years. Unofficially, since I could see over the ship's wheel."

She kept one hand on the wheel but glanced over at him. The windows were down and the breeze tossed her long, dark hair. Griffin felt as light as the small waves dancing out on the lake.

"Did you inherit the business from your parents? Violet said something about your generation of islanders sticking together in the difficult job of taking over family businesses."

"Did you like her shop?" Griffin asked.

"I bought three dresses. But you're avoiding my question."

The lightness of the dancing waves left him for a moment as he remembered the tough times of the past five years, beginning with his painful decision to drop out of college and come home. "When my father died and my mother moved to Texas, I bought the ferry line."

"You and your brother bought it?"

"Basically. He was wrapped up in something else at the time." Griffin didn't like the smooth interrogation Rebecca was conducting, even though he did admire her smooth treatment of the vintage car's gearbox. "Are you sure you never drove a standard transmission before?" he asked.

"I read some articles online and watched three different YouTube videos."

"Wasn't your laptop destroyed when your luggage fell in the lake?"

"They sent me a new one."

"They?"

Rebecca slowed the car, downshifted and drove around some pedestrians on the loop road around the island. She didn't look at him. "I ordered a new one online. It probably came over on your ferry."

"Let's stop up here," Griffin said. "There's a nice pull-off area."

When Rebecca put on the parking brake and cut the engine, she looked over at him and smiled. "How am I doing?"

"I would never guess you're a first timer."

"Believe me, I am. But I'm pretty brave about trying new things."

"Like being a lady's companion?" He hoped she might volunteer information about why she had taken that job and what she had done previously.

Rebecca pocketed the keys and got out of the car. "It's not very hard. I just pretend she's the grandmother I never had. She's really very sweet and easy to get along with." She leaned her elbows on a stone fence and looked out at the lake. "I see why you had me stop here. It's a beautiful view."

Griffin leaned on the fence next to her. "Why didn't you have a grandmother?" Griffin had a grandmother who lived out of state and one who had died long before he was born. Rebecca bit her lower lip and continued looking out at the lake. "Sorry," he said, lowering his voice. "It's none of my business."

"It's okay," she said, facing him with a thoughtful expression. "It seems as if everyone on this island has deep family roots. I just don't have any roots to speak of." She drew a deep breath. "Which is why no one ever taught me to drive a stick shift or a Bentley," she added in a cheerful tone, even though her eyes remained serious.

"Two more laps around the island with a few hills thrown in, and I think you'll know everything you need to know," Griffin said. He doubted he'd really taught Rebecca anything, and he certainly hadn't learned much about her despite his prying questions. It was probably better that way, he thought, as the sun glanced over her pretty dark hair before she got in the driver's seat and drove them back to the Winter Palace.

CHAPTER SIX

REBECCA CHOSE THE blue dress for her first night at the piano. "You'll knock 'em dead," Flora said. "Especially wearing that dress and driving the Bentley."

"I'll take the golf cart," Rebecca said. "I'm pretty confident about driving your car, but I don't want to take chances after dark."

Flora looked at the gathering clouds in the sky. "If it's rainy later, you have Griffin or Maddox drive you home instead of getting soaked in the golf cart."

"I'll be fine," Rebecca said. Even though her first instinct was always to reject help and handle everything herself, warmth spread through her chest at the older woman's grandmotherly concern. It was the first time she'd branched beyond politeness, and Rebecca felt as if she must have passed a test with her employer. She'd heard Flora Winter, the grand dame of Winter Industries, could be indomitable and opinionated, but had she softened with old age?

The company CFO, Jim Churchill, was worried about Flora being taken advantage of, especially after his golf partner had let it slip that Flora had called about changing her will at the golf partner's law office. The company leadership had made assumptions about Flora's nephew Alden inheriting everything, but was there a wild card in the deck? It was a massive company employing thousands across the country and around the world. Would its founder really make an impulsive change late in life?

Rebecca wished she could ask for details, but her job was to be observant and keep her cover as a lady's companion. Asking about Flora's will and if she was being unduly influenced wasn't exactly afternoon tea conversation.

"I hope you'll be fine this evening without me," Rebecca said. She held up her phone. "I'll check it often to see whether you need something. One of these nights you should come along. I'll play something you like."

Flora laughed. "I used to know everyone on Christmas Island, but that was two generations ago. I'm happy spending a quiet evening with Cornelius."

"Okay, but tomorrow I'm taking you for a drive in your fabulous car and we're letting Cornelius hang his head out the window."

Flora smiled and waved a hand. "We'll see what the weather does."

REBECCA PARKED BEHIND the hotel and made her way through the lobby. A man and a woman were having their picture taken in front of the Christmas tree. Rebecca paused and watched as members of the family took turns having their pictures taken with the older couple. She heard someone say it was a fiftieth anniversary. The two older people looked so happy, surrounded by their children, grandchildren and a toddler who was probably a great-grandchild.

"Can I take a picture of all of you together?" Rebecca asked.

Four members of the group handed her a cell phone at the same time. "I'll do my best," she said. "Smile!"

Rebecca took pictures with each of the phones. "Happy anniversary," she said to the couple. "Do you happen to have a special song?"

The woman gave her a curious expression.

"I'm the hotel piano player," Rebecca said, the words making her feel a little shot of pride and even belonging. She pointed at the baby grand visible through the double doors leading into the bar area. "I could play you something."

The woman asked for "Unchained Melody," and Rebecca waved for the whole group to follow her. She adjusted the piano bench and began playing the couple's song. Their daughter cried, but the older couple started dancing while the grandkids took pictures and video with their phones. Rebecca played a second verse and finished the piece to applause from the family.

"Happy anniversary," Rebecca said. "And many more."

"You made our night," the older man said. He dropped a bill in the piano's tip jar, and the group went back into the lobby. Rebecca watched them go, imagining what family celebrations and holidays must be like at a house with all those people, all that love. She remembered Flora's concern about her well-being and smiled. It was nice having someone care about her.

At that moment Rebecca glanced over to

the bar and realized Griffin was there, watching. He was intriguing, but there seemed to be something lurking beneath his surface. A piece of him that he didn't easily share—or at least not with her. His brother Maddox had a more open expression, as if he kept himself on a longer leash. Rebecca hadn't been on the island for a week, but she already realized it would take a long time to fit in with the locals, even though her friendship with Camille bought her a ticket into the group.

"They'll be telling that story for a while, about the piano player who knew their special song," Griffin said as he walked over to the piano. Rebecca kept her place on the bench and Griffin stopped short of putting an elbow on the piano as he had on the day of her audition. Was he keeping his distance for a reason?

"I hope so. They seemed like such a nice family."

"And they weren't bad dancers. If your playing doesn't work out, I may look them up and hire them to entertain my bar crowd."

Rebecca laughed. "I should get to work so I don't lose my job."

"Me, too. I'm the bartender for tonight since it's Hadley's day off. Rain is supposed to move in later, so I think we'll have a decent crowd."

Rebecca played "Raindrops Keep Falling on my Head," and Griffin smiled and went back behind the bar. A group of three men and a woman came in and they stood near the bar, ordering drinks and talking with Griffin as if they knew him. The group eventually sat at a table as the bar began filling up. Glancing at the people coming in, Rebecca saw raindrops on their shoulders and wet hair. One of the ladies carefully folded a dripping umbrella and put it in a stand near the door.

As it grew darker outside on the summer night, the bar lighting also lowered. Rebecca played through two dozen songs in her wide repertoire, but then she finally got out a thick, spiral-bound book she'd brought. No one was approaching to make requests, so the book served as inspiration. She knew all one hundred piano classics in it, and as she played through the book, the songs also reminded her of other ones she could play. A mix of songs from memory and songs with prompting from the book was how she usually got through a several-hour shift at the piano. She'd been doing it for years.

"How about a break?" Griffin asked. He

pointed to a swinging door behind the bar. "If you stop into the kitchen, Jerry will make you something to eat, and I can bring you a drink if you like."

"Maybe a soda water. I don't drink and play."

"Too dangerous?"

"Too sloppy. I don't mind improvising, but I prefer not to violate the laws of music."

He smiled. "Take as long as you need."

Rebecca stopped in the kitchen where the cook insisted on making her a sandwich to order, right down to exactly the right kind of cheese. "Gotta keep your strength up," the older man said. "And if you wouldn't mind, I'd love to hear 'The Christmas Waltz' when you get back out there."

"One of my favorites," she said.

When Rebecca returned to the piano, she noticed someone had put a small adjustable lamp next to her book of sheet music, and there was a glass of sparkling water on a coaster. She took a sip of the water and then played two verses of "The Christmas Waltz." Jerry leaned out the partially open kitchen door, listening, and she smiled to herself. It was nice bringing joy to other people. She had a keyboard in her apartment, but playing for herself wasn't the same.

People continued to enter the bar, all of them with rain-wet jackets and hair. She heard snippets of conversation all around her—people talking about the sightseeing and shopping they'd done, where they were staying on the island, and the rain.

At eleven o'clock Griffin politely saw the last guest out and closed the double doors leading to the lobby. Rebecca stopped half-way through the movie theme song she was playing. "You're not open until two in the morning?"

He shook his head. "A few bars on the island stay open that late, but we haven't found it to be cost effective on a weeknight. Fridays and Saturdays we'll stay open past midnight if people are still ordering drinks."

Rebecca stood, took her empty glass—which Griffin had replaced with a fresh drink—and left it on the tray behind the bar. Griffin wiped down the bar and took a tray of glasses into the kitchen. Rebecca picked up her piano book and tucked it into her shoulder bag. She went to the window and peered out at the rain-soaked night.

"I'll take you home," Griffin said.

"That's okay," Rebecca said. "I drove the golf cart."

He shook his head. "It's still pouring out."

"I'll be fine. You saw me submerged in the lake so you know I don't melt."

He smiled just a little, and Rebecca imagined she had been a pretty amusing sight that evening. "You'd be doing me a favor. If I hang around here I'll get roped into doing something. But seeing our piano player home is a great excuse for leaving."

Lightning flashed outside the windows, followed by a crack of thunder.

"Maybe just this once," Rebecca said.

He nodded toward a hallway in the back of the bar. "I'm parked out back."

"Did you drive to work tonight?"

"No, but I usually leave my truck in a spot behind the hotel because it's centrally located downtown. As you can imagine, I don't need a vehicle very much on this island."

"I'm surprised you have one," Rebecca said.

"I got it when I was at the University of Michigan because I lived off campus."

He paused in the doorway and pushed the button on his key fob. Headlights flashed on a dark-colored pickup truck. Rebecca clutched her bag to her chest and ran to the truck. When they closed the truck doors, rain pounded loudly on the roof but the cab felt like a safe haven as lightning flashed again, lighting up the night.

"What did you study at U of M?" Rebecca asked.

Griffin negotiated the narrow alley behind the hotel and pulled onto the main street downtown. During the daytime pedestrians and bicycles clogged Holly Street, but it was deserted late at night in the rain.

"Engineering," he said.

"Oh." Rebecca wanted to ask if and how that degree came in useful running a ferry and tourist hotel, but his tone didn't invite questions and he didn't elaborate.

"What did you study in college?" he asked.

Rebecca hesitated. Because she was on the island basically undercover, she had resolved to keep details about her personal life quiet. Not that there was much to say. She lived for her job at Winter Industries, a company that had given her belonging and a livelihood. But there was no reason to lie, and she imagined people knew she went to college with Camille.

Griffin jammed his foot on the brakes as a deer ran across the road in front of them.

"Oh my goodness," Rebecca said, her hand on her heart. "I'm glad you saw him first."

If a deer had run in front of her golf cart,

Rebecca was pretty sure she would have crashed into it.

"There are quite a few deer on the island. No one hunts them, but they usually keep to themselves when the tourists are here."

"Any reindeer?" Rebecca asked. "On Christmas Island?"

"Not that I've seen," Griffin said, flashing her a grin. "But anything can happen on this island."

He drove up the road to the Winter Palace and put the truck in Park but didn't cut the engine. It was definitely time for her to get out of the truck and call it a night. It was easy being around Griffin—too easy—and she couldn't risk letting her guard down. She wasn't on the island to make friends; she was here out of loyalty to Winter Industries. Getting too close to people could be a dangerous distraction, and she'd had years of practice keeping relationships in safe little boxes.

"Thanks for the ride," Rebecca said.

"Anytime."

"I'M ONLY HERE for the food," Griffin told his brother. "I didn't have time to eat all day, so you dangled the right bait tonight."

"You're welcome," Maddox said. "Maybe it'll be fun."

Griffin gave his brother a curious look as they approached the Santa Tavern, located on a back street in downtown. A free-standing blackboard outside advertised Trivia Night, Fifty-Cent Wings, Two-Dollar Beers.

"Is there any particular reason we're coming here when we haven't done this in almost two years?"

Maddox shrugged. "Might be someone interesting to team up with."

Griffin paused in the doorway and faced his brother, arms crossed over his chest.

"And we should support local business," Maddox said. "Since we own two of them."

Griffin gave his brother a mild punch on the shoulder. "You're not fooling anyone. I know Camille Peterson is back on the island."

"With a very interesting piano-playing friend," Maddox said. "Who might be here, too."

Griffin shook his head but followed his brother past the mistletoe hanging above the entrance to the Santa Tavern. Inside, strings of red-and-green Christmas lights criss-crossed the large room and there was a revolving plastic Santa at the end of the bar.

Pop-style Christmas music played and a big-screen TV in the corner rolled a Christmas movie.

Two horseshoe-shaped tables were set up in front of the large TV, and Griffin saw Rebecca and Camille at one table with two empty seats. At the other table four locals he'd known for years already had drinks and wings in front of them.

"Looks like they need two more players," Maddox said. "I'll let you handle the academic stuff and I've got sports."

"What if there's no sports category tonight?"

Maddox laughed. "It's bar trivia. There will be sports."

Griffin followed Maddox, who put a hand on the back of the chair next to Camille. "Can we join you?"

Camille looked up, flushed, and turned to Rebecca. "Do you want to let the May brothers on our team? We could turn them down and hope someone better shows up."

Her tone was light but the tension in her posture told a different story. Like him and his brother, Camille was working in a family business and Griffin knew all too well about the long, hard days involved in such a

legacy. She could be tired and hungry just as
they were, but there was also the matter of
her previous relationship with Maddox that
had sunk like an anchor years ago.

Rebecca tilted her head and studied Griffin
and his brother. Her expression was friendly
and teasing. "I don't know. Are they smart?"

"I'm smart enough to not fall off a moving
ferry," Maddox said.

Griffin held his breath for just a moment,
wondering if his brother had overstepped.
Maddox was always the joking one, but not
remembering what to take seriously had cost
him quite a lot. Griffin breathed a sigh of relief when Rebecca laughed and pointed at the
empty seats.

"Can't argue with that," she said.

"I want to win," Camille said, "so I expect you to pull your weight and not bail out
on us."

Griffin knew exactly what was beneath
Camille's words, which were directed at his
brother, but it was obvious that Rebecca didn't
know about Camille and Maddox's past. Rebecca stared openmouthed at her friend as if
she was trying to process Camille's rudeness,
and then she turned to Griffin. "I'll expect

you to answer any questions related to boats and navigation."

"And I'll expect you to get the music questions."

If Rebecca had other interests and talents, he was about to find out.

The bar owner turned off the holiday movie after both tables got their first round of drinks. He took their food orders, and then he used the remote to queue up the trivia game. "Good luck," he said. "Winning team gets buy one–get one coupons for burger night."

The locals at the other table—a man who worked on the docks, two women from the chamber of commerce and one of their husbands—rubbed their hands together and smiled at Griffin's table. "Gonna kill ya," Shirley from the chamber of commerce said.

"I hope so," Griffin said. "That way I won't have to keep working so hard to bring you tourists. They'll have to swim across if I'm not alive to run the ferry."

Rebecca laughed at the trash talk and briefly met Griffin's eyes before the first category flashed on the screen. Her dark eyes sparkled, and he felt a shot of warmth and attraction that woke something up inside him.

Sports, the screen declared in giant capital letters. "You got lucky," Griffin told his brother, who looked smug until the subcategories appeared. Synchronized swimming. Table tennis. Extreme skateboarding.

"Uh-oh," Maddox muttered.

"Courage," Griffin said. "Maybe the questions will be true and false and you'll have a fifty-fifty chance."

Neither table correctly answered the skateboarding or swimming questions. Rebecca answered two table tennis questions correctly in a row, and she didn't seem as if she was guessing. Griffin raised an eyebrow and she shrugged. "I lived with a family that was into Ping-Pong. We even watched the summer Olympics that year."

He wanted to ask why Rebecca had lived with a family, but considering she was a lady's companion, he assumed it had been a previous job.

The next category scrolled across the screen and the men at the other table groaned. The New York Stock Exchange. Griffin glanced over at Camille and Rebecca, and he could have sworn Rebecca sat up straighter and even squirmed with excitement. Had she lived with a stockbroker's family, too?

The scorecards in the upper corners of

the screen showed two-zero, with Griffin's team winning. Question one popped up and Rebecca nailed it before Griffin had time to finish reading it. When the second question regarding high-risk bonds came up, Rebecca paused a moment, swept her eyes over both tables of competitors and then answered it.

"Four-nothing," Maddox declared. Camille cut him a sarcastic glance and Griffin wanted to give him a solid elbow, but he refrained. Maddox didn't need his brother giving him crap.

The third question regarding blue-chip stocks came up and Rebecca again answered it after a brief pause. When the fourth question appeared on the screen—indexed mutual funds—Rebecca didn't even wait. She rattled off the answer and the score went to six-zero.

"Did you happen to live with a family of stock traders?" Griffin asked.

Rebecca considered his question for a moment. "No."

She turned back to the screen, where Cowboy Movies was the next category. "All right!" Shirley said. "Finally." Shirley was the first one to guess at all four questions and she got two of them right. Griffin tried to remember the last time he'd been to a movie.

There was a theater on the mainland, but he hadn't been since he was a teenager. He used his DVR to save up shows for winter nights, but he'd stayed busy the past two winters rehabbing the hotel. He was probably out of storage space and he didn't have time to do anything about it.

When he looked over at Rebecca's face, illuminated by a white string of Christmas lights that swept over her head, he wished he was a carefree person doing a summer job and enjoying the island. But he wasn't. He had two businesses to run, a brother who was rebuilding his life and no time for the mystery lady's companion who had suddenly appeared in Aunt Flora's life. Again, he wondered what had driven Flora to spend the summer on the island and hire a stranger to help her. Was she ill or just slowing down?

As interesting as he found Rebecca, he didn't know much about her and she deflected his questions smoothly, even as she answered question after question and led her team to victory. One thing he did know for certain was that she would be gone at the end of the summer, and he would be here when the snow fell over downtown Christmas Island.

CHAPTER SEVEN

THE DAY AFTER the trivia game Rebecca and Flora had lunch on the deck overlooking the lake. "So tell me about some of the companion jobs you've had," Flora said.

Rebecca kept her eyes on her chicken sandwich and tried to think fast. So far she'd learned that Flora was beloved on the island, pleasantly opinionated, devoted to her friends and her dog and as low maintenance as any octogenarian millionaire would be. She was also observant and perceptive. How much longer could Rebecca continue to fool her? Rebecca had crept into the library the night before because that was where Flora kept all her personal and business papers, but she had stalled out. Even though she was here to watch over Flora and to put her boss's mind to rest about the future of the company, she hadn't been able to make herself open the boxes of Flora's papers. It was creepy. Intrusive. And she wouldn't want someone prying into her own private life.

"The families you've lived with," Flora prompted. "There must be some good stories there."

Rebecca looked up and met her employer's eyes. "I have lived with quite a few families, and they were all interesting in different ways." This, she could do. Instead of detailing a job as a lady's companion, she could tell stories about the many homes she'd been in and out of throughout her teen years. Her early childhood had been in a children's home that she remembered fondly, but when the roof collapsed because of a heavy snowstorm, that part of the building was never rebuilt and the older kids had to be sent out to foster homes.

One of those foster homes had a piano, and it had changed her life. Another one had a mom who worked in finance and got every financial newspaper. Rebecca had taken them from the recycling bin at night and read them until her foster mom found out. After that the kind lady had slid the papers under Rebecca's door every night.

Moving on from those homes had been tough, but the county agency had been mismanaged with a revolving door staff, and teens were shuffled far too often. She had learned to guard her heart and not get too close to people no matter how much she liked them, because she knew a time would come when she would move on. In a strange way such a childhood had prepared her for her summer with Flora. It would be so nice to relax into a grandmother-granddaughter relationship with Flora, but she couldn't.

"I lived with a wonderful lady who worked in a bank and did day trading for fun," Rebecca said. "She also had the largest shoe collection I've ever seen."

Flora smiled. "Stocks and shoes."

"She was barely five feet tall and loved dangerously high heels," Rebecca said, remembering the woman fondly. She often looked back and wondered how different her life might have been if she'd stayed in one place, but things had turned out all right for her.

"Another family had quite a few children and I acted as a nanny for the younger ones. I even drove them to school sometimes, but they didn't have a fabulous car like you do."

"It appears your lesson with Griffin went well," Flora said.

"Very," Rebecca said. "I studied in advance, but he's also a patient teacher."

"He's a treasure," Flora said. "I've had my doubts about his brother a few times, but give a man enough time and he'll pull himself together." Flora grinned. "Of course there are exceptions to every rule."

Rebecca laughed, but she was tempted to ask Flora why she had never married. Building Winter Industries into a multimillion-dollar enterprise had certainly taken a lot of time and energy, but had there really been no one in Flora's life? She seemed too sweet and full of life to miss out on love. And her company's generosity to charitable causes, especially the full scholarships to the University of Chicago for foster-home kids like Rebecca, was a clear sign of Flora's kindness.

"And weren't there any tempting men at any of these jobs you've had?" Flora asked. "No one who interested you?"

"Not at those places," Rebecca said quickly.

"Hmm," Flora said as she wiped her lips with a purple linen napkin. "I'm delighted, of course, that you're free for the summer and there's plenty of time for romance."

Rebecca considered herself lucky that Flora seemed willing to change the subject. "Speaking of time," Rebecca said, "I prom-ised you and Cornelius a ride, and today is a great day for it. We could take a spin around the island and I'll show off my driving skills."

Flora looked as if she was thinking about something else as she gazed out at the lake. "I'd like that," she said after a long pause. "I need to go to the library and post office, and we could stop at both."

"Sure," Rebecca said. "Although I'd be happy to run those errands for you anytime."

"Let me put some things together and I'll be ready in half an hour."

Flora put down her napkin and pushed back from the table. Rebecca picked up their empty plates and watched as Flora went into her library and closed the door. Half an hour later they met in the foyer. Cornelius was on his leash and Flora had a folder full of papers. Rebecca looked at the papers curiously. Some of their edges were yellowed and tattered as if they were very old.

"Is that a map of the island in case we get lost?" Rebecca asked.

Flora smiled. "No."

She offered no explanation and Rebecca paused only a second before she launched into companion mode. "Ready for our adventure?" She dangled the set of keys and Cornelius yapped and hopped around. Smart dog that he was, he knew keys meant a car ride.

With Flora and Cornelius in the backseat and the windows down, Rebecca felt like a genuine chauffeur. She gingerly pressed the clutch and changed gears, anxious to make a good impression and let Flora know that she and her car were in good hands.

"You don't have to drive parade speed just because I'm old," Flora said. "I like the wind in my hair, and Cornelius is delighted."

Rebecca sped up and drove the road that circled the island until she got to the edge of downtown, where a small public library sat between the road and the lake. It looked as if it had once been a summer cottage, and its ornate woodwork—painted purple and yellow—made it seem like something straight out of a storybook.

"I like the new colors," Flora said. "It used to be blue and gray, but this is much more inviting and whimsical."

Rebecca parked and Cornelius hopped over the seat and sat in her lap. She scratched his ears. "Are you allowed in there, buddy?"

"Would you mind staying out here with him? I won't be too long," Flora said.

"Sure," Rebecca replied. "We can wander

on the beach for a minute if he gets tired of being in the car."

Flora took the folder of papers with her into the library. Was she planning to donate them as island history? Give them to someone? "What's in the folder, Cornelius?" she asked as the little dog sat in her lap and looked over the steering wheel. "And do you know anything about Flora recently changing her will? What will happen to her company?" Cornelius licked Rebecca's face and returned to watching seagulls through the windshield.

After only fifteen minutes Flora came out of the library with her folder and an additional envelope. It was a large mailing envelope, but Rebecca couldn't see what was written on it.

"Post office next," Flora said. "I have to see if my old friend Bertie King is still there."

"He is. I met him right after we got to the island and I had to pick up some packages. Nice man."

"I went to the island school with his father and he's always been just like him," Flora said. "Serious about his work and in love with this island."

"I can't blame him," Rebecca said. "I think I'm falling in love with Christmas Island."

She backed out of the parking space without stalling the engine and cruised downtown. It wasn't far, and if it was just her she would have walked. However, she didn't want to ask Flora to walk, and Flora seemed determined to handle whatever business she had at the post office herself.

What was in the envelope? Had she used the copier at the library and was she mailing those copies somewhere? But to whom?

"You didn't find any good books while you were there?" Rebecca asked.

"I wasn't looking. And besides, you've seen the library at my house. I've honestly read all of those books at least once, but it was such a long time ago that it seems like I'm reading them for the first time this summer."

There was silence for a moment as Rebecca drove slowly, watching out for pedestrians and families on bicycles. She passed the ferry docks, but the May ferry was out. Was Griffin in the pilothouse today or was he at the hotel? Did he ever take a day off?

"I'm having the most wonderful summer," Flora said from the backseat. "I wish summer lasted more than one hundred days, but I guess that's what makes each day so precious."

Rebecca felt a tug of sadness at the thought of time passing—perhaps too quickly for Flora, who'd already seen so many years. For herself she didn't think much about time or goals. She'd learned to live in the present without looking too far ahead, even though her job at Winter Industries was the best thing that had ever happened to her, and she hoped for long years of employment there.

Mercifully, two parking spots were open in front of the post office, and Rebecca parallel-parked squarely in the middle of them.

"Smart choice," Flora said. "It'll be easy to get out. I won't be long."

She again left Cornelius in the car with Rebecca and went inside. She didn't take the folder, just the mailing envelope. Rebecca turned her head and saw the folder lying on the backseat. It was incredibly tempting. All she had to do was lean over the seat, flip the cover open and take a quick peek at the contents.

But she couldn't. Being on the island under a false pretense had seemed okay initially because she was doing it to protect the interests of Winter Industries and, perhaps, Flora herself. Now that she knew and liked Flora, snooping in her business made Rebecca feel queasy. If she was going to find out anything, she was going to do it honestly, however that would work. Flora deserved respect for her private business, no matter how much Rebecca wanted to fulfill her own responsibility to the company.

CHAPTER EIGHT

"Now that you're so good with my car," Flora said after breakfast, "would you run down to the docks this afternoon and pick up my visitor?"

"Of course," Rebecca said. "Who am I picking up?"

"My nephew."

At first, Rebecca thought Flora might mean Griffin or Maddox May, whom she informally called her nephews, but there was no reason they'd need a ride from the docks. She quickly realized the visitor must be Alden Winter, who was only distantly involved in the running of Winter Industries but was known to be the only living descendent of Flora Winter's. Of course, Rebecca only knew that because she worked for the company, a fact known by only one other person on the island, Camille Peterson.

"His name is Alden and he isn't a lot of

fun," Flora said. "But I can count on him to be exactly the same way he always was."

Rebecca didn't think that sounded like a ringing endorsement of any human. She had never heard much about Alden, since he took a hands-off approach and was reputed to be mostly interested in horse racing and a casino he'd invested in. How close was he with Flora and did he visit her frequently?

"Will he be wearing a sign that says I'm Alden and I'm not much fun?" Rebecca asked.

Flora laughed. "He won't need a sign. He'll be dressed like he's going to a business meeting and he'll be coming alone."

"No family?"

Flora shook her head. "I had my housekeeper get a room on the third floor ready for him. He can have that floor all to himself for the two weeks he's staying."

"That's nice," Rebecca said. "Having family for a long visit." She felt a little twinge of jealousy about sharing the breakfast and lunch table with someone else because she'd started to love the time she spent with Flora. The older woman had funny stories and a warm heart, even though she was a lot more clearheaded than people realized and she tended to cut right to the core of a subject.

Rebecca was starting to wonder how long she could persuade Flora that she was just a friend of Camille's. Perhaps a visitor would be a good distraction, and his visit might shed light on the rumors that Flora had revised her will.

"He'll be on the one o'clock ferry," Flora said. "But don't let him drive my car. He treats everything like it's a racehorse."

When Rebecca drove to the downtown dock after lunch, she saw exactly what Flora had meant. A man dressed in a pin-striped oxford stood alone, arms crossed, on the dock. Unlike the tourists around him who were juggling kids, bikes and backpacks, Alden looked as if he was waiting for a taxi on a city street. And the taxi would be taking him someplace he didn't want to go.

Why was he here?

Rebecca parked the Bentley and as soon as Alden saw the car, he strode toward it, wheeling a large black suitcase behind him. Rebecca opened her door and stood, but she didn't relinquish her place by the driver's door. Just in case Alden had any ideas about popping behind the wheel.

As she waited for Alden, Rebecca looked over at the ferry that was tied to the dock, engines running. Griffin waved to her from the wheelhouse. She gave him a little wave and thought about how much had changed in just two weeks. When she'd arrived on the island, she was the stranger in town. But now she had two jobs, some new friends, had been to a locals' bar and was the designated pickup person for a visitor.

Her fitting in had been sudden, swift and… painless. Rebecca was a master at adapting to new places even though it was a reluctant skill. To find a permanent center of belonging—that was her idea of happiness. And she'd found it with Winter Industries. A good reason to be nice to Alden Winter, who would likely be taking it over.

"My aunt said she would send someone," Alden said. "Can you open the trunk?"

Rebecca realized she had no idea how to open the trunk on the vintage car. There was no button on the dashboard marked *trunk*.

"You need the keys," Alden said. "What happened to her usual driver?"

Rebecca took the keys from the ignition. "I'm Rebecca Browne. I'm not her official driver. I'm more of a summer companion. Her usual driver doesn't like boats, so he has the summer off."

Alden looked at Rebecca for the first time, as if he'd finally decided she was worth possibly knowing. "So you're staying at the Winter Palace?"

She nodded and tossed him the keys so he could open the trunk himself. Although he smiled politely, she suspected he was sizing her up. After he stowed his suitcase, she held her hand out for the keys.

"I could drive," he said.

"No, thanks," she said cheerfully. "I need the practice."

His polite expression faded and Rebecca suppressed a smile as she got back in the driver's seat. At that moment she was very glad Griffin had taught her to drive the car. As she pulled onto the island road, she wondered if Griffin knew Alden.

"Have you visited Christmas Island often?" she asked.

"When I can. It's not fun in the winter unless you really love Christmas. And my business interests usually keep me busy during the summer."

"But you made time this summer for your aunt," Rebecca said. "That's really nice."

Alden leaned an elbow out the open window. "How is the old gal?"

"She's wonderful," Rebecca said truthfully. "She gets along better than people who are only half her age. I hope I'm just like her when I'm eighty-five."

Alden seemed to be weighing her words in the silence that followed, and Rebecca was glad the drive wasn't very long. She glanced over. He was probably in his mid- to late-forties. Well dressed. Carrying about thirty extra pounds. While not exactly unpleasant, he didn't exude any of Flora's warmth or wit. Perhaps keeping his distance was his way of navigating the world. Rebecca could sympathize with that strategy. She'd tried living like that in her early teens, even though she wasn't very good at sealing off her heart. Each time, eventually, the kindness of her temporary family worked its way into her heart and moving on was tougher as a result.

She could already feel herself getting attached to Flora, Christmas Island and the new friends she'd met, and the feeling was dangerous but hard to resist.

"I suppose her dog is still alive?" Alden asked, interrupting her thoughts. His tone was bored, as if he didn't really care about the answer one way or the other.

"Cornelius is a sweet little dog," Rebecca said. "Immensely loyal."

"That's what Aunt Flora always says about him. I have no idea how old that dog is."

"Twelve," Rebecca said. "His birthday is next week, though, and he'll be thirteen."

"We'll have to have a party," Alden said drily.

"Already planning it. And now that you're here, you get to attend the party. I think there will be cake for the humans, and Cornelius is getting a special box of treats from my friend Camille's candy store on the island."

Alden didn't answer, but Rebecca decided to fill him in on the party details anyway. He should know how important the dog was to his aunt. She slowed and turned onto the road leading up to the Winter Palace. "Island Candy and Fudge is adding an entire line of pet treats to their inventory, and Cornelius got to be an early tester. He chose the Kringle Jingle with peanut butter flavoring."

Alden sighed.

"I love the Christmas theme everywhere," Rebecca added. "I can't wait for Christmas in July."

"Ho, ho, ho," he said quietly as Rebecca parked.

Flora waited at the door of the house with

Cornelius tucked under one arm. Rebecca watched as Alden approached his aunt. Instead of a hug, Flora tilted her cheek up for a kiss, which Alden bestowed on her. Cornelius squirmed and Rebecca thought she heard an uncharacteristic growl from the little dog as she opened the trunk. The black suitcase looked heavy, and Rebecca decided against wrangling it. She wasn't Alden's chauffeur. If Flora—or even Alden—had asked, she would have hauled it up to the third floor, but Flora and Alden seemed to have forgotten all about her as they talked while Cornelius ran a circle around their feet, yapping and putting up his little paws for attention.

CHAPTER NINE

THE NEXT EVENING, between requests from patrons in the crowded bar, Rebecca waved Griffin over to the piano.

"Flora asked me to invite you to the house tomorrow night," she said.

"Okay." His tone was half yes and half question.

"She's having a little birthday party."

"I thought her birthday was on the Winter Solstice?"

"You know her birthday?" Rebecca asked, genuinely surprised and also impressed. Maybe Griffin was closer to Flora than she realized.

"When she lived on the island year-round, she used to have a big party at her house for the brave islanders who stayed all winter. She'd have the driveway all the way up to the Winter Palace lined with luminaries in honor of the longest night of the year. Back when I was a kid, it seemed like we were going to a magical castle."

Rebecca imagined the scene, and a wave of longing washed over her. Wouldn't it be wonderful to spend winter on the island and be part of celebrations like that?

"I sort of miss those parties," he said. "So is it your birthday tomorrow?"

She shook her head. "Cornelius."

Griffin laughed. "Are you sure she isn't just looking for an excuse to have a party?"

"Could be. But she's been planning this for at least a week. Got him special gifts and treats and everything."

"Do I have to bring a gift?" Griffin asked.

"We don't want to spoil him. Just show up and bring your brother."

"As long as the party's over by the time it's dark," Griffin said. "Tomorrow night is the full moon. A bunch of us islanders have a summer tradition of doing a loop around the island on our bikes when there's a full moon."

"No lights?"

"Don't need them if you've lived here long enough."

And just like that, Rebecca felt like an outsider.

"You should join us," Griffin said.

Had her face betrayed her? Rebecca opened her piano book and flipped to a random page. She didn't want Griffin to invite her along because he felt obligated.

Great. The page she opened was the old Frank Sinatra song "Fly Me to the Moon." When she glanced up, Griffin was looking at the song title and smiling.

"Come along with us," he said.

"I'm not sure I could find my way in the dark."

Griffin leaned an elbow on the piano. "You could stick close to me."

Even though it was a bad idea to seek out a situation where she would be sticking close to Griffin, it might also be an opportunity to meet more people on the island. Could someone at the party or in the bicycle group provide the clues about Flora's plans she was looking for? Snooping was not coming naturally to her, but joining a moonlit bike ride might help her investigation. It was worth a try.

GRIFFIN HAD NEVER been to a dog's birthday party, but he couldn't argue with the quality of the food and drinks. And the company. Flora had invited a select group of people from the island. His brother Maddox, Camille

Peterson and her parents and sisters, Violet Brookstone and her brother Ryan, the island police chief and Bertie the postmaster. All people whose families had associated with Flora's over the years. Griffin knew and liked them all, but it was Rebecca Browne who made his heart hitch when she entered or left the room. As cohost, she was busy making sure the drinks were full and the guests had a place to sit.

He wanted to tell her to save some energy for the ten-mile ride around the island. In the dark it always seemed farther and it was a hot night with no wind. Already, his shirt clung to the back of his neck and made him feel hot all over.

"You'd think with a name like Winter Palace this place would be cooler," Maddox said as he came over and handed Griffin a cold drink.

"I'll turn on the ceiling fans," Rebecca said from behind them. "Flora doesn't mind the heat, which is why she's never added air-conditioning, but tonight it's a bit…close in here."

Close was a good way to describe it. The guests were assembled in the large living room where a baby grand piano sat in a place of honor near the windows. Griffin had seen it many times, and he'd even heard Christmas music played on it at those long-ago Winter Solstice parties. Who had been playing at the time? As a kid he'd never noticed or realized how much talent and work it probably required.

He glanced over at Rebecca. She could probably make that piano sound like magic, just as she did in the hotel bar. Business had picked up already and some guests had outright said they were drinking at the hotel bar instead of going down the street because they liked the pretty piano player.

She was pretty. And smart. But she was also a mystery that he shouldn't take time to unravel—not with two businesses to run and the summer days already flying past.

The sun was lingering close to the horizon, hovering over the lake with its last colors. It would be at least an hour until full dark, when the group of younger guests would leave on their traditional ride. Griffin had borrowed a nice bicycle from his friend Mike at the rental downtown, and he'd even installed a light on the handlebars. He hadn't told Rebecca yet, but it would be a nice surprise.

"I'm ready for cake," Flora said. "Alden, would you bring it out and put it on the table?"

Alden Winter, a man whom Griffin had seen a number of times over the years but never really known, went into the kitchen, his shoulders slumped as if he was being sent on a miserable errand. Griffin wanted to laugh. He'd have to ask Rebecca her impression of the visiting nephew who was almost certainly heir to a large fortune. Maybe being tasked with presenting a dog's birthday cake to a room full of islanders was the price Alden had to pay.

"And Griffin and Maddox, you two come sit by me," Flora said.

Griffin and his brother crossed the room. When Alden came back in with the cake, he noticed right away and glowered in their direction. Flora's nephew probably thought he should be the one invited to sit with Flora, but Alden had seldom visited his aunt and seemed like a fish out of water.

"Remember when you were little and you used to come to my Winter Solstice birthday parties?" Flora asked. She put one hand on Griffin's knee and one on his brother's as he sat on her other side.

"You had the best food," Maddox said.

"It was the cake I remember," Griffin said.

"You're the only person I know who had a tiered cake for her birthday every year. When I was really young I thought you were getting married every year because it looked like a wedding cake."

Flora laughed. "I had to have a tall cake because I had so many dear friends I wanted to invite for a slice. And I was always amazed that you boys never knocked it over as rambunctious as you were."

"Our parents gave us a lot of warnings," Griffin said. "And you always wisely set out sleds for us so we could go outside and take advantage of your hill."

Flora sighed. "I have such happy memories of you both and all the summers and winters I've spent on Christmas Island. I'll let you in on a little secret. I'm not sure if today is Cornelius's exact birthday, but I wanted a good reason to invite you here and have a party. Summer nights are just as precious as winter ones."

Griffin put an arm around her. "We're glad to be here. And glad you're spending the summer."

Maddox popped a kiss onto her cheek and she laughed.

"And now I'm ready for a song," Flora said. "Rebecca?"

Rebecca walked to the piano and sat on the bench. "Would you like a traditional birthday song or something nice like 'Who Let the Dogs Out'?" she asked.

Everyone laughed and Flora shook her head, grinning at Rebecca.

Rebecca beckoned for Cornelius to join her at the piano, and the little dog ran over. She lifted him onto the seat next to her. Cornelius had a reputation for being fussy with his affections, not unlike his owner, and he was impressed that the dog considered Rebecca a worthy companion. She had that effect on a lot of people, he thought. He tugged at the neck of his T-shirt. Man, it was hot.

When the birthday party finally concluded, Camille and Griffin helped Rebecca take everything to the kitchen and load the dishwasher. She covered the cake and put it in the refrigerator. "I chilled bottles of water earlier today," she said. "I thought it would be a good idea for our ride."

"I'm glad you decided to go along," Griffin said. Camille grabbed two bottles and left the kitchen, and Griffin was alone with Rebecca. She'd pulled her hair into a ponytail and she wore a bright green tank top. "And you wore glow-in-the-dark clothes."

She laughed. "I wanted someone to be able to find me in case I get lost. I bought this downtown today. Can you believe it was on the clearance rack at one of the souvenir shops?"

"Looks like a million bucks," Griffin said. "And you won't get lost if you stick with me. With us," he added. "We've never lost anyone and we've been doing this since we were about ten or twelve."

"I have some catching up to do," Rebecca said.

"Did you have crazy neighborhood traditions growing up?"

She hadn't said much about her life outside the island or her family. Griffin was tempted to ask Camille, who had been Rebecca's college roommate, but somehow it seemed dishonest to go behind her back.

"No," she said. "At least not that I know of." She turned away and picked up the bottles of water, handing him two. "I usually had my nose in a book or my fingers on a piano, I guess," she said. "We better get out there before they leave without us."

"They'll wait," Griffin said, but Rebecca was already heading through the back kitchen door toward steps that led to the lower driveway.

CHAPTER TEN

REBECCA APPROACHED the group of islanders standing near their bicycles with Griffin close behind her. There were only two bikes not claimed, but neither was the ancient clunky one Rebecca had been riding since she'd been on the island.

"I borrowed you something nicer for the evening," Griffin said. "From my friend Mike Martin, who has a rental downtown."

She approached the speedy-looking red bike. "It has a headlight," she said.

Griffin smiled. "Thought it might help since it's your first time doing this. You don't have to use it unless you want to."

"Thank you," she said. She realized everyone was looking at her and Griffin, and she felt a little embarrassed at the attention. She wasn't accustomed to people making a fuss over her or even noticing her.

"Rats," Camille said, smacking herself on the side of the head. "I forgot to put the samples of my new peppermint fudge in the box of treats I brought. I was going to ask your opinions when we got to our halfway snack spot."

"There's a designated snack spot?" Rebecca asked, grateful that her friend had drawn everyone's attention. After living together during college, Camille knew that Rebecca hated being the center of attention. It had taken an entire semester, but when Rebecca had finally opened her heart to Camille, they'd shared everything. Although Rebecca realized now that there were many things about Camille's childhood on the island she didn't know. It was as if the island was another world that outsiders might not understand. The inclusion of Maddox in the biking party also made her wonder what was behind Camille's ambivalence toward him. Did they have a past? And why had Camille never told her about it?

"An abandoned winery," Camille said. "It burned down about a hundred years ago, but the stone walls are, creepily, still standing. Locals go there to smoke, hang out, or scare each other with ghost stories, but there's also a nearby park with a bathroom and a vending machine. We rough it in style on this island."

Rebecca stowed her water bottle in the carrier on her bike, tested the headlight just to make sure she knew how to turn it on and straddled the bike. Violet and her brother led the pack down the hill to the island's perimeter road, and Rebecca and Griffin were at the back. Rebecca squeezed her brake handles experimentally, but then let them out and coasted down the hill. It was freeing but also scary because the faint glimmer of light on the horizon was blocked by thick trees.

A full moon suddenly lit the sky, and Rebecca chanced a look up even though she was afraid to take her eyes off what little road she could see ahead of her. A small cloud had passed by the moon but now the light was unobscured. When she looked back at the road, it seemed a bit brighter.

Growing up moving from house to house, she'd never owned a bicycle until she bought a used one during college. Residents of Christmas Island seemed as natural on a bike as on their own two feet, and already Rebecca thought her calves and legs were getting some muscle.

Living on the island for the summer felt so right. She was committed until Labor Day, but her company CFO had told her she was welcome to leave early if she found out what they needed to know about Flora's will. A shiver of guilt went through her. What was she doing making friends when she was really here to spy on a sweet old lady?

She should have said no to the assignment, but it was hard to regret with the wind in her hair and a handsome man next to her in a pack of friendly bikers. If she could gracefully get through the summer, watch over Flora and protect her interests, and return to her desk at Winter Industries, this would be a lovely summer memory she would take with her.

It seemed as if only minutes had passed when the group slowed and several of them switched on their headlights to illuminate a path as they pulled off the road.

"Are we sure we even care about these snacks after all the food at the party?" Camille asked.

"Let's see what you brought," Violet said. "I want to keep my options open."

They stowed their bikes and sat around a long picnic table. An outline of the ruined winery loomed against the starry sky, and Rebecca shivered. Griffin sat next to her with Maddox and Violet. Camille, her sister Cara and Violet's brother sat on the other side of the table with Jordan, a man the same age as Maddox, who worked at the Great Island Hotel.

"That was a great party," Violet said. "I remember going to the Winter Palace when I was little and thinking that the old lady there must be a fairy godmother."

Ryan groaned. "You just don't want to say that in front of our parents."

"He's right," Violet said. "One year we were in the car on the way home from the Winter Solstice party, and my brother made the mistake of telling our parents he wished we were rich like Flora Winters."

"It didn't go well," Ryan said.

"Wait," Cara Peterson said. "You guys aren't rich? Goodbye, Ryan. I'm never hanging out with you again."

Ryan laughed. "I got a lecture all the way home about judging people and making assumptions."

"And," his sister added, "about what it means to be rich. We got the standard lesson about having a loving family and how that was worth more than millions."

"It is," Griffin said.

"I know," Ryan replied. "And you know

what's funny? I'd never realized Flora Winter was a millionaire before that. I just thought she was rich."

"She was really generous to my grandmother when she needed a wheelchair ramp on her house," Jordan said. "We never officially knew Flora had paid for it, but we suspected when my dad overheard one of the workers talking. My parents wrote her a thank-you note anyway, even if she never acknowledged it was her. We aren't the only ones on the island with a story like that."

Rebecca took a piece of maple fudge from the box in the middle of the table. It was delicious and sweet and the maple flavor mingled with the night air and the scent of pine trees.

"I always thought she was lonely," Cara said. "I'd ride my horse past that house and see her sitting by herself outside. Of course, there were times I envied her because there was way too much drama in our house with Chloe as an older sister."

Camille laughed. "You're not wrong about the drama."

"Our parents always kind of watched over her," Griffin said. "Mom would bake bread or cookies, and me and Maddox would get the job of delivering it. Aunt Flora would invite us in and we'd get to play with her dog. She always had a little dog. I think Cornelius is probably her fifth one."

"I love Cornelius," Rebecca said. "He's a lot like her. Curious and perceptive, and once he decides he likes you he's very lovable."

"I think Flora likes you a lot," Camille said.

"I hope so," Rebecca said.

Griffin's arm brushed hers and he spoke quietly. "How could she not?"

Rebecca swallowed. Being included in the group of friends was like feeling warm and cold at the same time. They were so genuine and kind, but how would they all feel if they knew she was spying on the sweet old lady they'd admired all their lives?

After they finished the fudge and cookies and shared a few more stories about growing up on the island, the group got back on their bikes for the second half of the trek around the island.

"Is this speed okay?" Griffin asked as they rode in the back of the pack "We do a lot of biking on this island, but it's easy to forget some people have normal lives."

Rebecca laughed. "Maybe this is normal."

"I've always wondered," he said. "In the darkness everything is simple and all you have to watch out for is the bike ahead of you and toads."

"Toads?"

"They love to come out at night and cross the road, hunting for bugs. They don't all make it, of course, because there are some cars out here. And if you're not expecting them, you might crash your bike."

"Thanks for the warning," Rebecca said. She switched on her headlight and angled it down so it would illuminate the road several feet ahead of her. "Just for a little while," she said. "I don't want you to think I don't appreciate your thoughtfulness in borrowing me this bike and headlight."

He laughed, and the sound meshed with the waves caressing the rocks as the bikers finished their ten-mile trip around Christmas Island. Rebecca heard snippets of conversation about Camille's older sister's wedding, which was coming up at Christmastime. Griffin rode next to her, close enough that she could reach out and touch him for reassurance if she needed to.

She didn't need to. Rebecca was accustomed to fending for herself. However, each day on Christmas Island made her feel less alone, much as she had when she first joined

Winter Industries as an intern. The delicious sense of belonging was worth long days and unexpected assignments—even ones like being a companion to a grand old lady. She had to play the part and stay close enough to Flora and her acquaintances so she could help safeguard the older woman's property and interests, but there wasn't a person in the moonlit biking group who seemed like a threat.

Rebecca turned off her headlight.

CHAPTER ELEVEN

"You were quiet on the bike ride last night," Griffin said. He and his brother stood in the pilothouse on the ferry, which was secured at the mainland dock. It was two hours before their first run of the day and the sun had just lit the sky in the east. Griffin watched the gauges on the boat's dashboard while a mechanic went through the hydraulic inspection. Maddox stood, arms crossed, looking out at the lake.

"I had a lot to think about. Jennifer texted yesterday and told me she was getting remarried."

Griffin took a moment to absorb that before he responded. He'd always thought it was a mistake when his brother married Jennifer at just eighteen, but Maddox had believed he was doing the right thing. Their son had been born just months after the wedding, and the adorable boy had seemed to make up for the fact that his parents had married too young and too fast. Maddox had made a lot of sacrifices but had also grown up a lot.

"I guess that's good for her," Griffin said neutrally, waiting for his brother and best friend to share his feelings. Although Griffin was two years older and considered himself the wiser and steadier brother, he hadn't had the same experiences—having a wife and child—as his brother. Griffin had hardly even dated. He'd used all his energy to keep the family business going.

Things had changed, and the May brothers were working out their new normal of running two businesses and keeping their heads above water. Together.

"How does this affect Ethan?" Griffin asked. His nephew had become an important part of his life, and he couldn't imagine the boy going far away to live with a new stepfather.

"It'll be okay," Maddox said. "I think. The guy she's marrying is building a house right outside of town." On the island, Lakeside was known, unofficially, as "the mainland" because it was a medium-size town that offered basically anything the island didn't. It had supermarkets, a mall, a sporting goods store, a car dealership and a home improvement store.

Residents of Christmas Island went there to shop and stock up. Lakeside also had a tourist strip of souvenir shops and quick-serve restaurants near the ferry dock, and inexpensive chain hotels spread out along the shore.

Griffin breathed a sigh of relief. "Glad Ethan won't be going far."

"I wouldn't have agreed to that," Maddox said. "I have rights in the custody agreement."

The boy typically spent weekends and several week-long visits with Maddox, and Griffin loved having Ethan around, showing him the ropes on the ferry and playing with him in the downtown park. Someday, he hoped to have kids of his own. When he had time.

"Looks good," Maddox said, pointing at the gauge Griffin was supposed to be watching. "Glad one of us is paying attention."

Griffin laughed. In the past he'd been the responsible one. He'd been the one paying attention to every sound of the ferry's engine and every dime in the business accounts. Lately, it had been nice sharing some of the responsibility with his brother now that Maddox had recovered from his early marriage, unexpected fatherhood and then divorce a few years later. Tough years had tested Maddox, and he'd survived. Could the two of them pull off running both a ferry and hotel to ensure a solid future for themselves and the next generation?

"What happened when you took Rebecca home last night?" Maddox asked.

"I dropped her off, loaded both bikes on my golf cart and went home."

"And?"

"And nothing. She's a nice girl, but she's only here for the summer babysitting Aunt Flora."

"Who doesn't seem like she needs a babysitter if you ask me," Maddox said.

Griffin shook his head. "Maybe there's something we don't know. She could have serious health problems and she's the type who wouldn't tell anybody."

"So you're not interested in Rebecca?"

"I'm not interested in complicating my life any more than it already is," Griffin said.

Maddox slapped him on the back. "I guess you're the smarter brother, just like everyone says."

Griffin laughed. The previous evening with Rebecca at his side had made him wish he didn't have a ferry line, hotel and dozens of employees he was responsible for. It would have been nice to be…irresponsible. To do what he wanted, what felt right, for the first time in years. Instead, he'd been courteous and friendly to Rebecca. Ensured her safety on the bike ride and taken her home.

It had been the smart thing to do and just what everyone expected of him, but Rebecca made him want to do something unexpected…like kiss a beautiful woman under the stars.

CHAPTER TWELVE

"WHAT DO YOU think of my nephew?" Flora asked Rebecca at breakfast.

Rebecca poured a fresh glass of orange juice for Flora. "I think he seems very...hard-working. He was working on his laptop in the library last night after I got home from my moonlight bike ride."

Flora laughed. "Not Alden. My real nephew."

Rebecca cocked her head and waited.

"Griffin May, and his brother, too, of course."

"They're not really your nephews," Rebecca protested, hoping to avoid the question. Had Flora noticed something between her and Griffin?

"Not by blood, but I've felt like their honorary great-aunt all their lives. They're really sweet and wonderful boys."

Rebecca went over to the toaster and took her time spreading jam on two pieces of wheat toast. She kept her back to Flora as she processed the older woman's question.

What did she think of Griffin May? He was attractive, thoughtful, hardworking and…the flutter in her chest reminded her there was something else that was hard to define with words over the breakfast table.

"That's a long silence and a lot of strawberry jam on that toast," Flora said.

Rebecca turned to face her employer, whose grin was exaggerated by her many wrinkles.

"I like jam," Rebecca said. She sat down and took a big bite of her toast. She swallowed and then said, "I bought this jar downtown and I swear it's better than anything they sell on the mainland."

Flora waited, and Rebecca immediately realized she was outclassed by the wise and patient older lady.

"That's not a metaphor or double meaning," Rebecca said, laughing.

"Darn. I was hoping you and Griffin might hit it off."

"He's very nice," Rebecca said.

"He's a prize. I can't believe he's still single, but he's given up a lot for that ferryboat."

Rebecca sipped her coffee and considered asking Flora for details. Had Griffin given up college to come home and run the busi-

ness? Why? If she asked Flora, she'd probably find out quite a bit about Griffin, but she
would also run the risk of appearing to be interested. She was only on the island for the
summer, and her work would certainly suf-
fer if she let her mind get clouded by a summer romance—especially when Griffin was
technically her employer at the hotel. Nope,
she said to herself. It wasn't a good idea to ask
Flora questions, especially when the memory
of Griffin riding alongside her in the dark
was still fresh in her mind. When they'd arrived back at the Winter Palace, there had
been a moment where she'd thought he might
kiss her...

She shoved that memory right out of her
head.

"I'm thinking of preparing some fresh
music for this week at the bar. Any suggestions?" Rebecca asked. "Maybe something
classical?"

Flora smiled. "Love songs."

Rebecca picked up a prescription bottle
from the breakfast table and shook it. "Were
you supposed to get your heart pills in the
mail?" she asked. "I thought you mentioned
it last week."

"There was a mix-up at my doctor's office and they mailed them to my permanent address. The pharmacy at Lakeside has my information and they can send them over on the ferry tomorrow."

"But you're out of these," Rebecca said.

"I won't die without them for one day."

Rebecca glanced out the kitchen windows, which had a partial view of the lake. Blue sky and a lake so flat it probably functioned as a mirror greeted her. Griffin had offered her a free ride on the ferry anytime, and she hadn't left the island since she'd arrived.

"I could go pick them up today," Rebecca said. "I'm not playing until seven tonight, and you couldn't ask for a more perfect day."

Flora shook her head. "I don't want to put you to the trouble. I could always send Alden if I was desperate. He's usually looking for a way to prove he gives a darn about me."

"I'm sure he does," Rebecca said. "You're his only aunt."

"Unlike being the queen, being the *only* doesn't necessarily mean much. Unless, of course, you hold the keys to the family fortune."

Rebecca picked up plates and silverware and carried them to the dishwasher. Would Flora reveal any information about her will and whether she'd changed it over the winter? If so, was Alden the former or the current beneficiary? Rebecca had talked with Jim Churchill early that morning and she'd heard the disappointment in his voice when she told him she hadn't found out anything. She wasn't just working for him. Winter Industries was Rebecca's future, too. As she put forks and knives in the silverware carriage tucked into the door of the dishwasher, Rebecca hoped her silence might inspire Flora to say something more about Alden.

"It's a beautiful day for a ferry ride," Flora said.

Rebecca turned. "You could come along if you like. And Cornelius."

"No, thank you. Now that I'm here, I intend to stay put for the summer. If you don't mind, I'd rather send you than Alden because I'm more assured it will get done correctly. And could you pick me up some of those rose bath beads I like from the drugstore?"

"Happy to. While I grab my purse and sweatshirt, you make a list of anything else you need," Rebecca said. She bounded down the hallway to her room, brushed her hair into a ponytail and grabbed a hoodie and her bag. If she hurried, she could make the nine o'clock ferry and spend a little time browsing the shops on the mainland with plenty of time for lunch before the return ferry.

IF HE WAS LUCKY, the day would be exactly as it appeared, Griffin thought. An uneventful Tuesday, perfect weather, six trips back and forth across the lake before he handed the ferry over to his brother for the final two runs of the evening. Maddox had his son for the day, and he was taking him horseback riding at one of the island stables. Griffin envied his brother the unconditional love of a child, but he didn't envy him the careful dance he did every day to juggle his relationship with his ex-wife and his allotted time with his son.

Family wasn't easy. Growing up, their parents had made running the ferry line look effortless, and Griffin and Maddox had both been lulled into thinking that deciding to take over the family business would be an obvious choice. When Griffin had walked away, choosing instead a college degree and a career in engineering that would likely take him away from the island, his parents had been disappointed but supportive.

If only they had been honest about the financial condition of the business and his father's oncology reports. The steady decline of his father's health, his mother's refusal to deal with the financially sinking ferry line and his brother's preoccupation with a new and unexpected family had added up to a nightmare that brought Griffin home from college after spring break of his sophomore year.

He watched a few islanders boarding the ferry for the run to the mainland. The first morning run usually included the island residents who worked in Lakeside and made the daily commute. Among the regulars, though, he saw someone with a springy step and a bobbing ponytail. What was Rebecca Browne up to?

His first thought was that Rebecca might be leaving, and the jolt it gave his heart scared him. He hardly knew her, but she was a fresh face on an island filled with tourists who'd be gone by nightfall or residents he'd known all his life. Rebecca was a novelty.

And it was new for him to be interested in someone who might take him away from the important work of the May business. He'd put his personal life on a big block of ice for years. Could that ice be melting?

He took a closer look. Rebecca had only a small purse with her. He knew exactly how much luggage she'd brought to the island, he thought with a smile, so it was obvious she wasn't making a permanent move. As he watched her, Rebecca looked up at the pilothouse and waved. Griffin lifted a hand, but he didn't leave his station. The ferry was scheduled to depart in two minutes, and he only got off schedule when the wind or waves forced him to.

People needed predictability and reliability in their lives, right down to the little things.

He sounded the horn and maneuvered the ferry away from the dock. Lakeside was on the horizon, an easy twenty-minute crossing on a beautiful day. One of his experienced and reliable deckhands could watch the wheel if Griffin wanted to run down on deck and say hello, but he only left the wheel if he absolutely had to.

It was his boat, and everyone on it was his responsibility.

After they got underway, Griffin picked up the microphone for the ship's loudspeaker. Rebecca stood below, leaning against a railing and watching the distant shoreline. He said one word over the speaker. "Rebecca."

She turned and looked up at his pilothouse. With her head tilted, she raised both hands in a questioning gesture. Griffin signaled for her to come up to the pilothouse, and Rebecca nodded. She bounded up the short flight of steps and paused at the door.

"I was afraid you were going to declare a man overboard like you did the first evening we met," she said.

Griffin laughed. "It was only half true. You were a woman overboard."

"And you didn't even give me a chance. You counted me out before I hit the water." Her hands were on her hips, but her grin told him she wasn't mad. In fact, it was fun, sharing the memory from three weeks ago. A lot had happened since that night, and Rebecca had become an interesting part of his world.

"Sorry," he said, "but I saw it coming."

"I should have, but I hate giving up."

"Me, too. Usually."

Rebecca glanced around the narrow pilothouse, where an instrument panel spread out below a wide window. "Am I violating any maritime laws by being in here?" she asked.

"Only if you try to hijack this vessel."

She laughed. "I'm no threat."

Except, perhaps, to his heart, Griffin thought. He cleared his throat. "Are you spending the day on the mainland?"

She shook her head. "Just a little shopping. Flora needs her prescription and a few other things, and she doesn't trust Alden to get it right."

Griffin took a moment to absorb that as he watched the lake ahead. Alden, the nephew who was seldom around and had taken no part in life on the island even when he was here. Alden was a mystery to him, but the man was Flora's only living relative.

"I shouldn't have said that," Rebecca said. "It sounded mean. It's just that you don't send a man to pick out your favorite rose-scented bath beads."

"I should be offended on behalf of all men for your lack of confidence, but I think you're not wrong," Griffin said.

Rebecca moved closer so she was almost centered in front of the wheel. "You have the best view from up here, and I suspect you have the best job on the island."

"I doubt that," Griffin said. "Even though I wouldn't trade it. But your summer job comes with a mansion to ramble around in and an old lady who likes you more than anyone else, except maybe her dog."

Rebecca laughed. "She likes you and your brother."

"Good."

"Are you close because you grew up here, or is there something else?" Rebecca asked.

The question caught him off guard and seemed almost intrusive, but Rebecca's expression was pure friendly interest. If she wanted to know, why didn't she just ask Flora?

"She was close to my grandfather," Griffin said. "That whole generation was close-knit, I guess. And since she didn't have any kids or grandkids, I think she takes an interest in the kids and grandkids of her childhood friends."

Rebecca nodded, gazing at the approaching shoreline. "We're getting close. I should go down so I'm not distracting you while you're docking the boat." She smiled. "I'll see you tonight at the bar if you stop in."

"I'll be there. Maddox is out with his son today, but he has the evening shift on the ferry."

"His son?"

Rebecca's look of pure surprise told him she hadn't heard a word about the boy. Hadn't her friend Camille spilled the whole story? Griffin was momentarily stunned, but he decided to stick with facts. "Ethan is six and Maddox shares custody with his ex-wife."

"Oh," Rebecca said. Griffin could practically see her wheels turning as she processed something. *Had* Camille said something about her long-ago romance with Maddox that had screeched to an ugly halt? "I'll see you tonight," she said abruptly, turning and leaving Griffin alone in the pilothouse to think about all the things on the horizon that people don't see.

CHAPTER THIRTEEN

GRIFFIN STOOD ON Holly Street in front of his hotel as the July Fourth parade went by in a blaze of color and noise. Next to Christmas and Christmas in July, Independence Day was the island's favorite reason to throw a party. Downtown buildings wore flag buntings, glittery strings of foil stars caught the sun as they wrapped around posts and railings, and every piece of emergency equipment crawled past with lights flashing and sirens blaring.

Pedestrians waved flags, and island kids lined up with their decorated bicycles to ride in the annual parade.

"Uncle Griffin!"

He waved to his nephew who, at six, was finally old enough to manage his own bicycle and join the pack. Griffin had helped Ethan and Maddox decorate the bike with red-and-blue plastic spoke covers on the wheels and glittery star garland wrapped around the handlebars. They'd met up early before the first ferry run in the garage of the small island home where Griffin and Maddox had grown up—a two-bedroom house that was a former summer cottage. The boys had shared a room until Griffin went off to college. When their father passed and their mother decided to move, Griffin handed over his share of the house to his brother so Ethan would have his own room when Maddox had custody.

Ethan was managing, Griffin thought, although the low speed was tough on a novice rider. As he watched his brother prowl anxiously along the parade route, keeping a close eye on his son, Griffin remembered riding in the parade with his brother while their parents watched from the sidelines. For a moment he missed his father with an almost painful streak of longing. It was true that his dad had faltered and even failed toward the end, but Griffin and his brother hadn't known why. When the cancer finally became unmanageable, it was too late for secrets and sparing anyone's feelings.

Across the street Rebecca sat in a decorated golf cart with Flora and Cornelius. The cart was decked out in red, white and blue, and both ladies had wide hats and bottles of water. Leave it to Rebecca to take good care of Flora. Griffin wondered where Alden was and if he would come downtown for the street party or the bonfire later that night. More important, would Rebecca come?

"I swear it's exactly the same every year."

Griffin turned and found Camille Peterson, still wearing a bright pink apron with her family's candy company logo printed on it. Her business was just two shops down from his hotel.

"That's the beauty of it," he said.

Camille laughed. "Sirens, bikes and the whopping ten members of the high school band."

"And Santa," Griffin added.

Santa, in his red velvet suit and bright white beard, was magnificently portrayed every year by Bertie King—the official island Santa—who took the job even more seriously than his work at the post office. His wife, Anna, dressed as Mrs. Claus. In December's holiday parade, they traveled over the snowy streets of Christmas Island in a horse-drawn sleigh, but for the July Fourth parade they rode on the back of a fire truck.

"If you're lucky," Camille said, "you may get to take over the job of playing Santa one of these years."

Griffin laughed. "I never thought about that as being one of the hazards of living on the island all my life."

Camille waved to Rebecca and Flora across the street, and Griffin saw Rebecca's gaze fall on him. She wore a bright blue tank top and her bare arms were tanned from the island sunshine. When she smiled, Griffin forgot all about the loud, glittering parade for a moment.

"Are you coming to the bonfire tonight?" he asked Camille.

She nodded. "I talked Rebecca into it also, in case you were wondering."

He glanced over and met her eyes without answering.

"She was worried about leaving Flora alone with Cornelius, who hates fireworks, but I talked her into it by reminding her that Alden is there, too, and I highly doubt he'll be at the bonfire."

"You don't think so?"

"Alden has spent other summers on the island and he never mixed with the locals. He seems about as much fun as a semiannual dental checkup," Camille said. "I'm not sure why he's spending a month here when my sisters tell me he hasn't shown up in at least four summers."

Griffin shrugged. "Maybe he wants to spend time with his aunt before it's too late." When his own father had passed, Griffin was glad he'd spent almost every day of his life with his dad, working the ferry alongside him and spending quiet winters on the island doing maintenance and getting ready for the next summer. Even though he'd left to go to college and planned a future different from his father's, Griffin had always kept a piece of his heart on the island. Now that he was back, he doubted he would ever leave. There was too much keeping him here, not just for himself, but his brother and his nephew, too.

"I'm sure you like having your friend here for the summer," Griffin said. "You went to college together, right?"

Camille nodded, but she kept her eyes on the parade. Griffin had so many questions about Rebecca, including what she usually did with her time and why a summer job on an island seemed like a good idea.

"It was nice of you to help her get the job with Aunt Flora," he said.

Camille laughed. "I owed her. I was a history major, but even history majors have to take some math and statistics courses. I would never have made it through without her help."

"Why doesn't she work in math or business instead of hiring herself out as a companion to lovable but feisty old ladies?" he asked.

Camille handed fliers advertising her family's candy business to people around them, and then she gave Griffin her attention. "Not everyone is as lucky as we are and can inherit semisuccessful family businesses." She grinned and raised her eyebrows to show she was joking, but her words also made it clear that Griffin wasn't going to get any information out of her.

"Back to work," she said and went through the front door of Island Candy and Fudge.

As soon as the parade passed by, Griffin hurried back to the ferryboat for the afternoon run. The timing of the parade gave him a chance to watch it, but like Camille, it was time to get back to work. He heard a golf cart beep at him and waved automatically before looking up and realizing it was Rebecca and Flora. Cornelius yapped at him, and the cart glided past with its flags waving in the island breeze.

FLORA HUNG UP her apron and settled into a kitchen chair while Rebecca packed her items for the bonfire and wiped down the counters.

Working together in the kitchen had been fun, and Rebecca let herself pretend that Flora was her grandmother passing down family recipes and making a holiday special. It was something she'd missed out on in her youth, but it was never too late to make memories. When summer ended, she would remember Flora pulling out a yellowed index card with a typed recipe that someone had added notes to. It was hard letting herself get close to someone, but Flora had begun to warm up to her and she didn't want to push the older lady away. Whether she knew it or not, Flora Winter had changed Rebecca's life.

"Are you sure you don't want to come?" Rebecca asked Flora. "You've gone to all this trouble helping me make strawberry tarts and holiday punch."

"I'm much too old to go to a beach bonfire," Flora said. "But I did eat a tart and I'm taking a glass of that punch with me to bed tonight."

"It's pretty sweet," Rebecca said. "I think I'll have to limit myself to two cups at the most."

"Who needs limitations? It's a holiday," Flora said.

Hours later, at dusk, Camille rolled up in

her family's three-row golf cart. "I drove the big wagon tonight," she said. Camille's younger sister, her older sister and fiancé, and Violet and her brother Ryan were already in the cart. "We don't all have to go home together tonight, but I can at least make sure we get there safely."

Rebecca hopped into the front seat with her thermal jug filled with Flora's secret recipe holiday punch. On her lap she balanced a foil tray filled with strawberry tarts. She tapped her feet nervously on the floor of the golf cart.

"I'm not that bad a driver," Camille said.

Rebecca laughed. They'd been friends so long they could read each other's moods with the barest of hints. "I'm just excited," Rebecca said. "Flora told me all about going to these bonfires when she was young, and she made it sound so fun and perfect."

"It really is fun," Camille said.

"I like…belonging," Rebecca admitted. She didn't have to explain her feelings to the one person on the island who knew her background.

"You never mentioned the May brothers in all the time we've spent together," she added. She didn't name Maddox specifically because she didn't want to make her friend uncomfortable. There was certainly something between them that had left a trail.

"Did I ever tell you much about the island locals?" Camille asked. "I think we were a lot more interested in college life, which meant partying for me and kicking all our butts academically for you."

"I had fun, too," Rebecca protested.

"But you also made every single penny of your scholarship money count by going to every class and acing every test."

"Well, I would have had no one to disappoint except myself," Rebecca said. The thought had been her constant companion through college. There was no one to go home to during campus breaks, no one asking her if she was keeping up her grades. She did it for herself.

"I would have been disappointed," Camille said. She reached out and slid her arm around Rebecca for a quick hug and then put both hands back on the wheel. "And I'm glad to see you having some fun this summer. Flora seems to really like you, and you've fit in with the rest of us like you've lived here all your life."

"I wish I had," Rebecca said. She shocked herself by saying the words aloud, but every island tradition had drawn her in and made her wonder how different her life would have been if she had grown up making fudge or selling boutique clothing on Christmas Island.

"You better wait until you endure Christmas in July before you fall in love with the island too much. It's an agony of endless Christmas music, cookies, parties and tourists wearing ridiculously hot Christmas sweaters in the summer heat. You might decide this island is bonkers and never want to visit me as I grow old and need a companion."

Rebecca laughed and leaned back into her seat as her friend drove the group to the remains of the winery, where the July Fourth bonfire was taking place. What would her new friends think if they found out she was here to snoop into Flora's business, even though she was trying to protect her? The more she knew Flora, the more she suspected the octogenarian didn't need protection, just as she didn't need Rebecca to turn out the lights and put Cornelius to bed.

When they arrived at the old winery, it was nearly dark and the stone remains of the long-ago burned building rose eerily against the last light in the sky. Rebecca shivered.

"It's not really haunted," a voice from the darkness said. Griffin took her jug of holiday punch. "And if you tell me this is Flora's secret recipe, you're going to have to help me hide it from everyone."

"We made it together in the kitchen," Rebecca said.

"So you know the secret now? I may never let you leave the island."

Rebecca shivered again, but not because of the spectral remains of the winery.

"Come over to the fire," Griffin said. "It's just getting going, but there won't be any shivering over there."

"Are you the official greeter?" Rebecca asked, curious about why he'd emerged from the darkness just as her group arrived.

He flicked on a large flashlight and pointed out the path. "Tree roots. Watch your step."

Good, Rebecca thought. Nothing special between her and Griffin. Just a safety-minded guy helping a group of his friends along the dark path to the bonfire. For all she knew, Griffin had dated some of the members of their group. He'd be the same age as Camille's older sister, and hadn't Violet said they'd grown up together? Maybe he was nice and attentive to everyone equally. A very respectable characteristic, Rebecca thought. No wonder her eighty-five-year-old employer preferred him to the other men on the island.

Rebecca scraped her foot over a rock and jiggled her foil pan of strawberry tarts, which rustled in the dark.

"I'll carry the food and you can take the flashlight," Griffin said. He pressed the flashlight into her hand, making sure to fold her fingers around its handle, and then took her tray. It was friendly, gentlemanly and...a bit unnerving. Rebecca resolved not to sit too near him at the fire because the memory of his fingers on hers would keep her plenty warm.

A waist-high stone wall inside the winery ruins served as a counter, and all the partiers placed their food on it. Green-and-red battery-powered lanterns lined the wall, and coolers filled with ice and drinks sat below, illuminated by lantern glow.

"The Christmas theme is everywhere, just like I warned you," Camille said as she took Rebecca's arm and guided her over to some wood benches that someone must have brought for the occasion.

"I like it," Rebecca said. "What exactly goes on at this event?"

Camille shrugged. "The same thing that goes on at every bonfire. We talk, tell some stories, catch up and have a few drinks. Sometimes somebody sings the fight song from Christmas Island High School, but the words usually get mixed up with Christmas songs and everyone gives up."

"Sounds great."

"I've missed it," Camille said.

In the warm glow from the fire, Rebecca realized something. Camille looked happy. Content. As if Christmas Island was where she belonged even though she joked about the traditions and sometimes grumbled about the long days selling candy and fudge. The island was part of her in a way that no place had ever been part of Rebecca except, to a degree, Winter Industries. Walking through the doors and taking the elevator up to her office every day for the past several years had given her the stability and belonging she'd always wanted.

Christmas Island felt the same way.

Rebecca looked across the fire where Griffin and Maddox were seated with some other men their age, give or take a few years. Most of the people gathered were in their twenties, before marriage and children meant a late night out wasn't the best way to spend a holiday. Griffin was looking at her, too. In the firelight his handsome face took on a clarity and warmth that made her insides feel squishy. He got up and carefully put a log on the fire. He had sturdy, large hands. Capable ones. Griffin was the kind of man who took care of people and things.

Her fingers tingled with the memory of him pressing the flashlight into her hands. Griffin May was a temptation she didn't have words for in her job description.

"He's coming over," Camille said quietly. "Ask him to bring us drinks so I don't risk giving up my seat."

Griffin stood between Rebecca and the fire, temporarily cutting the heat but definitely not letting her forget about it. "Can I get you anything from the coolers?" Griffin asked.

"That's nice of you to offer," Rebecca said.

He grinned. "Not really. If I offer to serve everyone else, I can keep all of Aunt Flora's special holiday punch for myself."

"Where did that go?" Rebecca said. "I haven't seen it since I got here."

Griffin laughed. "It might be stowed under

my seat over there. If you'd like some, you could come over and join me."

Rebecca looked at the two empty seats near Maddox May and stole a quick glance at Camille.

"Bad idea," Camille said. "I speak from experience." She looked up at Griffin. "Why don't you bring us both a soda instead?"

He nodded and his polite smile didn't waver.

"Trust me on this one," Camille said. "That stuff is dangerous."

"I assume you mean the punch," Rebecca said.

"Of course."

When Griffin returned with the drinks, he sat next to Rebecca. There were about fifteen people at the fire, and everyone seemed to know each other so well they talked easily with no awkward gaps. Rebecca already knew Camille's family, the May brothers, Jordan, and Violet and her brother, but she also met Mike Martin, who owned the island bike rental, and Sophie, whose father was the mayor of the island.

Violet leaned across Griffin and touched Rebecca's knee. "You should come back at Christmastime. We do a winter bonfire like this, and it's cold but fun."

"We have to use snowmobiles to get here," Camille said, "and one year Griffin and Maddox had a little misunderstanding with a tree on the way here."

"Maddox was driving," Griffin said. "And I did suggest wiping the snow off the headlight, but he knew better."

"We made it," Maddox said from across the fire. "We were just afraid to go home that night and tell Dad about the…uh…adjustment we'd made to the front of the snowmobile."

Rebecca laughed and was glad to see a genuine smile on Camille's face. When there weren't so many people around, she really needed to ask her friend what was in her history with Maddox.

As the coolers emptied, someone started singing. No one attempted the school song, but a few beloved Christmas carols were sacrificed. "Violet has a gorgeous voice," Rebecca leaned over and whispered to Camille. "And Jordan. They harmonize like they've done this before."

Camille rolled her eyes. "The cutest couple that never was," she said. "Everyone sees it but them."

Rebecca laughed and then turned back to the fire, which had burned down to coals but still radiated heat. A few others got up to leave and started gathering their coolers and empty food containers. Camille's older sister and her fiancé went over and helped clean up the food counter.

"Go ahead," Griffin told Rebecca and Camille. "Maddox and I will stay and make sure the fire's out."

Although he was staying, Griffin walked with Rebecca's group along the path to the parking area. He illuminated their way with the flashlight and walked right next to Rebecca. She felt a bit off balance, as if the stars overhead weren't lined up with the horizon and were instead spread out, having fun however they wanted.

"Wait," she said. "I felt like I was forgetting something. Flora's jug."

She heard Griffin chuckle next to her. "I did such a great job hiding it I forgot it, too. Walk back with me and we'll get it, but you'll find it's a lot lighter now."

While everyone else got settled in Camille's cart, Rebecca retraced her steps with Griffin at her side. He took the jug from under a bench and handed it to her.

"I'm glad you came tonight," he said, standing close in the darkness on the far edge of the firelight. "It was fun."

Rebecca nodded.

"I've been so busy the past few years, I almost forgot what it was like to let go and relax," he said. "You make me want to let down my guard, Rebecca."

She breathed in the scent of lake water that always seemed to cling to Griffin and moved closer to him. "I think I know what you mean," she said.

They stood together in silence, and Rebecca had almost resolved to walk away when Griffin touched her cheek. His fingers were gentle, but the sensation robbed her of any thoughts except how his lips would feel on hers.

He leaned in, and she was certain he was going to kiss her, but instead he switched on the flashlight and pointed it at the ground. "I'll walk you back."

On the ride back to the Winter Palace, the fresh lake air mixed with the campfire aroma that clung to their clothes. The stars lit the night sky, and Rebecca was certain she'd never had such a magical Fourth of July. Cool air brushed her arms and face, but thoughts of

Griffin and that moment where she thought he might kiss her kept her warm.

"We'll have to talk tomorrow," Camille said. "I'd like to hear about what happened when you went back for the empty container."

"Nothing," Rebecca said, but she knew her friend wouldn't be easily fooled.

Camille elbowed her and laughed, but she clearly wasn't going to press for details with a cart full of people, even if it was her family. She'd always respected Rebecca's privacy and feelings, which was why Rebecca trusted her.

When the golf cart dropped her off at the Winter Palace, it was nearly midnight, but lights were on in the library. Had Flora forgotten to turn them off? Rebecca felt a quiver of fear. Was everything okay? Was Flora all right?

She went through the kitchen entrance and stowed her tray and drink container in the sink and then strode straight to the library. Alden looked up from his laptop with surprise and annoyance on his face. He quickly changed his expression to the usual bland neutral one Rebecca had grown accustomed to. Again, she wondered why he was visiting his aunt. Was it possible he knew about Rebecca's mission and he was keeping an eye on her? The thought made a chill run down her spine.

"You're up late," Rebecca said, stopping on the threshold. "I saw the light, and—"

"You're up late, too."

"I went to a holiday bonfire with some of the locals," she replied, even though she didn't owe him an explanation. She didn't work for Alden, although someday she might. Was he really going to inherit Winter Industries? He wasn't supposed to, according to Flora's previous will, but something had changed.

"My aunt has always seemed quite fond of people on this island, but I've never seen what the fuss was about," Alden said. "But then, I've traveled all over the world. Maybe my circle is that much broader." He closed his laptop and reached for the light switch on the wall behind him.

"Do you travel for business?" she asked. As a lady's companion, she shouldn't know anything about the part of Winter Industries Alden had inherited from his father. According to office gossip, WinterSon Corporation was poorly run and nothing like Flora's part of the business, but was that Alden's fault?

"I doubt you'd know anything about my business," he said.

Rebecca backed up a step and said goodnight. If she asked any more questions, she risked blowing her cover. Alden seemed like a savvy person who didn't trust easily. What if he researched her? She should have used a false name now that she thought about it. If he found out she worked for Winter Industries, her summer sleuthing was over.

CHAPTER FOURTEEN

THE FERRY WAS battened down and tied up for the night, all the luggage carts secure, and his dockhands departed until the morning. For once, Griffin could go home at ten o'clock on a Friday night and put up his feet. In the past he would have retreated to his apartment, pored over the ticket sales from his dock manager, read through maintenance records and considered ways to make sure the ferry line stayed afloat.

But the night was so still he could hear piano music from the hotel bar across the street. He listened. The song was familiar, but he couldn't name it. Like Rebecca, it was enchanting, fascinating, but defied definition.

He should put in a few hours of paperwork, but sitting down with a drink and listening to Rebecca won out. The books would wait, but summer nights like this weren't unlimited. It was still early in July and the slow season was far on the horizon, but he knew how fast the warm summer evenings would fly.

Griffin stopped by the hotel's front desk, checked in with the manager and asked if there were any issues. The man had done an internship at the Great Island Hotel the previous year, and his experience was already paying off. Both Griffin and Maddox felt confident about the hotel's management, which was a relief because they couldn't hand over the ferryboats to anyone else. They were the primary two captains, committing them to daily runs back and forth to Lakeside.

He didn't look at Rebecca when he entered the bar…at least not directly. Her dress was a vivid blue, obvious even from the peripheral glance he took. He wanted to get a beverage, find a table and then let himself drink in the sight of Rebecca bringing music and business to his hotel bar.

A man leaned over Rebecca and spoke into her ear as she continued playing without missing a note. She smiled and nodded at him, and a moment later she transitioned into a popular Christmas song that was played way too often on the holiday radio network. He usually cringed when its familiar notes started, but Rebecca added something—

was it depth or had she somehow altered the rhythm?—and the song took on a life he'd never expected. It wasn't just tolerable, it was appealing. He doubted he would ever hear it again without remembering this moment with Rebecca at the baby grand.

Maybe he was just tired, but the long, cold winter suddenly seemed lonely in a way he'd never thought about. What would Rebecca be doing at Christmastime? Would she move on to a new job babysitting a wealthy lady or did she have an entire life he didn't know about waiting for her?

"You look serious," Hadley said as she refreshed his drink.

"Tired," he said, smiling.

"Did you stay out late at the July Fourth bonfire?" Without waiting for an answer, she dropped into the chair next to him where she could still see the bar. "I used to love that, but my sister's kids were only in town for a day so I hung out with them."

"What did you do with them?"

"Sparklers. We let the kids wave them around and nobody caught on fire, so it was a successful holiday, and we celebrated with margaritas after the kids went to bed."

Hadley sighed and rolled her eyes. "He's

here again. He came in two nights ago when the bar was quiet because Rebecca wasn't playing. Something about that guy creeps me out."

Griffin was instantly alert. Was someone hanging around his bar bothering his friends and workers? He turned and saw the man lingering in the double doorway as if he was deciding if it was worth entering.

Alden Winter.

"He's staying with his aunt," Griffin said. Hadley knew who Alden was—he wasn't a total stranger to the island. "I don't know for how long, but Rebecca might." Griffin wondered if Rebecca and Alden talked much since they were living in the same house. He didn't like the thought, not that he had any specific case against Alden or claim on Rebecca's time. "He still doesn't seem interested in Christmas Island."

"Not the people," Hadley said. "But I bet he's interested in Flora's mansion and money."

Griffin nodded. Alden would be a fool not to want the Winter Palace and the reputed millions in Flora's accounts, not to mention Winter Industries, which she still took at least a remote role in running. Alden might be aloof and unfriendly, but he wasn't stupid.

"Maybe he won't stay long," Griffin said.

To his utter amazement, Alden crossed the bar and squeezed onto the piano bench next to Rebecca. Her look of surprise and—was it revulsion?—told him there was no way she'd invited Alden's attention.

"Ick," Hadley said. "You better toss him out."

Griffin rose from his seat.

"Or maybe just advise him to choose a table instead," Hadley said. "If you don't want to cause a scene. The guy likes martinis. I'll get behind the bar and make him one."

REBECCA DIDN'T see Alden enter the room because her back was partially turned to the door. She preferred seeing the bar area with its lively conversations and the tables of guests who nodded along with her playing or tapped a foot under the table. She'd quickly grown comfortable at the Holiday Hotel bar, and it was nicer than the bars she'd played in during college. Christmas Island guests were good tippers, too, and Rebecca always split her jar with the bartender and cook at the end of the night.

Her comfort and peace dissolved like a wet candy cane when Alden slid onto the piano bench with her. The bench was made for one person. Sure, she sometimes invited a kid or someone celebrating a birthday to sit with her, but that was different. Alden tucked in so close he restricted her movement and she had to move up an octave just to keep playing. The music was higher, matching the tension he created as she tried to finish her piece. As a cocktail pianist, she tried to never bring a piece of music to a hard ending.

She stopped abruptly when Griffin loomed over the piano, a tight smile on his face as if trying to be pleasant was physically hurting him.

"We've got an open table by the bar, Alden," Griffin said.

In the sudden silence, Rebecca was certain everyone in the bar heard the words. She tucked her chin and began playing one of her repertoire pieces that was so familiar she could have played it with locusts swarming around her head. Her fingers knew every note from muscle memory, but she couldn't keep the tempo from speeding up like her heart rate.

"I was just delivering a message from Aunt Flora," Alden said.

Rebecca stopped abruptly again. "Is she all right?"

"Sure," Alden said. "She just told me to say hello when she heard I was coming to the bar tonight."

Rebecca forced her shoulders to relax and she tried to pick up the melody she'd dropped. How dare he frighten her like that? She'd tried to like the guy because he was Flora's nephew, but this was just obnoxious. What was his game? Alden could talk to her at the Winter Palace any time he wanted.

Why was he bothering her now?

"I believe Hadley is making you a martini," Griffin said, arms crossed and jaw set. "I'll make sure it gets delivered to your table." He pointed with one finger toward an empty table without taking his eyes off Alden.

"I'll be right over," Alden said smoothly. "Right after I persuade Rebecca to play my aunt's piano like she plays this one."

"I do," Rebecca said. She smiled politely. "I've often played for Flora, but I guess you just missed it. Maybe tomorrow after breakfast I'll play for you both. Flora likes show tunes and rumba."

Alden opened his mouth but didn't say anything, and Rebecca wanted to laugh. Maybe

Alden hated show tunes and rumba. She had no idea what he liked or what he was all about. If she wasn't charged with watching out for Flora, she wouldn't be interested in learning a solitary thing about Alden. But she had to play nice for Flora's sake—and her own.

And so did Griffin. There was no use clashing with a guy who wasn't staying long and might never come back again. Rebecca gave Griffin a reassuring smile and then turned to Alden. "You should go enjoy your drink."

"Can I buy you one?" he asked.

She shook her head. "Thanks for the offer, but I like to stay sharp on duty."

"Well, then you can drive me home tonight when the bar closes," Alden said.

"Did you drive Flora's car?" she asked. She didn't intend to embarrass Alden, but he'd surprised her into asking the question.

"That's a beautiful car," Griffin said. "I drove it a few weeks ago and I swear it's only gotten better with age."

Alden's cheeks colored slightly, and Rebecca detected a hint of a smile on Griffin's face. Did he know Aunt Flora wouldn't let Alden drive her car, even though she was quite happy to let Griffin?

Alden got up from the piano bench but didn't look at Griffin. "No, I took the golf cart since you were kind enough to ride your bike and leave it for me. That's why I want to repay the favor."

Rebecca could think of nothing to say that wouldn't sound ungracious. She had no choice but to smile and accept. As Alden slid across the room and took up the martini waiting for him on an empty table near the bar, Rebecca caught Griffin's eye and he winked. She wanted to laugh and let out the tension from the past few minutes, but she smothered a smile and played a song that had absolutely nothing to do with cars or bars.

GRIFFIN HOVERED BEHIND the bar for the final hour of the night, only disappearing briefly to go out back or into the kitchen. Rebecca continued playing her mix of upbeat classical, pop and Christmas carols as she wondered what would happen at eleven o'clock. Alden had only one drink, but he hung around, clearly waiting for her.

Was Alden hoping to talk with her without the chance of Flora overhearing? Did he plan to reveal something that would be useful, or had he found her out?

Nothing about Flora's possible changing of her will made sense. Alden was her only living relative, he already ran WinterSon Corporation—which his father had spun off years ago—and there was no reason why he might have been disinherited. Sure, it took effort to warm up to Alden, but he wasn't a supervillain.

Unless there was something Rebecca didn't know. Her weekly phone calls with Jim Churchill back at Winter Industries had contained only updates on Christmas Island life. Flora seemed fine, there'd been no mention of a will and Churchill's worries about her physical or cognitive state seemed unfounded. Even with Alden's appearance, nothing interesting had happened. Yet.

She finished playing for the night and closed the piano's keyboard lid.

"You can take your time driving home," Alden said as he stood by the piano. "That will give me a chance to figure out why my aunt prefers your company to mine. You could give me some tips on winning her over since I've never been able to do that, it seems."

Rebecca smiled. "It's late, and Flora's an early riser. I should hurry home so I can be up early, too. I want to make sure the breakfast table is ready for her."

"Very dedicated," Alden said, but his expression implied mockery rather than admiration.

"Mornings are really beautiful on the island," Rebecca said. "You should get up early and take a walk or a bike ride. I always find it's good for thinking."

"Or planning?" Alden asked.

Rebecca had no intention of being drawn into any kind of conversation that Alden wasn't willing to have at the Winter Palace. Although, would she be wise to hear him out, or was it too great a risk to her own position?

She tucked her sheet music into her bag and slung it over her shoulder. Across the bar, Griffin waited by the back door that led to the parking area. Rebecca thought of the night he had driven her home in the rain. It wasn't raining tonight, and leaving with Alden produced an entirely different nervous sensation. He wasn't dangerous, he was just…unknown. She'd heard stories about his business style and the shaky ground WinterSon Corporation was on. No wonder there was trepidation on the current board at the thought of Alden inheriting Flora's empire.

Alden strode across the bar and barely nodded at Griffin, but Rebecca paused at the door.

"See you tomorrow night," she said.

His face was in shadow, but his expression was even darker.

"I could drive you home," he said.

"What about him?" Rebecca asked, pointing to Alden, who had gone ahead without looking back.

Griffin's expression relaxed. "He could ride in the bed of the truck."

Rebecca laughed. "I better take him home."

Griffin touched her arm. "I like to take care of my…friends."

The way his voice softened when he said *friends* weakened every bit of Rebecca's resolve. Being welcomed into the group of islanders was the greatest unexpected joy of her summer.

"Thank you," she said. She stole a glance at Alden, who was sitting in the passenger seat of the golf cart, one leg crossed over the other and his arm slung across the back of the seat. "But you have no idea how good I am at taking care of myself."

She wasn't saying it to brag but to reassure Griffin. Even dark island roads with an awkward and off-putting houseguest as her companion didn't compare to the times she'd pulled herself through with her own determination.

Griffin nodded quickly and went inside, but Rebecca's heart was torn. Would she rather take a summer night's drive with Griffin May instead of Alden Winter? No doubt. But she had her cover to keep, and making an enemy of Alden might jeopardize her summer work.

When Rebecca got to the golf cart, she saw that her bicycle was secured on the back. It was Griffin's good-night gift to her. She was certain he would have done something just as thoughtful and courteous for any of his employees, but it felt sweet and personal anyway. Maybe because she wanted it to be.

CHAPTER FIFTEEN

REBECCA'S TOES WERE squeezed into a pair of high heels, but the sunshine, sparkling blue water and lake breeze wiped away any discomfort.

"Thanks for being my plus one," Camille told Rebecca as they lined up on the ferry dock with two dozen residents of Christmas Island. "My sisters both have a date, and I didn't want to be the *lonely* Peterson girl at the party."

"You're doing me a favor by including me. I don't know the groom, but I love weddings," Rebecca said. "As long as the dress is pretty and the cake delicious."

Rebecca wore her blue cocktail dress and Camille had on a flowy, floral, knee-length dress. The weather was perfect for a summer wedding, and Rebecca had promised she would send pictures to Flora through the late Saturday afternoon ceremony and evening reception in Lakeside.

"You'd like Patrick," Camille said. "He's one year older than us, and I always thought he'd grow old and die on Christmas Island, but he fell in love with a girl from the mainland." Camille shrugged. "What can you do when it's true love?"

"His bride doesn't want to live on the island?" Rebecca asked.

"I guess not. Her family has come out for day trips or the weekend. That's how they met. But she's a French teacher at the high school on the mainland and our little island school doesn't offer French."

"I bet it'll be hard for Patrick to give up the island," Rebecca said. She sighed as they found a seat on the ferry's open deck. "I'm already sad about leaving at the end of the summer."

"Really?" Camille asked. "I could offer you a job with the Island Candy and Fudge Company. You'd never have to leave."

Rebecca laughed and tilted her head back. As she did so, she saw Griffin in the ferry's pilothouse. She wasn't surprised to see him there, but she was surprised by his attire. Griffin wore a suit and tie, and he looked so handsome Rebecca caught her breath. He waved to her and broke the spell, and Camille nudged her.

"Not taking me up on the offer?"

"I love it here, but I belong at Winter Industries."

"You're outrageously loyal, which is something I love about you." Camille leaned close. "I'm not prying about your summer job, but have you learned anything yet?"

The hum of the ferry's engine created background noise so they couldn't be overheard, but Rebecca was still nervous about saying anything. She trusted Camille completely, but she felt an uneasy sense of betrayal because she liked and respected the people on the island.

Was Jim Churchill wrong to think Flora's change to her will had anything to do with her decision to spend the summer on Christmas Island? Was someone on the island unduly influencing her, or had she gone there to get away from someone? Nothing about the change to her will made sense. Yet. Rebecca got closer to Flora every day, and they were developing a friendly bond. It was one more reason she hoped to be successful, and also the reason she felt guilty.

"I was stuck in a golf cart with Alden a few nights ago and he didn't tell me a thing," Rebecca said lightly. "I was hoping he'd confess he was on the island to beg his aunt to leave all her money to a pet shelter, but he just talked about his racehorses instead. I got a crash course on horse breeding and choosing the right trainer and jockey."

"Fascinating," Camille said. "Maybe I should throw myself at him and try to marry into the Winter fortune."

Rebecca shook her head. "Those millions wouldn't be worth spending all your time with Alden. You're worth more than that."

Maddox May, wearing a suit and tie like his brother, strode past their bench, walking steadily on the moving ferry. Both brothers were tall, broad-shouldered and handsome, especially wearing a suit. Did either of them have a date for the wedding?

"I am worth more than that," Camille said.

Maddox leaned on the railing at the front of the ferry and talked with his friend Jordan, who worked at the Great Island Hotel. Rebecca could tell her friend was looking at Maddox while being careful not to appear like she was.

"What's your deal with Maddox?" Rebecca asked. "I know you grew up together, but I've noticed some…layers between you two."

She'd wanted to ask, but the time had never

seemed right. It was strange that she and Ca-mille had shared so much, but she could not remember hearing the name Maddox May one single time in all the island stories her friend had told her throughout college.

Camille smiled sadly. "One of these days I'll tell you the whole pathetic story. Don't hold your breath, though. It's not the stuff romance novels are made of."

"No happy ending?"

"Definitely not."

"Darn," Rebecca said. She put an arm around her friend. "Let's hope this wedding is a romantic's dream. Patrick gave up the island for his bride, so it must be the real thing."

Camille laughed and they both leaned back into their seats as they faced the lake breeze. Rebecca loved weddings, probably because they were a rare treat for her. With no family of her own, she'd missed out on going to the weddings of cousins and siblings. She'd never been a flower girl or a junior bridesmaid. The few coworkers' weddings she'd been to had been lovely and made her long for someone to walk her down the aisle and go wedding-dress shopping with. Someday.

"I'm surprised both brothers are going to the wedding," Camille said. "They have a backup captain, but they don't usually trust anyone but themselves to run the ferry."

"Would you let someone else run your family business?" Rebecca asked.

"Totally. I'd give it away right now along with a lifetime supply of maple fudge."

"Sold," Rebecca said, laughing. "And I know you're kidding. There's a reason you came home."

"True. Because my perfect older sister Chloe is getting married in six months and leaving the island. This is my big chance to be number one."

"You're my number one best friend," Rebecca said, even though she wasn't sure Camille heard her because she seemed intent on watching Maddox May deftly swinging a rope as they approached the mainland dock.

Rebecca stood and teetered a moment on her high heels. The ferry horn blasted behind her. Startled, she dropped back into her seat with her hand over her heart and shot a glance at the pilothouse. Griffin smiled broadly at her and she couldn't help smiling back.

As they exited the ferry, Griffin stood by the gangplank and advised all the passengers to watch their step. Rebecca paused as she passed him.

"Was that your revenge for me turning down a ride with you so I could drive a millionaire home?" she asked. The festive occasion made her feel free and fun. Did she know Griffin well enough to tease him?

"I always blow the horn when we approach the dock. Maritime law," he said seriously.

"Oh."

Griffin smiled. "There is some leeway on the exact timing, though."

Camille was several steps ahead and Rebecca and Griffin were the last two people to step off the boat. A charter bus waited on the dock to take the island wedding guests to the ceremony.

"We'd better hurry," Rebecca said. She nodded toward the bus.

"Will you do me two favors?" Griffin asked.

"Of course." She knew her voice sounded reasonable and businesslike, but inside she was an aviary of birds flying in chaotic freedom. Griffin was the first islander she'd met a month ago on her initial ferry trip, and their paths crossed so often it no longer surprised her to find him at her side.

"Ask the driver to wait one minute while I turn over the ferry to my stand-in captain."

"Okay," she said. "And what's the other thing?"

"Save me a dance at the reception."

Rebecca smiled in answer. "As long as I don't stay too late and miss the ferry back to Christmas Island."

"I wouldn't leave without you," Griffin said.

BY CHANCE OR LUCK, Griffin and Maddox were seated right behind Camille, her family and Rebecca. He tried to pay attention to the vows of his childhood friend Patrick and Michelle, the mainland girl he was marrying, but Griffin kept getting distracted by Rebecca's long brown hair, which fell in waves just past her shoulders. The outdoor garden ceremony was hot, but the waterfront location came with a breeze.

"Wish I could take this jacket off," Maddox whispered during the ceremony.

Griffin nodded. "Reception," he said. At least the venue, a lakeside mansion now dedicated to weddings, had an air-conditioned ballroom large enough for the reception. It would be a relief to take off his jacket and enjoy some food, but something else contributed to the heat under his collar.

The dance. If he was going to dance with

anyone from the island, he wanted it to be Rebecca. For one thing, he'd grown up with everyone else, and dancing with Camille, her sisters, Violet, or any of the rest of the group would be like dancing with a relative.

Rebecca was nothing like a relative. She was fresh, different and more interesting than he let himself dwell on. There was no use getting involved with her because she was only here for the summer. His life was on Christmas Island, and she was a temporary visitor, like a beautiful season that would come and go. A romance between a mainlander and an islander wouldn't work. He'd seen the sacrifice it would require, and watching his friend Patrick marry Michelle and prepare for a new life in Lakeside was a powerful reminder of the two worlds separated by a ferryboat.

It didn't matter that he owned that ferryboat. He was a realist not a romantic, as life had required him to be, and he'd already given up a lot for the family business.

But still, he watched Rebecca's profile when she turned and exchanged a glance with her friend Camille, and he resisted the desire to reach out and curl a lock of her hair around his finger.

He was in trouble.

He should never have prearranged a dance with her.

The ceremony ended, and the newly married couple proceeded down the aisle. Ushers released the rows of guests from the front to the back of the seating area. When Rebecca stood with the rest of her row, including Camille, Griffin noticed his brother shift in his seat and pull out his cell phone. He stared at the screen even though it was dark. Camille and Rebecca filed out and Maddox put the phone in his suit jacket's pocket.

"I don't want to go through with it," Maddox said quietly as wedding music played in the background.

"With what?"

"The speech. Patrick is having his best man say something at the reception, but he asked me to make a toast, too, since we've been friends all our lives."

"He should have chosen you for his best man," Griffin commented.

Maddox shrugged. "His new brother-in-law is a good guy, and it made his wife's family happy."

Griffin wondered how happy Patrick was to be moving to the mainland and changing his entire way of life. Would he get used to the sound of trains and cars? Miss the quiet of the island in winter? Feel nostalgic for home every time he heard Christmas music?

"You'll be fine with the speech," Griffin said. "I assume you wrote it down, right?"

"I typed it into a notepad on my phone a few days ago, but I don't think I can do it."

"You're not afraid of public speaking," Griffin said. "I've seen you talk in front of a crowd on the ferry dock, at our hotel and in bars sometimes."

"It's not that," Maddox said, but his explanation was interrupted when the usher returned to send their row to the reception area. Camille and Rebecca were already waiting in the receiving line with Camille's family, and Griffin realized what his brother was probably afraid of.

"You don't want to talk about true love and commitment with Camille listening, right?" Griffin whispered to Maddox.

Maddox raised his eyebrows and nodded slightly. He looked a little pale under his summer tan.

"You're going to have to. Just don't overthink it. Hold up your champagne glass in one hand, read whatever it says on your phone and get it over with," Griffin said. "You're not a villain just because you made a mistake in love, and that doesn't rob you of the right to wish your friend the best."

Griffin thought about his own mistakes in love, few though they were. A brief flirtation with Camille's older sister lasted one week and one prom date, and they parted with an agreement that friendship was the only thing they had in common. When he was nineteen and home for the summer after his freshman year of college, he fell hard for a girl who waitressed at a downtown restaurant. She was only there for the summer, and she politely but firmly broke his heart when she got on the ferry at the end of the season. After that he wasted some melancholy days in the autumn of his sophomore year of college, but when he learned that the family ferry line was in trouble, that news supplanted his summer romance.

He should have been paying closer attention that summer instead of filling his time with the beautiful red-haired waitress. If he had, he would have known sooner that his family needed him.

Griffin rolled his shoulders and tugged at his collar. The late-afternoon sun was hot, and all the talk about love and regrets made him wish he was on the deck of his ferry, face turned toward the cool lake breeze. Some days he felt the heavy weight of responsibility, but most of the time he appreciated being the captain of his own ship, free to live as he chose even if that meant owning weighty decisions and, sometimes, mistakes.

An hour later, after the bridal party took pictures outdoors and finally rejoined the guests inside the cool ballroom of the former estate, Griffin and his brother were enjoying drinks and appetizers with two friends from the island. Rebecca and Camille were several tables away with Camille's family. Did Rebecca have a family on the mainland? She never mentioned anyone. It might be a good topic of polite conversation while they danced.

Griffin drank his soda slowly. He'd be piloting the last ferry back to Christmas Island that night, and he didn't mind filling the role of designated driver for dozens of islanders. His brother was on his second cocktail, and Griffin hoped he'd make it through the toast.

"Game time," Griffin said as soon as the best man had given a short toast. He nodded toward the microphone and gave his brother an encouraging thump on the shoulder. "Just read what it says and don't overthink it."

As soon as his brother took the microphone, it occurred to Griffin that he should have read his brother's speech. Just in case. But it was too late.

"Growing up on the island is like having a giant family," Maddox said. "You know the other islanders so well you can predict what time they'll mow their lawn or what drink they'll order at the bar. Patrick, you've always been a close friend and I wish you the best." He raised his glass an inch, and Griffin let out a relieved breath. It was going to be okay. "Also," Maddox said, "we see a lot of people come and go from the mainland. Most of them don't measure up to our island family."

Griffin glanced over at Camille's table and he knew from her white, strained expression, that she was thinking the same thing he was. Oh, man. *Maddox, stop talking.*

"But sometimes the right woman comes in on the island ferry, and makes you forget all the islanders you've grown up with." He raised his glass higher. "To Michelle and Patrick."

Griffin took a long drink of his soda. The speech was mercifully short and wasn't a total disaster, as long as no one was reading between the lines. Servers came around with plated dinners, and Griffin happily forked into his food. He noticed that Rebecca and Camille left the table and disappeared through a side door. Assuming they were going to the restroom, he finished his dinner and enjoyed a piece of wedding cake for dessert.

But Rebecca and Camille hadn't returned. Their plates had been cleared away, and a slice of wedding cake sat at each of their places. Maddox noticed, too, and they exchanged a glance.

"Was it something I said?" Maddox asked. He tried to smile, but they both knew it wasn't much of a joke.

"You might have gone a little too far with the comments about someone from the mainland being perfect. Especially given how that turned out for you."

Maddox's face fell and he blew out a breath.

Griffin glanced at his watch. Rebecca and Camille would probably be back soon. The empty places at their table nagged at him like a missing puzzle piece. He ate the last bite of his wedding cake as he considered that summer was half over—a summer that Rebecca had affected in so many ways. He consulted his watch and found another ten minutes had elapsed.

The band began playing and the bride and groom had their first dance. Rebecca was missing it. Would she mind? He wished he knew more about her. Did she like weddings? Traditions?

The band played "The Way You Look To-night," and many couples joined the newly-weds on the floor, but there was still no sign of Rebecca and Camille. Griffin was accustomed to being responsible for others, caring about them, assuring their safety on his boat, accounting for them on the passenger manifest. And he cared about Rebecca. He wouldn't bother denying it, even to himself.

He approached the Peterson table and put his hands on the back of the empty chair where Rebecca had sat thirty long minutes ago. He exchanged a pleasant hello and comments on the wedding with Camille's parents.

"I see you're missing someone," he said, not sure how to approach the subject.

Camille's sisters exchanged a glance, and Chloe, her older sister, said, "Camille and Rebecca left."

"Left?" Griffin did a quick calculation. His stand-in captain was running the usual evening schedule, so there would be at least two ferries Rebecca and Camille could ride back to the island before the last run, which he would captain.

"Camille," her younger sister began. "She, uh, turned her ankle in the high heels she was wearing, so they decided to go back early."

"I'm sorry to hear that," Griffin said. "I hope she's okay."

"She'll be fine," Chloe said. Although Griffin had only dated her for one week and one prom, he knew her like she was family. Her expression said, *I know you know I'm fibbing, but please let it go.*

If he thought Rebecca or Camille was in need of any help, he'd chase them down to the ferry dock. But he suspected the real reason for their retreat was Camille's reaction to his brother's toast. And he couldn't fix that, no matter how much he wanted to.

He rejoined the group at his table, but his thoughts were on Rebecca. She'd be boarding the ferry right now. Maybe she was sitting below the pilothouse. Would she jump when the stand-in captain blew the horn? There were hours of daylight left, but the low sun would begin sending color across the lake and deepening shadows as the boat approached

Christmas Island. Griffin could picture every channel marker, wave and inch of the nautical miles between Lakeside and the Christmas Island dock.

With every nerve of his body, he wished he was the one in the pilothouse assuring Rebecca's safe passage back to the island. Instead, he had almost three hours of wedding reception to endure while he waited to return his fellow islanders home. He went to the bar and got a fresh soda.

Reception out on the lake was spotty, but a message would be waiting for Rebecca.

I hope you had a smooth crossing, he texted.

He emptied his glass, waiting for a response. The band finished playing an upbeat song and launched into a love song he'd heard Rebecca play on the baby grand in his bar. She did it better. His cell phone buzzed as he thought of her.

Thanks, Captain. We're shipshape.

He smiled. The message was friendly and light, as if he was just checking up on a friend. Did she think it was more? Had he shown her that he felt more?

We never got that dance.

After he sent the line, he made himself breathe while he waited for a response. It was a simple statement of fact.

You can take me and Flora dancing sometime.

Griffin laughed even though it wasn't the response he was expecting. What was he expecting?

That sounds like an invitation, he responded. Did he want to risk an official date with Rebecca? His heart said yes even though the practical demands on his life and time told him to be cautious. Was he ready to do something for himself for once? And what would Rebecca say? She'd kept him at arm's length at first, but she'd slowly lowered her arms and allowed him closer. Maybe a dance was exactly what they needed.

CHAPTER SIXTEEN

TWO EVENINGS LATER Rebecca put on her black dress and some sparkling jewelry Flora had insisted on lending her. When Rebecca had protested that the silver gemstone necklace looked far too expensive, Flora had said it was older than Rebecca and deserved to be taken out and shown a good time.

Griffin had kindly invited Flora to join them for dinner and dancing at the Great Island Hotel, but the older woman had laughed and responded by insisting Rebecca borrow the matching earrings, as well.

Rebecca entered the elegant lobby of the Great Island Hotel with Griffin at her side, and she felt like an epic fraud. What was she doing going on a date with an islander who made her heart feel larger than the usual space it occupied? Wearing family jewels from someone who wasn't her family— someone she hadn't been honest with?

It was better than she deserved.

She was here to spy on Flora and sleuth out any undue influence on the island. She could try to justify her behavior by saying she was going for an insider view. And the view was excellent. It was the second time that week she'd seen Griffin wearing a suit, and the effect had not worn off.

"They have a jacket and tie policy for dinner," Griffin said.

"You caught me looking," Rebecca replied, laughing.

"I hope you were looking because you approve and not because I have dog hair stuck to my lapel or my suit smells like the engine room of the ferry."

"Did you wear this down into the engine room?"

"Only for five minutes. I wanted to show Maddox the filters we should get changed within the next week."

"The work never rests," Rebecca said.

"He had his golden retriever Skipper with him," Griffin said. "That dog loves boats, kids and basically everything."

Rebecca picked a piece of golden fur off Griffin's sleeve and they both laughed.

At the door to the dining room, the greeter recognized Griffin and checked off his name without asking a single question. "Mel will seat you," she said.

Rebecca and Griffin followed Mel across the spacious dining room, where every table had fresh flowers and each diner was elegantly dressed. An orchestra played just loudly enough to be heard over the chatter from the tables and the faint clinking of silverware on china plates. Griffin waited for Rebecca to be seated and then moved his chair close to hers instead of sitting across the table from her. Without a word, Mel rearranged the plates, silverware and glasses as if this happened every day.

"I have to shout over ferry engines all day long," Griffin said. "I wanted to be able to hear you during dinner."

Rebecca's heart attempted a cartwheel. Was she that interesting?

"And since we're on the edge of the room, I won't be in anyone's way here," Griffin added.

"You didn't have to do this," Rebecca said. "Dinner, I mean. I only stood you up for a dance, and we could have just shown up later for the orchestra."

Griffin cocked his head and studied her for a long moment. "You didn't really stand me up."

"I left the party early." Was he going to insist on being so adorable?

"Only because you were a good friend and Camille twisted her ankle."

Rebecca felt the flush rise up her neck and creep across her cheeks. Although she was excellent at lying to herself and talking herself through tough situations with a hardy sense of optimism, she was lousy at lying to other people. Concealing her real reason for being on the island was slowly eating a hole in her ability to sleep at night, especially as she fell more and more in...tune with the pace of the island.

"She didn't twist her ankle."

Griffin opened his mouth and put his hands on his cheeks. "You're kidding."

Rebecca laughed and swatted him with her napkin. "It's not funny. We had to leave but there was another reason."

"Was it about my brother?"

Rebecca took a moment to consider her answer. Of course Griffin knew the story. But did he know the extent of the damage to Maddox and Camille's relationship?

"Did you know about Camille and Maddox before this summer?" Griffin asked instead of waiting for Rebecca's reply.

She shook her head.

"I didn't think so. The few times we've all been together, I noticed you seemed a bit confused by Camille's attitude toward Maddox. You two are close and you lived together in college, right?"

Rebecca nodded, absorbing his words and wondering how much she should say.

"I think there's only one good reason why Camille never told you."

Rebecca swallowed a flash of irritation. If Griffin thought it was because Camille was still in love with Maddox, he was wrong.

"Maddox screwed up bad," Griffin said. "And if Camille wanted to write him out of her history, I couldn't blame her." He smiled. "You're a good friend, especially because you've revealed absolutely nothing about Camille's private business. Not many people have that kind of discretion."

"I let you fill in the blanks better than I could have explained it," Rebecca said.

Griffin picked up both dinner menus and handed Rebecca one of them. "My brother has learned a lot, and he's going to be fine. Let's hope the same for Camille in her new venture, taking over the family fudge empire. And let's choose our appetizers. I'm starving."

Rebecca laughed. "Flora told me exactly what I should order from the menu, but I think it's possible her information is a few years out of date."

"At any other place I'd say that's true, but traditions seem to last forever on Christmas Island."

Rebecca ran her eyes over the appetizers and smiled. She looked up. "Flora was right about half of these choices. She surprises me every day."

Griffin grinned. "Nothing my dear aunt Flora does would surprise me."

Rebecca desperately wanted to ask him how much he knew about Flora's financial affairs and Winter Industries, but there was no way to do that without revealing what she knew.

Griffin was perusing his menu, and without looking up, he said, "I think she's so sharp because she ran her own business all her life. She's a woman who misses nothing, and she's probably the shrewdest person I know."

"I've noticed that," Rebecca said.

"I should probably ask her advice about my ferry and hotel empire, even though I'm small potatoes compared to Winter Industries," Griffin continued.

"You should ask her."

Griffin laughed. "She'd probably tell me I better figure it out myself, and she'd be right. Anyway, I had it mostly figured out a few years ago, and we're getting over the hump where maybe our hard work will pay off."

Rebecca knew the correct term for that situation—return on investment. But she was a piano player, friend and companion for the summer. Not a financial analyst.

"Do you and Maddox share the work equally?"

"Just about. He's had some things to work through, and it's not easy being a single dad. He has our family home now so he can start raising the next generation of boat captains."

Their waiter took their appetizer, salad and entrée orders. Rebecca had seldom eaten at such a luxurious restaurant. Even business dinners back in Chicago, where Winter Industries' headquarters were located, were never this focused on pure elegance and refined choices.

She listened to the five-piece orchestra playing through a repertoire similar to her nightly cocktail piano lineups. Some old classic love songs, light classical that was easy to identify, a hidden gem like a beautiful movie theme or a pop song dressed up with violins.

"You know every song, don't you?" Griffin asked. "And I'd guess you're an excellent dancer since it's pretty obvious you have rhythm."

"With my fingers," Rebecca said. "Sadly, I'm a very average dancer, no matter how much I love the music."

"We'll see. My mom attempted to teach me and Maddox to dance so we'd know how to behave the one or two times a year we came to the Great Island Hotel for events like the annual Christmas party. Did your mom teach you to dance?"

Rebecca shook her head. She seldom told her childhood story to people. Not because there was anything to hide, but because she didn't want them to feel bad for her. A lot of orphans and foster kids had had a tougher childhood than she had, and things had turned out okay for her.

"I don't have a mom or a dad," she said. "I grew up in an orphanage until I was ten and then in foster homes after that."

"You're kidding," Griffin said. His eyes were sad and his surprise showed in his parted lips.

"Not kidding," Rebecca said.

"Where did you learn to play the piano?"

She smiled. That was his first question? Most people who heard she'd lived in an orphanage wanted to hear horror stories, not real anecdotes about the decent but understaffed place she spent her childhood.

"Public school when I was in fifth and sixth grade. I had to wait for one of the later school buses at the end of the day, and I would hang out in the music room. A very nice teacher stayed late every day and got me started. Luckily, when I moved to a different school in seventh grade, they had an orchestra and needed a piano player, so I continued studying."

"You must have been determined," Griffin said.

"I'm a very determined person."

"One of the many things I like about you."

If she had the luxury of allowing herself a summer romance, Rebecca might have asked what else he liked about her, but she was trying to remember to keep things light and her heart free.

"It wasn't all glamorous, though," she said with a smile. "I thought I had it together enough to play in a talent show at the end of sixth grade, and it might have gone all right if the third page of my music wasn't upside down."

Griffin laughed. "Was it a good thing you changed schools the next year?"

"Very."

Rebecca sipped her wine and felt its warmth spread through her, even though it was Griffin's words that caused much of the heat. People were nice to her at work and valued her contributions to the company, but it was a delicious treat to sit down and talk with someone who seemed to value…her.

"And did you learn any special talents in the Christmas Island public school system?" Rebecca asked.

Griffin laughed. "The one-building school system?"

"But you learned enough to go to college," Rebecca said. "It must have been a good school."

Griffin's expression turned wistful, his eyes on the tablecloth.

"You haven't told me what happened halfway through college," Rebecca said. She waited out a long pause while Griffin looked around the dining room and then returned his gaze to her. "You don't have to," she added.

"I know," he said quietly.

"But I did tell you about the recital disaster."

He smiled. "I was one of those lucky kids who could do the academics but I also liked working with my hands. The guidance counselor they sent out from the mainland suggested I become an engineer. I'd never thought of leaving the island and going to college until that moment, but something about it grabbed my attention. I was determined just like you were."

"And so you went to the University of Michigan?"

He nodded. "And even though I missed the lake and the island, sometimes so much it hurt, I was doing well in my classes. I came home for the summer after freshman year and focused on having fun instead of really paying attention at the dinner table. If I had, I might not have been surprised later that year when my mom called and asked me to come home."

Rebecca reached over and put her hand on his as he toyed with his silverware. She could see the pain in his expression. "I'm sorry you had to give up your dream."

"It was more than that," Griffin said. "Dad was sick, Mom was overwhelmed and Maddox was a senior in high school. Someone had to come home and pull things together or we'd lose it all."

Rebecca tried to feel what Griffin did, the pull of family and the sacrifices required. She wanted to understand the choice he'd made, even though she'd never had to choose between herself and her family's wishes. She'd only had herself. Was that a bonus she'd never appreciated before?

"You've done a wonderful job," she said. "I read the online reviews before I booked a ticket on your ferry for my first trip to the island."

Griffin laughed. "We're the only ferry service to Christmas Island."

"The reviews were good anyway," she said.

"You know what's getting rave reviews these days?" he asked. "Your piano playing. In fact—" he tapped her wineglass with his "—I think we should drink to that."

Rebecca sipped her wine. "I've come a long way since the sixth grade."

"Haven't we all?"

After dinner they sat in the lobby while the orchestra reassembled and tuned up in the ballroom closed off by ornate doors. When the doors opened, Griffin offered Rebecca his hand.

"I've been waiting for this dance," he said.

They entered the ballroom, and Rebecca paused in the doorway. The hotel was over a century old, so she'd expected ornate gilded decor. She had been looking forward to feeling like a princess in a fairy tale. Instead, the room was done in an Art Deco style that made it romantic without being too serious. It was more modern than she'd expected, but something about it seemed just right for an island.

"What do you think?" Griffin asked.

"It wasn't what I was expecting, but Christmas Island has been full of surprises this summer."

They walked over to a table on the edge of the dance floor. A candle glimmered in a glass lamp and couples were filling the surrounding tables. A waiter stopped by for their drink order.

"Hey, Griffin. I don't usually see you here unless it's a special occasion," the waiter said.

"It is," Griffin replied. "I'm here with Rebecca, who has doubled my bar business three nights a week with her cocktail piano playing."

"If he's treating you to a night out," the waiter said, "I'd order the Great Island cocktail."

"Maybe just one," Rebecca said.

"Same," Griffin said. The waiter left and Griffin took off his jacket and hung it over the back of his chair.

"Should we dance while we wait for our drinks?" Rebecca asked. "I like this song."

She held out a hand, took a moment to enjoy the feeling of his large hand enveloping hers and led him to the dance floor. Only a few couples were dancing, and she might have felt conspicuous, but she knew only a few people on the island and none of them were likely to be at the hotel. The people in the ballroom were probably hotel guests, staying only for a transient but wonderful time.

She was only here for a short time, too.

"What else has surprised you this summer?" Griffin asked as he put his other hand at the small of her back. "Aside from the Art Deco ballroom we're in."

The truth was that she was surprised by the rush of excitement she felt being close to Griffin and moving together on the dance floor. She was surprised by her friendship with him that seemed to have the makings of a summer romance. And she was surprised that she'd let herself make a huge mistake that could jeopardize her goal of watching out for Flora's interests and the future of Winter Industries.

It was very easy to take her eyes off her goal when the tempting Griffin May was right in front of her.

"I'm surprised by the people," she said. "Everyone is so nice—especially Flora—and I feel like I'm part of a family for the first..." She hadn't meant to add the part about family, even though it was the truth.

"You fit right in," Griffin said. "With the island family."

"Like a visiting relative?" she asked.

Griffin pulled her a little closer, or maybe she swayed toward him. It was hard to say. Rebecca felt the music swirl around her, saw the tiny lights from the table candles and heard layers of conversations on the dance floor. It all made her feel giddy, as if she was a carefree girl enjoying an island fling. She looked up at Griffin, and his dark eyes seemed to reflect her feelings. Could she have a romance, even if the summer was half over and her job wasn't even close to being done? What would it hurt?

"Not a visiting relative," he said. "Like

someone who likes it here and sees the beauty in island life."

"I do," she said. "I honestly think I could live here if I didn't have to go back."

"Why do you have to go back? Do you have another job lined up?"

Rebecca tilted her head so her cheek touched his shoulder and she didn't have to look at him when she avoided telling him the whole truth. Not that looking away made it feel better.

"I do have another job," she said truthfully, even though she left out details. "I have a commitment, and I can't back out."

"As a lady's companion?" he asked. He leaned back so he could see her face. "You seem overqualified somehow."

"I'm qualified," she said. "I make sure Flora's comfortable, entertained and happy. Just like any good companion or friend would do. Plus, I can drive a stick shift and play the piano." She smiled at Griffin. "You know, maybe you're right. I am overqualified."

He leaned in and touched his cheek to hers. "I think you're just right."

After only one Great Island cocktail and two more dances, they paused on the expansive front porch of the hotel. The sun had long set and only a pink glimmer on the horizon marked where it had been. Griffin reached for her hand, and she turned toward him with the lake forming a dark background that suggested endless possibilities.

"I know you only promised me a dance, but a kiss would make this the most perfect evening I've had in ten years."

"I think you're exaggerating," Rebecca said. "Ten years is a long time."

"It sure is," he said, his smile reflected in the romantic lighting on the porch.

Rebecca put a hand on his cheek and lifted up on her toes to touch her lips to his. He deserved more than just a brief brush of their lips, even if a romance with him couldn't have a future. She breathed in the scent of the lake and the flowers in boxes along the porch as she kissed him.

"Even better than I imagined," he said when she broke the kiss.

When he drove her back to the Winter Palace, Rebecca almost gave him a good-night kiss as he held open her door, but she'd already invested so much in the evening she might find herself out of balance.

She slipped through the kitchen door and was surprised, again, to find Alden in the library. Instead of working on his laptop, though, he was going through boxes of old photographs and papers stored on the library shelves. When he saw her standing in the doorway, he jammed the lid back on a box.

"Out with the locals again?" he asked, his expression more sneering than curious.

"Just one," she said. She stepped farther into the room and eyed the boxes stacked on the table. "If you're looking for something, I'm sure Flora would help you. She knows where everything is. Sometimes I think she has a filing system in her brain."

"I'm not looking for anything. Just killing time on a long, boring evening on this island."

Rebecca had questions, but she didn't think late at night in a lamplit library was the best time to get to the bottom of Alden Winter's motivation. That would be better done by daylight.

CHAPTER SEVENTEEN

THE NEXT AFTERNOON Alden was out of the house and Flora was beating Rebecca at a game of gin rummy in the library. An afternoon rain shower kept them inside, and Rebecca popped a tray of cookies into the oven between hands of cards. So far that day she'd stayed busy addressing envelopes for Flora using her extensive address book. The stack of red envelopes sat on a nearby table.

"Can you believe I've never heard of sending Christmas in July cards?" Rebecca asked.

"Yes, I can," Flora said, smiling. "My parents used to do it because they thought it was clever to have them mailed with postmarks from their summer home on Christmas Island. I took up the tradition because it gives me an excuse to buy boxes of cards from the clearance rack after the actual holidays."

"I think it's fun."

"And proactive. At my age I never know if I'll still be around in December."

"Please," Rebecca protested. "After spending a month with you, I'm convinced you'll outlive me."

"I hope not."

"Do you think Alden will continue the family tradition of Christmas in July cards?" Rebecca asked.

Flora considered it for a moment as she picked up the playing cards Rebecca had dealt and rearranged them in her hand. "I think he'll only do it if he wants an excuse to show off pictures of a horse or boast about himself."

Rebecca didn't answer. She didn't want to say something negative about Flora's only living relative, and she hadn't been able to decide exactly how Flora felt about Alden. She treated him almost with pity instead of affection. Maybe she was missing something important that would pertain to Flora's will?

"I know that sounds harsh," Flora said. "Alden's not a bad young man, but he's a lot like his father, my late brother. He was also easily distracted from his duty to the family business, which was why we split it years ago when I was about your age."

Rebecca already knew that the two branches of Winter Industries had diverged a long time ago, but with Flora's passing, they would certainly be reunited in the hands of Alden Winter. Wouldn't they?

"Alden was in here last night when I got home from my evening out with Griffin," Rebecca said.

"Which I've heard far too little about aside from what you ordered for dinner and how many couples were on the dance floor. I'm still waiting for details on that kiss."

"How did you—"

Flora interrupted her, laughing. "So there was one. Good."

Rebecca concentrated on her hand of cards and carefully selected one to play. "Can I get you a glass of something to go with the cookies?" she asked.

"Don't worry," Flora said. "I've had a grand romance, too, so I won't press you for details."

"There's not much to tell."

"I certainly hope that's not true," Flora said, grinning at Rebecca over her glasses. "So tell me what Alden was doing up late last night."

"I think he may stay up late most nights," Rebecca said. "I've seen his lights on when I come home from playing piano, and one other night I found him up late in the library."

"Snooping around?" Flora asked.

Rebecca froze for a moment and then rested her wrists on the edge of the table so her hand holding the cards wouldn't shake.

Did Flora suspect her own nephew of deceit? Could this be the clue she was looking for?

"I don't know what he was doing," Rebecca said. "But I did see him looking through those old boxes." She nodded toward the shelves where the boxes were stored.

"Which one?"

Rebecca shook her head. "I don't know. He put the lid on and put it back as soon as I came in. I guess he didn't want company."

Flora sighed. "I suppose he was looking for a way to make sure he'll inherit my millions."

Rebecca counted to ten slowly in her head, willing herself not to appear too interested.

"Would you like to hear a secret?" Flora asked.

"I already know how to make the holiday punch," Rebecca said. This could be her big moment, her chance to help Winter Industries. Her own heartbeat thudded in her ears as she tried to keep her interest light and play the role of lady's companion instead of what she really was.

"It's not about the punch. It's about my fortune," Flora said, laying an ace on the table. "I'm leaving my island property and my personal millions to Griffin and Maddox May."

CHAPTER EIGHTEEN

GRIFFIN HELD ONE end of the measuring tape while his brother held the other. The breeze off the lake caught the tape and flapped it, making a metallic sound in the quiet early morning.

"It's long enough," Maddox said as Griffin walked toward his brother, reeling in the tape.

They stood together as the sunrise turned some low clouds near the horizon the color of wild roses that grew along the perimeter of Christmas Island.

"I thought it had to be," Griffin said. "I remember measuring this off with Dad when I was about fifteen. He always wanted to add an extra dock and ferry."

"Think we can pull it off?"

"The dock won't be a huge expense since we already own the land," Griffin said slowly. "Concrete and reinforced steel here." He pointed to the water's edge where some reeds grew in the unused area adjacent to their current dock. "That'll set us back maybe fifteen, twenty thousand."

Maddox whistled softly. "And then we have to buy another boat."

"If we do the dock this fall, it will show the bank we're committed and improve our chances of a business loan for the boat. I think it'll pay off, but we have to be all in," Griffin said.

The brothers locked eyes for a moment, and Maddox nodded slightly. "I'm all in. I have a son to raise on this island and I'd like for him to inherit a thriving business instead of a just-break-even one."

"We'll need another captain for the ferry runs to Saint Harper," Griffin said. "But that's a problem for next year. Right now we have to pull together money to build a new dock before winter." He grinned at his brother. "Think there's any chance of us winning the Holiday Hustle this year?"

Griffin and his brother had entered the island-wide race every year since they were twelve and fourteen years old, when they were finally old enough to get out of the junior level competition. The combination of physical and mental feats drew contestants from all over, especially since the winning prize was twenty thousand dollars, sponsored every year by Flora Winter.

"I wonder what the race committee has on this year's agenda," Maddox said. He didn't look at his brother as he spoke.

"Top secret and sealed until race day, as always," Griffin said. "We're running it together this year, aren't we?"

"Ethan is six this year, and technically we could be a team," Maddox said. "Ever since he watched the race last year, he's been talking about being big enough for the junior events."

"Oh," Griffin said, disappointment settling into his gut even though he understood his brother's need to be a good dad and start a tradition with his son. That was how he and his brother had started, on a team with their own dad. "Sure, that's a good idea. You don't want to disappoint him, and it will be fun for him to get his first chance at the kid prize. Five hundred bucks is huge to someone that age."

"I'm sorry," Maddox said.

"Don't be. Being a good dad comes first, and maybe I'll find someone smarter than we are to partner with." As soon as he said the words, Rebecca's face popped into his head.

"If Ethan and I win, I'll put the five hundred bucks into the first load of concrete," Maddox said.

Griffin laughed. "No, let him blow it on video games and candy. Or something else fun."

"He's been talking about getting a kayak so we can go out and paddle together. Have to get a tandem one," Maddox said.

Maddox tucked the tape measure on his belt and walked over to the ferry tied at their dock. He'd have the morning run, which left Griffin a few hours of free time. Griffin turned and looked up the hill toward the Winter Palace. Would Rebecca agree to be his partner for the race? He had no idea what kinds of challenges the Holiday Hustle race committee had in store for the Christmas in July event. Every January they came up with the challenges, both physical and cerebral, and kept them under lock and key so no island participants could prepare or have an advantage.

He pulled out his phone and hovered over Rebecca's name in his contact list.

Can you meet me downtown this morning? I need to ask you something important.

As he waited for a reply, he tried to imagine the scene at Flora's mansion. Were they having mimosas on the terrace? Cutting roses to fill the vases on the breakfast table? Taking Cornelius for a morning ramble along the cliff?

His phone buzzed and he swiped away the lock screen.

I could ride down in half an hour. Meet you... where?

Shade tree by ferry ticket office? I have coffee.

See you soon.

Griffin waved to his brother, who sounded the horn as the first morning ferry departed the Christmas Island dock. He went inside the ticket office, checked on the workers and ticket sales and found two paper cups by the coffee machine in the break room. He grabbed two packets of cream and sugar and swiped two donuts from the bakery box he had delivered every day for his employees.

Griffin didn't know if the coffee and donuts would be enough to tempt Rebecca into a competition where anything could happen, but he was going to try.

It HAD BEEN two days since Flora dropped the stunning news about her heirs over a hand of cards, and Rebecca hadn't seen Griffin during that time. It would take all her fortitude not to kiss him as she had on the porch of the Great Island Hotel or tell him their fledgling summer romance was over.

It had to be over. She couldn't know this secret about Griffin while also having a relationship with him. How she wished she could have asked Flora a million questions after she laid her ace on the table, but she'd been brave enough to ask only one: Did Griffin and Maddox know?

Flora had told her that the only other person who knew was her attorney, and she asked Rebecca to keep the secret and take it with her when she left the island. Flora said she planned to tell the May brothers when the time was right.

"Why did you tell me?" Rebecca had asked.

"Because I trust you," Flora said. "And the secret was killing me. I had to tell someone."

The logic was both wholly inadequate and

wonderfully simple, yet Rebecca felt cursed with the secret.

As she rode her bicycle toward the ferry docks and downtown Christmas Island, she dreaded her first glimpse of Griffin. Now that she knew he would be a millionaire several times over, would it change the way she treated him? It didn't change how she felt about him, but it did mean she couldn't go dancing with him again or kiss him in the moonlight. When he eventually found out that she knew about his impending wealth, he'd always wonder if that was part of her interest in him this summer.

Although she had agreed to tell Jim Churchill anything she found out, she hadn't yet called him to tell him about the surprise inheritance. Flora's personal fortune was not tied directly to Winter Industries, so Rebecca didn't think she was violating her work agreement. Unless the May brothers were going to inherit the company, as well, which didn't seem likely. They were grounded on Christmas Island, wholly unequipped to take on the management of an international company. Flora hadn't offered any information about her company, and there was no way Rebecca could ask.

Griffin was waiting under the shade tree, and Rebecca felt her heart lurch when she thought about what she had to do. She had to break it off, neatly and swiftly, before things went any further. It was for the best, anyway, since she'd be leaving at the end of the summer.

She put down the kickstand and Griffin stood on the other side of the bike, steadying it. Something about the simple action said everything about Griffin. He was steady and dependable. But did his dark eyes have to look at her that way, as if she'd somehow made his day by riding up on an ancient bicycle?

"I have something very tempting for you," Griffin said.

"Maybe I should go," Rebecca said, grinning despite her resolve to be cool and businesslike.

Griffin put a hand over hers on the handlebar of the bike. "Please don't."

He pointed to the bench, where two cups of coffee and a plate covered with a napkin waited.

"What's under the napkin?" Rebecca asked.

"Donuts. You get first choice."

"Is there a special occasion?"

Griffin blew out a long breath. "I have something important to ask you, and I'm nervous about your answer."

Rebecca was certain he could hear her heart thudding. It was louder than the gentle waves brushing the nearby ferry dock. Was it possible he knew about the inheritance—or suspected—and he wanted her to confirm the truth? But how did he know? *Oh, goodness. What if Flora thinks I told him?*

"Please sit," he said. He waited for her to be seated on the bench. She took the lid off a cup of coffee and peeked under the napkin. Rebecca didn't think she could possibly eat or drink anything, as nervous as she was, but she needed something to do other than look at Griffin's handsome, eager face. Although the chocolate one did look good… She picked it up and took a tiny bite. The sugar flooded her with a brief rush of confidence. Whatever he said, she would think of the right answer, no matter what. She owed Flora and Winter Industries her loyalty more than she owed Griffin May—even though she wanted to lean in and touch her lips to his and feel that sweet rush she'd felt at the Great Island Hotel.

"I should probably give you some backstory first," Griffin said. "So you know that

I'm bringing up the somewhat awkward subject of money for a good reason."

Rebecca took a larger bite of chocolate donut so she wouldn't have to answer that statement. Holy Christmas, this was going to be rough.

"My brother and I basically bought the ferry line from our parents, which I think you know. It's been reasonably successful over the years, but we both want more. It's true that it's the only ferry line serving the island, so that's in our favor, but we're thinking of investing in another ferry and running service to Saint Harper in addition to Lakeside."

Rebecca chewed slowly, waiting for his explanation to circle around to the inheritance from Flora. Why else would he be telling her this?

"To do that, we need capital. We have to improve this dock and make room for another ferry before we can even think about buying another boat."

She nodded. It was logical, and making practical financial decisions and projections was second nature to her. "Do you think you'll get enough return on investment?" she asked.

Griffin smiled. "I do. We've done some

market research this summer that gives us hope and something to take to the bank."

"The bank?"

"For a business loan. We poured a lot of our earnings into the hotel, which is starting to pay off, but we're still putting our necks out there. Which is what I wanted to ask you about."

"I don't—"

"How are you with solving riddles and thinking on your feet?" Griffin asked.

"I'm...usually really good at that."

"I thought so. I saw you in action at bar trivia night. I think you must have some ace up your sleeve that no one knows about. Which makes you perfect for what I'm asking."

Rebecca thought of that ace Flora had laid on the table. The chocolate donut stuck in her throat, and she wanted to jump on her bicycle and pedal as far and fast as she could. Living a double life was a mistake. She wasn't cut out for all this subterfuge.

"Every year the island has a major Christmas in July event," Griffin said.

Rebecca nodded. The change of subject was disconcerting but welcome. Where was this going?

"And the big event is the Holiday Hustle, where teams compete in a challenge that is part athleticism and part brains."

"That sounds fun," Rebecca said.

"It is. I've competed with my brother for years. We've never won, but we came in second when I was seventeen and he was fifteen."

"What knocked you out of first place?" Rebecca asked.

"Memorization. We were given a list of historical dates involving the island and five minutes to memorize it. We got smoked by the town librarian and her marathoner stepson."

Rebecca smiled, picturing the librarian's triumph and thinking how fun that must have been.

"Maddox has a different partner this year," Griffin said.

Camille flashed into Rebecca's mind and she wondered if somehow the old friends had made peace.

"His son," Griffin said. "There's a junior level and Ethan is just barely old enough. Which leaves me without a partner."

Rebecca had almost forgotten about the will

and the inheritance, but the thought returned. "Is there a big cash prize for winning?"

Griffin grinned. "Huge. Twenty grand, sponsored by your boss."

"Flora?"

"Every year. She says she's enough of a capitalist to enjoy a good competition," Griffin said. "But she doesn't know what the challenges will be because she appoints an anonymous board who plans in secret so no one has an advantage."

"Interesting," Rebecca said.

"So what do you think?"

"About the race?"

"About being my partner," Griffin said. He got up and motioned for her to follow him. He led her to the edge of the water near the ferry dock. There was only a rough wall of stones along a length of shoreline. "Here's where the new dock will go, and ten thousand dollars—my half of our winnings—would give me enough of a start on improving the seawall to show the bank that Maddox and I are serious about another ferry."

"You want me to help you win the Holiday Hustle so you can put the money into your business?" Rebecca asked. He really didn't know he was in line to inherit millions from Flora?

"I know it sounds crazy."

"It's not crazy," Rebecca said. "It's a short-cut to getting what you want, and I like the idea of it, but I don't know if I'm the right partner for you."

"You're smart, and we seem to…get along. I think we could work well as a team if we put some time into training and preparing."

Too well, Rebecca thought. Every minute she spent with Griffin was exponential, making her want to add more. She would never break her promise to Flora, but being with Griffin made that secret seem like a towering burden.

"Tell me more about the event," Rebecca said, hoping to buy time to consider her decision. She watched the waves wash in and out, sparkling in the island sunshine. Six months ago she couldn't have imagined that she'd be spending summer on an island, carrying out a secret assignment that got more complicated every day.

"I can tell you some of the past events, but I can't predict exactly what the challenges will be this year," Griffin said. "There's some biking, of course, as you go from obstacle to obstacle, and sometimes you have to run between them. At least, it's best to run because time matters in addition to the number of points you earn.

"One year we had to figure out who was the oldest inhabitant of the island and get our picture with that person." He laughed. "You can imagine there were hilarious mistakes when some ages were wildly misjudged. We had to count the pillars in the downtown marina, estimate the lengths of all the boats on one of the piers and add them together, fry a burger to perfection at an outdoor restaurant, make a perfect rum punch at an island bar and climb a tree at the island school to retrieve a kite."

"Is that all?" Rebecca asked, laughing. "You didn't have to fly over the island spelling out your name with an airplane?"

"Don't give them any ideas," he said. "Those are just some samples, but you see what I mean about the combination of brains and brawn?"

"I'm not sure I bring any brawn."

"But you're brave and determined. Do I need to remind you about the ill-fated leap onto my boat?"

She shook her head. "I can't believe you'd want me on your team after that."

"I definitely want you," Griffin said. He took her hand. "Even if we don't win and I have to get a paper route to save up money for building my dock, it will be fun spending time with you." He leaned close and Rebecca was certain he was going to kiss her.

"You're too old for a paper route," she said. "And I don't even know if Christmas Island has a newspaper."

"Is that a yes?"

It was foolish to spend more time with Griffin, given how attracted to him she was and the magnitude of the secret she could never reveal. The irony of helping him win a small pot of money when she knew he was in line to receive millions almost made her laugh. Oh, how she wished she could have asked Flora why she was leaving her money to Griffin and Maddox. What had they done to inspire her to disinherit her own nephew? Was she definitely leaving Alden the company then since her personal wealth was going elsewhere? Rebecca knew she should get to the bottom of the question, and she should also turn down Griffin's very tempting offer.

But there was no graceful way to say no. And her heart was saying yes. Hadn't she known what it was like to fight her way to success and work for every dollar and accomplishment? She owed Griffin a fighting chance, even though he didn't really need it. What price would he put on his pride when he eventually found out about Flora's millions?

"Yes," she said.

CHAPTER NINETEEN

FLORA TOOK OFF her sunglasses, closed her eyes and let the air coming through the open car window ruffle her silver curls.

"You look like an advertisement for summer," Rebecca said as she smoothly shifted gears in the 1954 Bentley.

"I can't believe July is already half over," Flora said. She kept her eyes closed and stroked Cornelius's tiny chin as he sat on her lap. "When I came out here for the summer, I promised myself I would enjoy every single moment."

"I hope you have."

Flora nodded. "Completely. And drives like this are part of the reason. I feel as if I'm sixteen again."

Rebecca laughed. "I'm not sure I'd want to be sixteen again, although if I could redo the last ten years with the knowledge I have now…"

"What would you do differently?"

Rebecca considered the question. The blue lake sparkled as she drove in and out of shade provided by the lovely old trees circling the island. She was spending a magical island summer, having an interesting flirtation with a handsome man and she had a luxury car to drive in addition to the companionship of a fascinating lady. Could she really do any better than this? A strange feeling that she was meant to be on the island hit her, and for the first time since her arrival she wondered… what if? What if she stayed on the island?

Her loyalty to Winter Industries was rooted in the fact that they made her feel like part of a family. Christmas Island felt that way, too. But would the feeling last beyond summer? Flora would go home, and then the crowds would thin. Who would she play the piano for?

"Such a long pause," Flora commented. "You must have quite a list of things you'd do over, but you're not saying. I can tell you what I'd do over again."

"You?" Rebecca asked. "You seem like a person who's done everything right."

"Ha," Flora said. "In business, maybe. But my greatest regret was letting love slip through my fingers when I was younger than you are now."

Flora's eyes were wide open. She leaned forward in her seat as if there was something she could see just around the bend in the road ahead. "I was utterly and completely in love with a man named William. I'd seen him over and over when my parents came out to the island for summer vacations when I was young. We were the same age, and I was lucky enough to get invited along on some of the young people's events. Much like you've been doing this summer."

Rebecca nodded. They were less than halfway around the island, and she hoped they wouldn't run out of road before Flora told her story. A tale of a long-ago love affair? This was the kind of thing Rebecca had missed out on growing up in different homes. She never delved into anyone's family history or stories.

"We went to bonfires and on boating trips. Every year, when my brother and my parents and I came over for the month of December, we ice-skated on some of the frozen lake inlets. It's hard to believe those teenage years were almost seventy years ago now. It seems like another time."

Rebecca bit back the emotion that swelled

up her throat and stung her eyes. She blinked and focused on the road ahead.

"William and I fell in love, but there were several years my family didn't get to the island because of my father's business and some international travel. For me, going to Europe was never a substitute for coming to Christmas Island, even though I did love seeing the grand capitals over there. When I was twenty we came back, and that's when I realized how much I had missed. In my absence, William had fallen in love with an island girl and married her."

"Oh," Rebecca said. "How terrible."

"For me," Flora admitted. She carefully ran a finger over Cornelius's nose and between his eyes, just how he liked it. The little dog was in heaven, blissfully unaware of the sad story his owner told. "But William seemed very happy, and what could I do? I'd missed my chance, and I feared I'd never love anyone as I had loved him."

"Did you keep in touch with him?" Rebecca asked. "He lived on the island and you continued to come back every year. Did your paths cross?"

Flora nodded. "All the time. I remember when he and his wife had a child. I sent gifts and attended the christening as an old friend along with half the island, but I can still feel that old slice of pain."

There was a long silence as they passed by the ruins of the winery.

"It's not the same, but I was in love with a boy in ninth grade," Rebecca said. "The family I lived with at the time was very strict, so I couldn't go on a date with him, but I went to a homecoming dance at school because my foster sister was going, too. I remember dancing and thinking nothing could ever keep us apart, but I moved on to a new foster home before Christmas that year and I never heard from him again."

"I wish I'd known you at the time," Flora said. "You could have lived with me instead of being bounced around like that."

Rebecca let out a long breath. "It made me resilient and grateful. So what ever happened to William and his family?"

"His wife died young, only in her twenties," Flora said.

Rebecca glanced over quickly.

"I know what you're thinking. It should have been a second chance for me, but it wasn't. He was devastated over her loss, and never wanted to love someone again. He wouldn't give me a chance to get close to his heart, even though he was part of mine and that hope never faded."

Rebecca sighed, thinking about lost love and how it had changed Flora's life. The older woman had never married and had, instead, devoted herself to building her business empire. Was she happy? Was that Rebecca's future if she continued to put her loyalty to Winter Industries in front of her heart's desire?

Ridiculous. Her summer crush on Griffin wasn't comparable to the great love of Flora's life and the ripples of consequences radiating out from it.

"I do take consolation in loving his grandsons as if they were my own," Flora said. "Sadly, I've had much more time with them than their own grandmother had."

"Are they still on the island?"

Flora reached over and patted Rebecca's knee. "You're so smart I was certain you had already guessed. The great love of my life was William May, Griffin and Maddox's grandfather."

Everything clicked into place, finally, and Rebecca understood the inheritance. There was no undue influence, no great mystery to why Flora was leaving her millions to the May brothers. But…why had there been a recent change to her will and why was Alden hanging around the island, overstaying his original plans?

The longer she spent on the island, the more convinced Rebecca was that nothing was simple. Was she succeeding or failing at her assignment from her CFO? She would call him later and report this information, even though she almost felt she was betraying her own family.

"Now, let's talk about you and Griffin," Flora said. "Cheer me up with your summer romance, and then we'll get ice cream downtown. At my age, that's a perfect afternoon."

"There's nothing to tell," Rebecca protested.

"Fiddlesticks. And if you tell me you can't date him because you know he'll be a millionaire, I'll have to accuse you of being a snob," Flora said.

Even though that was absolutely part of the reason she couldn't date Griffin, especially since he'd eventually find out that she knew about the inheritance before he did, it wasn't the entire reason.

"I'll be moving on at the end of the summer," Rebecca said. "And moving on is a lot easier when you're not leaving a piece of your heart behind." She didn't add that she'd learned that lesson over and again growing up, but Flora knew about her foster-home childhood and she would certainly figure it out. "However, I do have entertaining news for you involving Griffin."

"Good."

"He asked me to be his partner for the Holiday Hustle on Christmas in July."

Flora laughed. "I just love that wacky race. Do you know it's been going on since I was a kid? The tradition almost died about twenty years ago, but I kicked in enough money to keep it going long after I'm gone."

"Do you ever help plan it?"

"No. I leave that to people with much more devious minds than mine. It also makes it more fun to watch when I don't know what's coming. So Griffin chose you over his own brother?"

"Maddox's son is old enough to enter the junior race, so he's doing that. Starting in on the island tradition early, I guess," Rebecca said.

"Excellent," Flora said, nodding. "I can't wait. I may even stay out late the night before at the Christmas in July party. It's given at the Great Island Hotel, and they don't spare any expense." She laughed. "When I was younger, I loved the dancing and drinking, but I'm happy to watch everyone else now."

Rebecca pulled into a parking spot in front of a downtown ice cream store. Tourists streamed past them on the sidewalk and on bicycles in the street. Cornelius put his paws on the door frame and wagged his tail, sensing adventure.

"One time, when we were in our midthirties, William and I danced together at the Christmas in July party." Flora's voice trembled. "There were Christmas trees and white lights surrounding the dance floor, and everything about that night was pure magic. He was in my arms, finally, and it was every bit as good as I'd imagined and hoped."

Rebecca let a long pause hang in the air, punctuated only by the sound of the dog's tail slapping the dashboard in his excitement.

"What happened?" Rebecca asked quietly.

"After one wonderful kiss, he came to his senses. Or lost them," Flora said. "I went home alone to the Winter Palace and he went back to his little house on the island, where I'm sure the memories of his wife tortured him." Flora turned her intelligent eyes on Rebecca. "Living with regret for the things you didn't do seems to me to be worse than living with the things you did." She gathered herself up. "Which is why I'm going to have a double fudge sundae right now, and I suggest you do the same."

Rebecca hopped out of the car and circled it to help Flora over the curb and into the ice cream parlor. But she couldn't shake the weight of Flora's story, even as she enjoyed a fluffy milkshake and watched the vivacity of Christmas Island through the plate-glass window of the ice cream parlor.

CHAPTER TWENTY

GRIFFIN STEADIED THE canoe as Rebecca put one foot in, wobbled and then sat abruptly on the front seat.

"I don't know about this," she said. "Are you sure this isn't a pointless exercise?"

"I'm not sure about anything," he said. He stepped in, took the rear seat and cast off from the city dock, where he'd borrowed the canoe. "The more oddball things we practice, the better our chances for winning the Holiday Hustle."

"Has rowing a canoe been part of the challenge in the past?"

"At least three times that I can remember. It was a kayak one year, and there was a paddle-boarding attempt last year that didn't go very well. It was funny, though, watching some of the contestants lying on the board and paddling with their hands like they were surfers going out to the big waves."

"Maybe we should work on our biking

or roller-skating skills instead," Rebecca
said. She dipped a paddle into the water and
splashed Griffin without turning around to
see her target.

"We'll do that, too," he said. "Just in case."
He splashed her back and laughed when she
shivered and wiped a cold drop of water off
the back of her neck.

"Okay, truce," she said. "Am I steering or
are you?"

"I can steer if you want to be the muscle,
or we can just see how it goes. Maybe we'll
work so well together it won't matter who's
in charge."

Rebecca didn't answer, but he saw her nod.
They paddled into the large harbor, where
rows of docks jutted out from the island. Sailboats, powerboats, kayaks and personal wa-
tercrafts bobbed peacefully, bathed in the July
evening's light. It was still almost eighty de-
grees, and the blue water was inviting even
though Griffin knew it was cold.

"It's so clear," Rebecca said. "I swear I can
see the bottom."

"You can. It's deceptive, though. Looks
like it's only a few feet deep but it's more
like twenty."

"What's that cable?" she asked, pointing with her paddle.

"It's the power that comes over from the mainland. I've heard stories about the year they installed it and how complicated it was. That was before I was born. When I was a kid, we used to dare each other to dive down and touch it," he said. "Somehow we thought we could get electrocuted so it had the thrill of danger. Shows how much we knew when we were kids." He chuckled, remembering summer nights diving off the break wall and searching for the underground cable, sometimes in the dark. He and Maddox had been among the braver kids, but they weren't alone. Growing up on the island had been amazing, the kind of freedom most kids never get to experience.

"I went to summer camp one time," Rebecca said. "I had a foster sister about my age, and she was afraid to go away from home unless I went, too, so my foster family paid for me to spend a glorious two weeks in cabins with other kids." Her voice was soft. "It was the only time during my childhood I didn't feel like an orphan, because we were all there without our parents."

"Was it fun?"

"Very. I actually did paddle a canoe, although that was twelve years ago. And we hiked and built campfires and told ghost stories. All the things you read about in books and see in teen movies."

"I'm glad you got to do that," Griffin said.

"Me, too. If telling scary ghost stories comes up on the Holiday Hustle, I'm your woman," she said. She turned and smiled.

Griffin felt his heart hiccup in his chest at her words. If only there was a world in which Rebecca could be his instead of this fleeting summer romance with a clear expiration date. Her face was lit by the evening light as she smiled at him, and then she turned around quickly, like a firefly whose light was here and gone.

"Do you remember those stories?" he asked, trying to think about a steadying topic instead of how much he wanted to repeat the kiss they'd shared on the porch of the Great Island Hotel. Did Rebecca want that, too?

"The framework is always the same," Rebecca said. "Creepy location, unsuspecting friend, smarter and more cautious friend, an unexplained sound in the dark forest and a lingering mystery haunting an entire village going on for decades."

Griffin laughed. "I think that sums it up."

"Any ghost stories on Christmas Island?" Rebecca asked.

"A few. Being an island, we have the classic shipwreck stories involving sightings of a foundering ship during storms and mysterious moanings from caves along the shoreline."

"Creepy," Rebecca commented as they paddled past a luxury yacht with an artificial Christmas tree on the back deck.

"And we have mysterious lights that appear on the lake or on the shoreline just out of reach. If you try to chase them, they keep moving ahead of you," Griffin said.

"Have you tried getting someone to come around the island from the other direction so you can trap the carrier of the mysterious light?" Rebecca asked.

"That's a practical idea, but it would take all the fun out of it. The other enduring island story is the mad woman at the hotel, who is sometimes seen with her dogs in the hallways late at night. The Great Island Hotel doesn't like anyone telling ghost stories about it, but you have to figure there are some good stories involving a hotel that's been there over a century."

They paddled in unison, venturing out of

the harbor and along a rocky wall that ended in a lighthouse. The lighthouse was painted with red-and-white stripes, and the top was a Christmas green. Its windows shone with the sunset.

"Are there any ghost stories involving the Winter Palace?" Rebecca asked.

"There are none that I know of. I love Flora, but I think we all assumed that if there were any ghosts, she would scare them away. She's not a person you mess with."

Rebecca laughed. "She's sweet."

"Like the grandma you smoke cigars with instead of baking cookies," Griffin said.

"We bake cookies, too," Rebecca said.

Griffin laughed. "I don't know of any actual hauntings involving the Winter Palace, but if you wanted to tell Alden there were ghosts, it might be fun to mess with him."

Rebecca shrugged. "Maybe he already thinks there are. He tends to leave the lights on late at night. Or maybe he's a night owl." She paused and paddled. "He's gone now. Flora said he had something he needed to do, some business thing involving his race-horses I believe, but he'll be back."

"Is he prowling around the house late at night?" Griffin asked. He didn't like the sound of that because Alden had never inspired his trust somehow. There was something just…off…about the guy.

"He, uh, seems to be reading or researching in the library," Rebecca said.

"I don't know much about his business, or Aunt Flora's for that matter, but I wonder why he's spending so much time here this summer," Griffin said. "We've seen him on and off over the years, but never for this length of time."

Instead of answering, Rebecca pointed to the beach near the lighthouse. "Can we pull up the canoe and explore here?"

"Unofficially, yes. This little island with the lighthouse belongs to the government because it's a navigational aid, but the no-trespassing sign has been faded and unreadable since I was a kid." He steered their canoe toward the lighthouse with long strokes of his paddle.

"Are you sure we won't get in trouble?"

"I'm sure," he said. "I think you'll like this, and one year there was even a Holiday Hustle clue hidden at the base of the lighthouse. We can call this research."

REBECCA DISEMBARKED FROM the canoe with only the toe of her shoe getting wet. It was exhilarating and a bit rebellious paddling to an off-limits lighthouse with a handsome man who was equally off-limits.

Not that she could tell him that. He must think her reason for keeping him a canoe paddle's length away was that it was a light summer romance, destined to end when she departed the island right after the Labor Day holiday.

He took her hand as they walked over pebbles on the edge of the water, the stones grating and slipping under their feet. "The sand is shifty here," he said as if explaining why he had her hand in his. "And we have to step over some big rocks to get to the path to the lighthouse."

Rebecca had navigated her life by always doing the sensible, forward-thinking thing. But as they approached the long shadow of the lighthouse on a summer evening, she didn't want to follow her own rules. Griffin's fingers toyed with hers as they crossed the soft sand, and he tightened his grip as he helped her over large rocks meant to protect the lighthouse base from storms.

No one had ever protected her from storms. She'd been her own beacon until the scholarship from Winter Industries had come along. When she graduated from college at the top of her class, Winter Industries had swept in with another offer—they would pay for her Masters in Business and she would have a future home with the company. It was the closest thing to security she'd ever known.

She considered Griffin's profile as they stepped onto the smooth sidewalk surrounding the lighthouse. He would inherit millions, all Flora's personal wealth. But he hadn't played dirty for it. He couldn't have. He didn't even know about it. Would he be working so hard to compete for the prize money if he knew what was waiting for him when Flora passed?

Of course the time they were spending together now was about the competition and the need to prepare and train. Wasn't it?

"You should tell me something about the history of this little island in case it comes up in the race," she said. *Focus on the safe practicalities.* Not how nice it would feel to have his arms around her in the balmy evening air.

"I think I have a book back at my place with the island history. Maddox and I studied it last year, and it helped us with a few of the challenges. Contestants aren't allowed to take books or cell phones on the course, so you have to rely on what's in your head."

"Then I'd better study," Rebecca said. "I know the island has a website because I looked up some basic information before I committed to this job. There's probably a history page on the site."

"I assume," Griffin said. He paused under the lighthouse where some seagrass grew along the base. "Are you glad you took the job?"

"Absolutely," Rebecca said without the slightest pause. "This is the nicest summer I've ever had—with the exception of those two weeks at camp when I was a preteen."

"Because you feel like you belong somewhere?" he asked.

Rebecca's breath caught in her chest. That was exactly the feeling, but it was a strange surprise to have someone understand.

"The island makes me feel that way, too. Don't get me wrong, I liked living at college for the three and a half semesters I stayed, but I sometimes wonder if I would have gone through with my plans to become an engineer and live wherever the work took me." He smiled wistfully. "Would I have been happy somewhere else?"

"People can learn to be happy wherever they are," Rebecca said. "I'm sure of that. But living in a mansion with a baby grand and a nice lady who likes mimosas at breakfast sure makes it easier."

"I'm glad you like it here. Flora might decide to stay throughout the fall and maybe even until Christmas. She's done it before, although not for a long time. Maybe you'll end up being a Christmas Islander longer than you planned."

The thought evoked a happy rush before Rebecca could remind herself that she was only here to gather information. Had she already gathered enough that she could go home? Maybe the change to Flora's will—which her attorney had revealed over a golf game—had a very simple explanation: she had finally made her choice to leave her money to Griffin and Maddox. Perhaps she should just come right out and ask Flora if that was a recent decision. Was there a way to bring it up?

But then, if she found out the whole truth, she wouldn't have a reason to stay on the island any longer. The man who held her hand as they walked a grassy path along the shoreline made her want to overstay her plans.

"Unless you have something better waiting for you somewhere else," Griffin said. His words jolted her back to their conversation even though she'd drifted away to imagining autumn leaves turning and snow falling on Holly Street.

"I doubt there's anyplace better than here," she said.

"I could offer you a permanent job playing piano at my hotel, and Camille might need some help, too."

Cocktail piano and candy making. Rebecca considered for a moment how ridiculous it would be to give up a sizable salary as a financial analyst and take part-time jobs on an island. Griffin's expression was so hopeful. Of course, he didn't know she had a corporate-level job waiting for her back in Chicago.

Not that she had anyone to answer to back home. No parents or family to tell her she was crazy to give up a good job and move to Christmas Island. But that was a double-edged sword. She also had only herself to rely upon, and being tempted to change course based on emotion and feelings seemed like a betrayal of everything she'd worked for.

"Tempting," she said honestly. It really was. "But I have commitments." They stopped and looked across the water at downtown Christmas Island. "Do you think we should paddle back before it starts to get dark?"

"We'd find our way using the lights downtown and I know from experience there's nothing to run into between here and there, but if we go back now we can get that book from my place and maybe study it over a drink. You've never been to my bar as a guest."

She smiled. "I'm used to being on the other side of the piano and letting my fingers do the talking."

"I like hearing you talk," Griffin said.

His dark eyes were sincere and his voice low and soft. The man was irresistible and so far off-limits that she couldn't even tell him why. Just her luck, she'd find herself falling for a man destined to be a millionaire, and that fact would prevent her from letting herself fall the rest of the way.

If things had been different and she'd arrived on the island without the shadow of pretense hanging over her, would she have had a chance at a relationship with Griffin? No matter how much she wanted to kiss him in the day's dying light, it was too dangerous a question to answer.

"I could have a glass of wine while you tell

me every challenge you remember from previous Holiday Hustles and we make a plan of attack." She smiled cheerfully. "I wouldn't mind winning a cut of that money myself."

"What would you buy with it?" he asked.

She had turned to walk back toward the canoe beached on the shoreline, but his question brought her to a stop. "I don't really need anything," she said. Material possessions were a luxury she'd never allowed herself because of her nomadic childhood. Even with her generous salary, she kept her clothes and housewares in her studio apartment to a practical bare minimum. She didn't currently own a car because she took public transportation from her apartment to the Winter Industries office building, and she didn't need a car for trips to visit family or to go on vacation. Christmas Island was the first real vacation she'd ever had.

"Maybe I'd invest it in a company bottling and selling Flora's secret recipe for holiday punch."

Griffin laughed. "I can't believe she told you that. I've asked her for the recipe so many times." He shook his head. "When you told me a few weeks ago that she was like the grandmother you never had, that really sank in with me because that's how Maddox and I have always felt about her. Our real grandmother died very young, a long time before we were born."

"Oh," Rebecca said. She already knew the story, but she couldn't let him know that.

"And so I was always sure that if she ever bequeathed it to anyone, it would be to Maddox or me. Funny, isn't it?" he asked, his smile genuine as he held the canoe for Rebecca to step in. "At least it's nice to know the secret's safe with you."

CHAPTER TWENTY-ONE

GRIFFIN RETURNED THE canoe and thanked his friend at the rental shop on the harbor. "Sure I can't pay you?" he asked.

Jackson shook his head. "You can give me a free ride on the ferry one of these days. I need to take one of my boat props to a shop on the mainland to have it machined."

"Ferry runs every day," Griffin said as they shook hands, and he turned back to Rebecca, who waited on the dock. The sunset lit her face and her long, dark hair blew out behind her. How was someone so lovely inside and out not already in a relationship? He'd noticed she was keeping him at arm's length on their lighthouse trip. Friendly, but with some long pauses in their conversation. Willing to take his hand, but only to climb over rocks or navigate shifting sand. And a kiss? He wasn't sure it would be welcome.

"Are you sure you want to have a drink?"

she said. "I know you don't get much free time, and you probably have things to do."

"Nothing that's more important than having a drink with you," he said.

Rebecca looked away, as if his words were too powerful to look at directly, like the sun.

"Strategizing how to win the Holiday Hustle could be my ticket to getting the new dock project rolling," he added, sensing that sticking with the practical was the safest route through unknown waters.

"We do have studying to do," she said, her expression brightening. "Can we borrow paper and pens from the hotel front desk?"

Griffin smiled. "I'll see what I can do."

They walked down the dock and turned onto Holly Street, nearly bumping into two women coming from the other direction. Camille and Violet had bags over their shoulders and wore flip-flops. They smiled as soon as they saw Rebecca.

"We were just about to text you and see if you wanted to come downtown and get a drink with us," Camille said. She held up her phone with the half-written text and laughed.

"No way," Rebecca said, smiling. "I can't come downtown and goof off. As you can see I'm very busy."

"You can bring Griffin, too," Violet said. "As long as he's buying."

"I'd be happy to buy drinks," Griffin said. "We were actually going to my bar, and I hope you won't consider it cheaping out since I do own the place."

"Even better," Camille said. She pointed to the life jackets Griffin had slung over his shoulder. "Were you just out in a canoe?"

Rebecca nodded. "We practiced paddling in case it comes up in the race."

"You were out at the lighthouse," Violet said. "We were sitting on the lawn down by the Mistletoe Hotel, and we saw you."

The group crossed the street together, hardly bothering to look for cars on the quiet Thursday evening.

"We thought it was very romantic, whoever it was that had rowed out to the lighthouse," Violet whispered to Rebecca.

Griffin desperately wanted to turn around and see Rebecca's face or at least overhear her reply, but the front door of his hotel opened and a group of guests whooshed past them and drowned out their conversation. Had Rebecca thought the trip to the lighthouse was romantic?

He had.

Their group paused at the front desk while Griffin said hello to his manager and borrowed some paper and pens. He handed Rebecca the supplies with the Holiday Hotel logo on them—an outline of the hotel with a Christmas tree in one window. In the bar a table for four near the front window was available, and Griffin motioned his group over to it.

"Have a seat and give me your drink orders," he said. "Would you like anything to eat?"

"We don't want you to go to any trouble," Camille said.

"No trouble. I'm ready for a late dinner, and I can put in four orders just as easily as one."

Rebecca smiled at him, and his efforts to be gracious—even though he would have preferred having her all to himself—were rewarded. Camille and Violet were old friends, and he was glad Rebecca wasn't having a lonely summer. He'd be happy to help her pass the summer evenings, but it would be a mistake. She wasn't staying, and he wasn't leaving.

All three women gave him their food and drink orders, and he promised to be right back. Hadley winked at him as he passed the bar. "Three dates? That's triple your usual."

"Friends," he said.

She smiled. "I know. You're married to your ferryboat, so I've given up on dancing at your wedding anytime soon. Let me take care of your drink orders while you tell Jerry in the kitchen what you're eating."

"Thanks," he said. He popped into the kitchen for a moment, and then passed the silent piano on his way back to the table by the front window.

"So who are all the teams this year?" Violet asked as he sat down. "The usual match-ups? I swear, if a team comes over from the mainland and wins it this year, we're going to have to cut off ferry service on race day for all future races."

"It was one time," Griffin said. "Those two guys didn't look like athletes or brainiacs, but I heard later they were some kind of professionals traveling the country and funding their trip by entering local races. I hope they won't be back."

"I follow them on Facebook," Camille said.

All eyes swung toward her and she held up both hands in surrender. "Hey, sue me. I thought they were pretty interesting. But they're out in California for the summer hiking the mission trail. No threat to us."

"So you're in the race?" Griffin asked.

Camille nodded. "With my sister Chloe. I actually wanted Rebecca for a partner because she's the smartest person I know."

Rebecca laughed and shook her head.

"But my sister is being dramatic about her upcoming wedding. She seems to think that since she's marrying a guy from the mainland and moving at Christmastime, she'll never be back to the island again."

"It's a big move," Violet said.

"Please," Camille said. "I told her she was making a big deal over nothing. The ferryboat runs every day, and she's getting married not moving to Antarctica. I went away for a few years, but now I'm back."

Griffin had seen relationships come and go between islanders and people from elsewhere, and the track record wasn't encouraging. Still, he knew how close the Peterson family was and he doubted Chloe would ever truly be separated from her family, even with a marriage and life on the mainland.

"I'm sure you and Chloe will be a great team," Rebecca said. "How about you, Violet?"

"My brother and I have a tradition of running together. We never come close to winning, but it's fun. One year we teamed up with Griffin and his brother, unofficially, and that was the closest we've ever come to not disgracing ourselves."

Griffin laughed. "I think you carried us that year. Remember that challenge when we had to follow a set of blueprints and build a birdhouse? It would have been utter humiliation for me and Maddox."

"Ryan can build anything," Violet said. "So we're hoping we have to build a cabin or an outhouse or something. I have a feeling that you and Rebecca are going to be tough competition this year."

Griffin and Rebecca exchanged a smile across the table, and he felt his heart flip. Spending time with her would be worth it even if they came in last place.

Rebecca held his eyes for a moment and then picked up the Holiday Hotel paper and a pen. "So what do I need to know?" she asked.

Hadley brought over their drinks, and Griffin took a sip of his while he tried to quiet the emotions swirling through him. Was the island life he'd chosen, the responsible path for the future of his family business, worth giving up everything else? When he'd been forced to give up college, he'd brooded about it but a tiny part of him had been relieved to have the choice made for him. He wasn't sure he really wanted a life off the island, and the decision had been taken out of his hands.

This felt different. Being forced to abandon any thoughts of a relationship with Rebecca because he was *married to his ferryboat* as Hadley put it raked up all the old feelings from five years earlier, when he'd come home to the island for what he thought would be the last time.

"Ten events, usually," Violet said. "Almost always a water obstacle of some kind like rowing out and grabbing a clue from a floating buoy."

"Or a race with kayaks," Camille added. "That was a fun one."

"The main mode of transportation is by bike or foot, no golf carts or motorized vehicles allowed," Griffin said. "And we usually cover a lot of the island."

"Which is all uphill if you haven't noticed," Camille said.

Griffin laughed. "It's only uphill if you're tired or it's really hot."

Rebecca paused with her pen over the

paper. "What kind of challenges have there been in the past?"

"Memorization every single year," Violet said. "Memorize a list of original founders of the island, a list of boat names currently docked on the pier downtown—in order, of course—or recite from memory the first paragraph of the island-governing charter."

Rebecca smiled. "I like the sound of that."

"You would," Camille said. "You'd probably also kick all our butts in the math obstacles. We had to count ridiculous things like the number of steps carved into the hillside on the way up to the sunset lookout or the number of flags displayed downtown. And then there are sometimes actual math problems like using an equation to figure out the volume of water in the Great Island Hotel's swimming pool."

"That sounds easy," Rebecca said.

"You have to do all the math in your head," Camille said. She sat back in her chair. "Dang it, I wish you were on my team. Griffin, any chance you'll give me Rebecca and you can have my sister, who will probably get weepy about halfway through the race?"

He laughed. "No way. I sat next to your sister in math class, and I don't think the two of us together could come up with the formula for volume."

That was his official answer, but no way was he giving up his time with Rebecca.

"The skill challenges are the real wild-cards," Camille said. "They are often basic things that a lot of people sort of know how to do, but not many people can do well. The one year we had to pull taffy was the only time my sister and I nearly made the podium."

"We had to sew a row of buttons exactly matching a military costume from the island museum once, and I did great with that," Violet said. "Clothes and fabric are my super-power. Sadly, we had to find clues hidden in the skull cave right after that, and my terror of bats completely undid my earlier triumph."

"So," Rebecca said, pen poised over paper, "practice sewing buttons, pulling taffy and tiptoeing through creepy caves." She grinned at Griffin. "Looks like we're going to be busy for the next few days."

"Maybe I'll get lucky and we'll have to line up nautical flags to spell out a coded mes-sage," Griffin said. "It's too much to hope there will be a ferryboat driving challenge."

Camille cocked her head. "That would seem too stacked in your favor."

A little girl ran in from the lobby and pounded on the baby grand's keyboard before her mother chased her down and grabbed her hands. "No," the mother said. "Don't touch."

The girl turned a pouty face toward her mother and squirmed onto the empty bench. She looked as if she was about to have a complete meltdown. Griffin knew the expression from helping with bedtime when his own nephew was a toddler. Once the little guy had been past a tipping point, rational conversation was out the window.

The little girl spread her fingers over the keys and tried playing what almost sounded like a song. The mother put her hands over her daughter's. "That's enough now, honey. These people are enjoying the quiet and it's bedtime for you." The mother glanced apologetically around the bar, which was mostly empty.

Griffin got up and walked to the piano. "It's okay," he whispered to the mother. "I own the hotel and bar." He made a show of looking at his watch and then spoke seriously to the little girl. "My guests here do enjoy piano music, so I have a job for you. Can you play for two minutes exactly, and that will be our good-night song?"

The little girl nodded.

"Okay," Griffin said, consulting his watch and holding up one finger. "Start. Right. Now."

He stood next to the piano and exchanged a smile with the mother while the girl pressed random keys with her little fingers. She didn't pound the keyboard and instead was clearly trying to play something that sounded pretty. Griffin glanced over at Rebecca, who was staring at him as if he'd just saved the universe from destruction. Were those tears in her eyes?

He swallowed and looked at his watch. "Halfway done," he told the little girl. "You're doing great." Griffin risked another look at Rebecca and saw that her face had relaxed into a beautiful smile, as if she was remembering something happy. She'd told him the story about the music teacher who encouraged her talent. Who knew if this kid would grow up to be a wonderful piano player someday?

Camille and Violet were chatting at the table, but Rebecca continued to watch the little girl at the piano.

"I'm sorry, but it's time to say good-night," he told the girl. "But there's one more thing you have to do before you go."

"What?" the girl asked.

"You have to stand up and take a bow. Your audience expects it."

The girl slid off the bench and bowed so low her ponytail touched the floor. Griffin clapped, and the other tables also clapped and cheered, but Rebecca was the first to leave her seat and give the little girl a standing ovation. The other bar patrons also stood up and the girl bowed again.

"Sorry," the mom whispered. "And thank you."

"Thank you," he said. "Maybe your little girl will come back and be my piano player someday."

The mom led her daughter out and Griffin saw them through the lobby doors as they climbed the staircase to their rooms on the second floor. He waved to the little girl and then returned to the table.

"You're such a softie," Violet teased him.

"I'm a businessman," he said. "Always on the lookout for talent."

"That's the other thing," Camille said. "The race always has some challenge that requires talent like drawing a sailboat to match a picture or—oh, God, do you remember that year we had to play 'Jingle Bells' on a plastic recorder?"

Violet laughed. "I almost felt sorry for the judges. If they thought they were coming up with horrible challenges to make people really work for the cash prize, they were right, but they were only hurting themselves."

Jerry leaned out the kitchen door and signaled to Griffin, and he jumped up and retrieved a tray of food, delivering it to his table. As they ate, Violet told funny stories about island residents and also summer people, as the locals called them.

"Rebecca already heard some of the stories about this island when we were in college, so I'm surprised she was willing to come out and live here for the summer," Camille said. "You probably thought we were a bunch of nuts."

"Not at all," Rebecca said. "This island is even better than I ever imagined." Her eyes strayed to the piano and then back to Griffin, and hope fluttered in his chest.

When they finished their late dinner and their drinks, Camille and Violet headed down Holly Street toward their family homes just off downtown. Griffin and Rebecca stood on the sidewalk in front of his hotel. A streetlight near them buzzed and there was music and laughter from a bar down the street. Someone rode past on a bicycle and rang the bell as they passed another person on a bike.

"That was so sweet what you did for the little girl," Rebecca said. "I hope she remembers it all her life."

"She actually played all right," Griffin said. "It could have gone either way."

Rebecca rose up on her toes and kissed him on the lips, a soft, sweet kiss that caught him by surprise and was over too soon. He put a hand on her shoulder and felt her soft hair under his fingertips. The streetlight over them buzzed again and then went dark.

He laughed. "It's a sign you should kiss me again," he said.

"You're such a good guy," Rebecca said. "You deserve happiness."

Her words were wistful, almost as if they were a goodbye.

"A kiss would make me happy," he said playfully.

Rebecca jingled the keys to Flora's golf cart, which was parked across the street. "Only temporarily," she said. "And you deserve the kind of happiness that lasts."

She walked across the street and got behind the wheel. Griffin waved, watched the red taillights disappear into the night and stood for a moment by himself, wondering what would bring him lasting happiness if the woman he cared about was out of reach.

CHAPTER TWENTY-TWO

REBECCA TOOK FLORA'S arm as they climbed the steps to a platform rising over the downtown dock. As soon as Flora was firmly installed behind the podium, Rebecca stepped back discreetly and sat behind a flag bunting, where she would be out of sight for the opening ceremony of the Christmas in July Sailboat Race.

"I'm honored to be here for the eighty-fifth running of the Christmas Island to Lakeside sailing regatta," Flora said. "Because I am also eighty-five, I can tell you that's a very long time." She smiled and the assembled crowd laughed and applauded.

As Flora continued her short speech, which launched not only the yacht race but also all the Christmas in July weekend festivities, Rebecca enjoyed her bird's-eye view of the harbor and part of downtown. A huge evergreen grew in the sloping lawn at the top of the harbor. Rebecca imagined it was planted on purpose to be the island's sustainable and permanent Christmas tree. It was decorated with bright lights—visible even on the sunny day—and huge ornaments that sparkled.

Garlands and lights had greeted them as Rebecca drove Flora through downtown in her vintage car. Fake snow had swirled down and Christmas music added cheer to the shops, restaurants and tourists navigating the busy street. Rebecca had laughed at the Christmas sweaters and Santa hats people wore despite the heat.

Flora wore an elegant red suit with matching lipstick and a sparkling star pin, and Rebecca admired her ease and grace even with hundreds of people listening to her speech. No wonder she was a venerable force on the island, a patron of local events, a leader of a huge company, and, apparently, a softie for her two pseudo-grandsons who would inherit millions.

Griffin and Maddox had no idea how lucky they were to have family and the admiration and love of someone as wonderful as Flora. Not to mention the fortune they would get when the sweet, strong lady passed on.

Flora finished her speech and waved a flag, and a horn sounded, officially launching the sailboats that waited at the edge of the harbor. The crowd cheered, and Flora turned to Rebecca.

"Now we celebrate with some good, old-fashioned shopping."

"Oh," Rebecca said. "Sure. I didn't know you needed anything or I would have gotten it for you."

"I don't need anything, but I do need to get a Christmas in July gift for someone special."

Rebecca offered her arm and walked slowly down the six steps to the ground at Flora's side.

"Who are we shopping for?" she asked.

Flora turned a smile on her. "You. You're going to the ball at the Great Island Hotel, and you'll be wearing a new dress befitting the occasion."

Rebecca laughed. "I haven't actually decided if I'm going, and I have a dress that will work if I do."

"A girl doesn't go to a fancy party in a dress that will work," she said, "especially a beautiful girl whom I've grown quite fond of."

"Are you going to the party?" Rebecca asked.

"Maybe for a little while," Flora said. "But I don't want you fussing over me. You need to have fun. Life is short, and summers on Christmas Island are even shorter."

When they were on the sidewalk just across from the Island Boutique, Flora looked both ways and stepped brightly into the street, as if she were forty years younger. "I always loved this store and bought more than one Christmas ball dress in here," Flora said. "I just hope Violet has continued her family's tradition of stocking dresses that are fabulous and not just dresses 'that will work.'" She made little air quotes on the last three words and Rebecca laughed.

"We can at least look," Rebecca said.

"And I'm buying," Flora said.

"You don't have to do that."

"I know."

"Are you getting something for yourself, too?" Rebecca asked.

Flora laughed as Rebecca waited for her to enter the store first. "No one cares what an old woman is wearing. But I will wear some jewelry befitting my stature as a glamorous patron of the island." She grinned at Rebecca. "I don't want to let people down."

Violet greeted them before they made it three feet into the shop.

"This young lady needs a party dress," Flora said. "Something sassy that sparkles."

Violet's smile didn't even flicker. "You're absolutely right," she said. "Come to the back, where I have a stash of party dresses just waiting for the right person."

Rebecca followed Violet and Flora past summery dresses, flowing linen trousers and skirts, pretty straw hats, elegant handbags and a rack of shoes that were island casual mixed with resort style. The back of the store had the more serious dresses, as Rebecca already knew from her three cocktail purchases weeks ago. She loved those dresses, but wearing them each week—blue on Tuesday, black on Friday, plum on Saturday—had, admittedly, gotten a little old. Maybe Flora was right and a new party dress would be fun. If she chose carefully, she could add it to the rotation for her cocktail piano nights— definitely a Friday or Saturday night choice.

"Here we go," Flora said. She turned to Violet. "I'm buying, so don't let Rebecca even consider the price."

"Ooh," Violet said. "I'm so glad you came in because I have at least six dresses that deserve someone as beautiful as Rebecca to wear them." She held up a black dress that was floor length, off the shoulder and had a slit that would show a lot of leg. It had black lace sleeves that flared at the wrist.

Rebecca gasped. "I can't wear that."

"You certainly can," Flora said. "If you don't try it on, I just might."

Violet hung the black dress in front of a mirror and fished another one from a rack. This one was deep burgundy velvet with a plunging neckline and a long, body-hugging skirt. The velvet shimmered and a row of sparkling beads rimmed the neckline, cuffs and hem.

"I'm trying that on, too," Flora declared. "Unless Rebecca claims it first."

"Wait," Violet said. She put the burgundy velvet next to the black one and held up a dress so beautiful it was a work of art. The white satin bodice had a lace overlay with silver threads that caught the light, but the skirt was long and full, the silver satin needing no embellishment.

"Oh, goodness," Rebecca breathed.

"Try that one first," Flora suggested. "I have a ruby-and-emerald necklace set in silver that will look beautiful on you."

"I can't," Rebecca said. "It's too beautiful,

like a snowflake met a champagne glass and they're getting married."

Flora and Violet laughed, and Flora settled into a chair. "I'm ready for the fashion show."

"Is the Christmas ball really this formal?" Rebecca asked.

Both Violet and Flora nodded.

"No one told me."

"We're telling you now, and there's plenty of time before the ball."

Rebecca tried on all three gowns, even though her heart was definitely bought and sold by the silver satin one. She texted Camille and asked her to pop across the street from her candy store to give her opinion.

"You're my date, right?" Camille said. "I already bought that dress." She pointed to a white figure-hugging dress with a red lace overlay.

"Did you really?" Rebecca asked.

Camille grinned. "Totally did. It's my way of announcing I'm back on the island and I'm not burying myself at the fudge shop."

Rebecca wondered if showing Maddox what he was missing was any part of Camille's decision to show up in a dress that would drop jaws, but no way would she insult her friend by asking. "You'll be stunning," she said. "It won't matter what I'm wearing because everyone will be looking at you."

Camille shook her head. "They may be looking at Violet, who has not revealed her dress. As the purveyor of fine party dresses, the expectations are high."

Violet made the lips-zipped gesture. "You'll just have to wait."

Rebecca turned to face the mirror in the dress she'd known she was going to choose the moment she saw it. In the mirror's reflection, she could see Violet, Camille and Flora, and her heart swelled with love for her old and new friends who were like family.

"I feel like you're my fairy godmother," she said, turning to Flora.

The older woman smiled. "Maybe I am."

Rebecca felt tears in her eyes and she swallowed the lump in her throat.

"Shoes," Violet declared. "You can't wear sensible black pumps with that dress."

When Rebecca and Flora climbed back into the Bentley, Flora put a hand on Rebecca's arm before she put the car in gear. "Take the long way home by looping around the island. This day is too perfect for us to go straight home, and I'll give you some pointers so you and Griffin can pull off a win."

No matter what happened in the Holiday Hustle, Rebecca felt she had already won just by spending the summer on Christmas Island. She tried to push away the thought that summer would end all too soon.

GRIFFIN WENT THROUGH his usual meticulous closing down of his ferryboat—the William May, named after his grandfather—and his office and dock. He secured the vessel's heavy ropes and double-checked them. Next, he checked the presale tickets for the next day to see if there were any large groups scheduled. The Christmas in July weekend was notoriously busy, and Griffin and Maddox had hired their stand-in ferry captain for the Saturday night and Sunday runs for the past several years.

They needed the extra help on the holiday weekend, but it also gave them the freedom to attend the Saturday night formal ball and compete in the Holiday Hustle. As Griffin closed and locked the windows in his ticket office, he thought about how strange it would be not to run the race with his brother. They'd done it together for twelve years, and as junior competitors before that. He shrugged off the melancholy. Maddox had a son to consider, and Griffin had done all right with his own partner.

Rebecca was the perfect partner for him. She was book smart, but also savvy. Resilient and dedicated, she likely had hidden reserves of talent he didn't even know about. For all he knew, she spoke three languages and had an eidetic memory.

Even if she didn't contribute a single point to their team's standing, Griffin relished the thought of spending hours with her. He closed the office door and looked down Holly Street. Strings of colored lights crossed the street, and music was pouring from all the bars and restaurants. The lake behind him was peaceful and silent, but the party scene in front of him was one of the aspects of Christmas Island that he loved.

The whole island seemed to glow with holiday warmth. His hotel had a Christmas tree covered in vivid, shimmering lights on its porch roof. He and his brother had carefully secured it in place in case a breeze came off the lake and swept up the street. He paused, hearing a hint of piano music soaring over the downtown scene. Rebecca would be playing at his bar tonight.

Without thinking about how tired he was

or how long the weekend would be, Griffin ran his fingers through his hair, took off his boat captain's jacket and strode toward the hotel with the shining tree on the roof. It was piano music. A Christmas song…something about letting it snow. He hummed along as he took the hotel's front steps two at a time and then paused in the lobby. It smelled of cinnamon and evergreen, and the artificial tree that usually graced the lobby's corner and invited guests to take family pictures was even more decked out than usual.

Griffin nodded to the manager behind the front desk and followed the music. He wasn't a dancer—although he could manage slow-dancing with someone he cared about in his arms—but his feet felt light as Rebecca's playing filled all the spaces between the tables and bar patrons.

How long had she been playing? It was after nine-thirty, so she must have been at the keyboard over two hours. He encouraged her to take breaks on nights he was in the bar, but he suspected she short-changed herself most nights. As he watched her, she glanced over, and he noticed a distinct hiccup in the holiday song. Usually, no matter what was happening in the bar or who was talking to her, she didn't miss a beat.

He walked straight to the piano. "Can you take a break?" he asked, leaning close so she could hear him over the music and conversation in the room.

"When my boss says so," she said, flashing him a grin and then looking back at the sheet music in front of her. He suspected she didn't even need that music, as she played a Christmas song she probably knew by heart. He closed the book and she continued playing as if nothing had happened.

"I'll get us drinks while you finish Frosty's fascinating tale, and then meet me at a table," he said.

"You're the boss."

Griffin laughed and went to the bar, where Hadley already had a soda water ready for Rebecca. She stood waiting, head cocked, for his order. "I'll have what she's having," he said.

"Keeping it light tonight," Hadley commented.

"Long weekend," he said. "I'm saving myself for the big events."

"You're asking her to the ball, right? Or have you already?"

He opened his mouth. Why had he pictured himself dancing with her under the tent on the Great Island Hotel's lawn, but he hadn't gone the extra step of securing her company for the evening?

"I plan to," he said.

Hadley squeezed her eyebrows together in disapproval. "It's tomorrow night. You better hope someone didn't beat you to it." She put his soda on the tray and shoved it toward him. "Hurry up, ding-dong."

Griffin grimaced at her, but he was gratified to notice that the piano music ended. Gracefully, but definitely ended. He turned and met Rebecca at a table between the bar and the piano. She sat first while he put the tray on the table. Suddenly nervous, he didn't know how to say what was in his heart. *Dance with me tomorrow night, race with me on Sunday, stay on the island even after the nights get cold—especially when the nights get cold.*

He cleared his throat, sat down and drained half his glass.

"Thirsty work on the ferry tonight?" Rebecca asked.

"Always. Are we ready for this weekend?"

Rebecca sipped her drink and then smiled.

"I'm the outsider here, so even if I think I know what's coming, I'm probably wrong."

"You don't seem like an outsider."

She swallowed and glanced over at the silent piano. "I'm only here for the summer and I'm sure you know how fast the summer flies."

"Too fast," he acknowledged. "We make three quarters of our yearly income in only one hundred days and it usually seems like a whirlwind I wish would stop."

"Usually?"

"This summer I don't want it to end." He leaned back in his chair and considered Rebecca for a moment. She appeared more relaxed than she had been when she'd arrived on the island. Was it the pace of island life? Was she happier?

"I've told you so much about the race, but I've forgotten to get to the subject of something else," he said.

Despite her tan and the low lighting in the bar, he noticed pink stealing across her cheeks as she looked up. Did she suspect he was going to ask her to the dance or was there another reason?

"What subject?" she asked.

"The fun part. The Christmas in July Ball at the Great Island Hotel."

She smiled. "I know about it and even bought a new dress yesterday. Actually, Flora bought it for me as a gift. She's the sweetest person."

Griffin nodded. She had a dress. This was going well.

"Camille and Violet helped me pick it out, and I promised Camille I'd be her date for the party," Rebecca said.

"Oh," Griffin said, knowing his disappointment was obvious. She'd promised to go with someone else? At least it wasn't another man, but still. He'd imagined them dancing together under the holiday lights. Rebecca bit her lip and there was an uncomfortable silence between them despite the hum of bar conversations around them. "I thought maybe, since we're a race team, we would go together," he said.

Rebecca's smile faded and he knew he shouldn't press her about it. After all, they'd shared one dinner, dancing and two kisses he doubted he would ever forget. But they weren't officially…anything. Rebecca was leaving at the end of the summer, and his time and dedication had to belong to his island business.

But was it wrong to want another taste of a sweet romance, no matter how clear its end date?

"I can't let Camille down," Rebecca said. "She's my best friend."

And Griffin well knew Camille would want someone in her corner because of the likelihood she'd run into Maddox at the dance. If only those two would patch up their differences, it would remove a layer of tension hanging over the island like morning fog.

"If there's some last-minute race strategy you wanted to discuss," Rebecca said, "you could tell me now or, of course, I'll see you at the dance."

He shook his head. "No race details. We've been all over the island, and you've probably memorized more facts about Christmas Island than I know from living here most of my twenty-seven years. I think we're as prepared as we can be."

If only there was a way to prepare for the way he felt about Rebecca. Looking at her across the table, he recognized the half-joy, half-agony tug-of-war in his chest. When had he fallen in love with her? He tried to compose his expression, but he was afraid his feelings showed on his face. He was in love with Rebecca, but there was nothing he could do about it.

Rebecca finished her drink. "I should get back to work. Island guests on Christmas in July weekend want to hear all their holiday favorites, and I'm only halfway through my big book of Christmas carols."

She stood and started to walk away, but then she turned and came back to the table. Griffin's heart leaped. Had she changed her mind about the dance?

"Can I play something for you?" she asked. "A favorite Christmas song, maybe?"

His thoughts fast-forwarded to Christmas, when Rebecca would be gone, just a summer memory as beautiful but impermanent as a sunset.

"'I'll Be Home for Christmas,'" he said.

She drew her eyebrows together and looked a little sad for a second before she smiled just as she would at anyone making a request. "Of course," she said. "It's a classic."

Griffin sipped his nearly empty drink as he listened to Rebecca play the familiar song redolent of past Christmases. She played it with more emotion than he'd ever heard it performed. He should have chosen something else out of consideration for her. She'd grown up in various foster homes. What did the song mean for her? Was it painful? He wanted to know about all the holidays she'd spent, and if there was sorrow, he wished he could kiss it away.

But he might never get the chance to be part of her life. He listened to her playing and tried to imprint it on his heart, knowing he'd never hear the song again without picturing this night.

When she finished the piece, Rebecca glanced over at him and he smiled at her. As she launched into a song about sleigh rides, Griffin took their two empty glasses to the bar and slipped out the door into a night filled with holiday lights that twinkled like a shooting star that burned brightly and was gone.

CHAPTER TWENTY-THREE

REBECCA KNEW SHE needed sleep, but instead she lay awake watching the moon through the wide window of her bedroom. The partially open window brought her the peaceful sounds of island life. Waves, a boat horn from across the lake, night insects letting the universe know they were there.

Where was she...and did anyone really care? That had been the hardest part of drifting through the foster home system. She had always tried not to think about the fact that if she suddenly disappeared, no one would really notice. Only when she became a Winter Industries scholar—the most successful one they'd ever had—had she felt the belonging and connection she craved. And now she longed to be part of the Christmas Island family.

Her summer romance with Griffin hovered so close to love that it would only take naming it to tip the balance, but she couldn't say the words. Even if she believed he felt the same way, their relationship existed because of a lie. It would be wrong to encourage his feelings or give him false hope.

She sat up in bed. Flora was her family now. As the matriarch of Winter Industries, the older woman had been an important part of Rebecca's life for a long time, but they'd never met until this summer. Flora had certainly never heard of her before, since the scholars program was run by a committee under the direction of Jim Churchill. How could Rebecca say goodbye to Flora and never see her again? It would be like leaving a piece of her heart on the island.

There was only one way out of the hole she'd dug for herself from her first ferry ride. If she wanted to have a relationship with her new friends on Christmas Island, she had to risk losing them completely by telling them the truth. Rebecca flopped back onto the soft pillow in her luxurious bed and closed her eyes, steeling herself for what she had to do the next day before the ball. If she had to pack her suitcase and leave the island, she'd miss the ball and let Griffin down as his race partner, but he'd be fine. A man who was inheriting millions didn't need ten thousand dollars.

Whether or not he needed her, he deserved someone truthful.

THE NEXT MORNING Rebecca fussed over Flora's breakfast and had nearly worked up the courage to tell her the truth when Flora put down her napkin and looked at her elegant silver wristwatch.

"May I ask you something?"

"Of course," Rebecca said.

"My nephew is returning today on the ferry. Either he discovered how much he missed me or he wants to enjoy the holiday spirit, but he's coming back."

"That's really nice," Rebecca said. She'd wondered why Alden had left and if he would return. Did his coming and going have anything to do with his involvement in Flora's will? She was almost out of chances to find out because of her resolve to tell Flora the truth before accepting the gift of a ball gown. She could no longer lie to her fairy godmother.

"I'd like to spend time with him," Flora said. "But I find we quickly run out of topics."

"You haven't been...close over the years?" Rebecca asked.

Flora laughed. "I'm sure you can see we have not. He's a reckless spendthrift like his father, my dear but foolish brother. I think the sense in the Winter family must be in the female genes." Flora smiled at Rebecca. "You are more like me than my own nephew."

Rebecca drew in a breath. She was both immensely gratified and miserably horrified. Flora had just given her the ultimate compliment, and the only repayment was the truth.

"Flora, there's something I have to—"

"I know it's an imposition," Flora said, interrupting her, "but would you take the car and pick him up?"

"Yes, I'd be happy to."

Flora got up. "Excellent. I'm going to sit in the sun with Cornelius and read. I need to rest up before the busy weekend really gets going."

The older woman left, and Rebecca sat back and sipped her coffee. She'd missed the opportunity, but there could still be time before the ball.

Rebecca picked up Alden from the noon ferry and returned to the Winter Palace, where she went to her room and paced the floor, agonizing. An hour later, after Rebecca had doubted her resolve a thousand times, she knocked on Flora's bedroom door. She didn't usually visit Flora in her private room unless requested, but she wanted a quiet place to tell the older woman the truth she deserved.

"Come in," Flora said. "Although I should send you away and advise you to have a luxurious bath and a nap before tonight's ball. You won't believe how marvelous it is until you see it for yourself, and I want you to be the most lovely girl there."

Rebecca smiled, even though her heart twisted with guilt. "The dress you bought me will probably be the loveliest one there."

Flora pointed to the easy chair next to hers. Both chairs sat in a sunny alcove with a view of the lake. Rebecca picked up Cornelius from her chair and put him on her lap when she sat down.

"You've come to talk about something serious," Flora said.

Rebecca nodded and let out a long breath. "It's about why I'm here this summer."

"I know why you're here," Flora said. "To be my wonderful companion and collect a decent salary for living in an island mansion and playing my Steinway."

"You've never asked me how I heard about the job," Rebecca said.

"From your friend Camille."

Rebecca shook her head. It was time to drop the pretense. "Jim Churchill sent me."

Flora sat back in her chair and folded her hands on her lap. She studied Rebecca, and Rebecca sat very still, afraid even to squirm. She knew she deserved whatever was coming. "Finally," Flora said. "I wondered when we were going to stop dancing around that inconvenient fact."

"You knew?" Rebecca felt blood rush to her face, heating her cheeks.

Flora tilted her head. "I know Jim worries about me and thinks I've gotten a bit too old to manage my affairs. That's why he plucked you from the finance department at Winter Industries to come here and keep an eye on me."

Rebecca couldn't breathe. She methodically rubbed Cornelius between the eyes with one finger how he liked. *Flora knew.* Why hadn't Jim told her?

"I looked you up on the company website after a quick internet search," Flora added. "And I was very impressed. You graduated in the top ten from the University of Chicago and became our first scholar to go on for a masters. Which you also finished at the top of your class. No wonder Jim Churchill trusts you to do his dirty work for the summer."

Rebecca wanted to cry. Her accomplishments meant nothing in the face of the utter betrayal she'd caused. "When…when did you find out?"

"Before I came to the island."

"But…but you never said anything," Rebecca said.

Flora laughed. "Why should I? It was entertaining at first, waiting for you to blunder into my business and show your hand. But you didn't blunder. In fact, I discovered I liked you a whole lot."

Rebecca swallowed. "I discovered I liked you a whole lot, too," she whispered.

"And I also realized you were very good at keeping secrets."

"I'm sorry," Rebecca said, looking up and meeting Flora's gaze.

"Keeping secrets is a double-edged sword. It means you can't trust someone…or the opposite. You can trust them very much, depending on where their loyalty lies."

Rebecca knew that only the absolute truth would save her. "I'm loyal to Winter Industries. The scholars program changed my life."

"Is that the only reason you're loyal to the company?"

"No," Rebecca said. Cornelius rolled over on her lap and she ran a hand tenderly along his belly. "It feels like a family to me. I was in love with belonging somewhere."

"Was?"

"I've made a mess this summer. I haven't succeeded in doing what Jim Churchill asked."

"What specifically did he ask you to do?" Flora asked.

Rebecca sighed. She was about to commit the ultimate betrayal of her boss, but it was even worse to confess the truth to the company's matriarch. She felt she'd betrayed everyone. There was no way out but the truth.

"He heard a rumor that you'd recently changed your will. On top of that, your decision to spend the summer on the island, when you hadn't in several years, made him think there was something going on with you."

"Going on?"

"He was afraid someone might be unduly influencing you or taking advantage of you," Rebecca said. "He's very worried about the future of the company because he cares about it and all the people who work there. He wanted me to sort of…watch over you."

"Spy on me, you mean," Flora said.

Rebecca wished she hadn't eaten lunch. She felt sickness rising up her throat, and her eyes stung with tears. She had to keep it together and face what she'd done, no matter how pure her intentions had been.

"You didn't do a very good job of spying for the company," Flora said. "I talked to Jim Churchill last week, and even though I dropped the names Griffin and Maddox May several times in the conversation, it didn't seem as if they meant a thing to him. I'm guessing you didn't tell him what I was doing with my personal fortune."

Rebecca shook her head.

"And you sure as heck didn't tell Griffin or he wouldn't be hustling to make a few bucks for his ferry dock."

Rebecca shook her head again.

"You kept my secret," Flora said. "Just as I thought you would. But I do wonder why."

"You asked me to," Rebecca said. "And my loyalty is totally tangled up right now. I care about the company almost desperately and Jim Churchill has been like a father figure to me. But I care about you, too, and you have a right to do whatever you want with your money."

"I do," Flora acknowledged. "And I can do what I want with my affection, too." She reached over and put her hand on Rebecca's knee. "I've grown to like you so much this summer that I'm glad Jim sent you out here."

"You don't have to be so nice about it," Rebecca said, her voice shaking. "I should pack up and get out of your way."

"Absolutely not," Flora said. "I hired you for the whole summer."

"But you can't really want me to stay."

"Nothing has changed. I knew why you were here from the start and I'm glad you finally confessed it. I told Cornelius this morning that I thought you were finally ready. And Jim Churchill doesn't have anything to worry about. He'll run the governing board that controls the future of my company when Cornelius and I are strolling the streets of the afterlife. That has not changed."

Rebecca set Cornelius gently on the floor and stood. Relief mixed with a powerful sense of sadness and regret flooded her. "This has been the best summer of my life, and I think of you as the grandmother I never had. No matter what, I want you to know my affection for you is real."

Flora smiled. "I believe it is. And I think you also care about Griffin."

Rebecca nodded, unable to speak past the lump in her throat.

"I put you in an impossible position when I told you about his inheritance," Flora said. "I am sorry about that now that I know how you feel about him. It was my way of testing you."

Rebecca shook her head and one tear slid down her cheek. "I put myself in this situation. And I should tell him the truth about my summer job before anything goes any further."

Flora leaned forward in her chair. "Not tonight. Have a wonderful time at the ball. You deserve that. And Griffin does, too. Why not have tonight?"

The question lingered in Rebecca's mind long after she returned to her room to pass the rest of the afternoon. Then it was time to shower and dress for an evening ball at which she would feel like an imposter.

GRIFFIN AND HIS brother stood by the punch bowl while the Great Island Hotel's orchestra played the tenth Christmas song in a row. People were already dancing, and men in dark suits mixed with women in sparkling, colorful gowns. Under the giant white tent on the lawn of the hotel, hundreds of strings of white lights illuminated the faces of locals and visitors. It was the biggest event of the year. In December the hotel hosted a Christmas party in its ballroom, but only locals attended because of the bitter lake winds and limited ferry service dependent on lake ice.

This event had everything. Music, guests, food and drinks, holiday cheer. But it was missing the one thing that had his pulse throbbing. Where was Rebecca?

"Second time in a suit this summer," Maddox grumbled. "Although the food and drinks are better at this party than they were at the wedding."

"The wedding was fine," Griffin said. Or at least it had been fine until Rebecca and Camille had disappeared. He hoped his brother would stay out of Camille's space tonight so she wouldn't leave early and take Rebecca with her.

"At least you'll have someone to dance with tonight," Maddox commented. He nodded toward the tent's entrance, marked with an archway of red ribbons and white lights. Camille and Rebecca stood for a moment, arm in arm, and Griffin smiled at the expression on Rebecca's face. Her friend had probably told her the party was spectacular, but he doubted she was prepared for the over-the-top holiday extravaganza. It still wowed him every year and he'd been coming since he was officially an adult at eighteen.

Camille's dress was red and she looked very pretty with her blond hair put up. But Rebecca shimmered in a silver gown. Something around her neck sparkled even from across the tent.

"Wow," Maddox said.

Griffin let out a long breath. "You're not kidding." Without waiting for his brother, Griffin put down his punch glass and strode toward the entrance. As he approached Rebecca, he noted every detail. Her long, beautiful neck was bared by her upswept dark hair. Was that a string of red-and-green gems around her neck? The low neckline of her sleeveless dress showed off her skin tanned from a summer of island life. The glittery hem of her dress stopped just above a pair of red high heels.

She looked like the Christmas gift he'd been waiting for all his life. The feelings swirling through him weren't just about her appearance. Anyone else wearing that same dress and those red shoes wouldn't move him. It was Rebecca. He loved her. He thought the words as his feet kept propelling him toward her and he couldn't stop. Didn't want to stop. What would happen if he told her tonight?

Rebecca laughed at something Camille said and then she turned her head just enough to spot him moving out of the crowd. Her smile broadened and she held out both hands. Should he take her hands? Hug her? Her body language was an invitation he couldn't refuse. He gave her a brief hug and kissed her cheek. She smelled like flowers as always, and he didn't want to let her go.

"Look at you all dressed up," Rebecca said. "I like the vest."

Griffin wore the same black suit he'd worn to the summer wedding and their date at the Great Island Hotel, but he'd added a red vest and bow tie to make the suit more appropriate for the black-tie ball. At least that was what his mother had suggested several years ago when she presented him with the red vest and his brother with a silver one.

"Christmas only comes…twice a year," he said.

"You're such a goofball," Camille said as she gave him a hug.

"Thank you," he said. "You are both beautiful."

Camille laughed. "Especially Rebecca. That dress was the prettiest one in Violet's collection this year and no one else could have pulled it off. Flora insisted on it."

"She went shopping with you?" Griffin asked.

Rebecca nodded. "And she loaned me this jewelry from her personal collection. She got it out of the safe, so I'm spending the entire night panicking about losing one of the earrings."

"I think they're just priceless emeralds and rubies," Camille said. "No need to worry."

"Flora loves you," Griffin said.

He'd noticed Flora's affection for Rebecca and had, at first, felt suspicious of it. But as he'd gotten to know Rebecca, he'd learned for himself that it was impossible not to love her. His words were light, but when he said them, he thought he saw Rebecca's smile falter for a moment. Was it hard for her to accept love because of the way she'd grown up?

"She came with us tonight," Rebecca said. "Alden is in charge of finding her a nice chair and then taking her home whenever she wants to go." Rebecca cast a glance behind her as if she was waiting for Alden and Flora. "I hope she enjoys it."

"Let's get a drink," Camille said. "I can't dance until I've had at least one so I'm not so worried about my mediocre dancing skills."

Griffin offered an arm to both Camille and Rebecca, and the three of them crossed the tent to the long bar set up on tables draped with green-and-white linens. A string of old-fashioned Christmas bulbs swooped low over the uniformed waiters and bartenders standing behind the wineglasses, punch bowls and colorful liquor bottles.

"I'm having something that won't stain if I accidentally spill it," Rebecca said.

"Good call," Camille said. "Champagne."

"Three glasses of champagne," Griffin told the bartender. As he waited for the bottle to be opened and bubbly poured, he glanced around for his brother. Had Maddox found someone to talk to or dance with? He hoped so. He didn't want to abandon his own brother, but Maddox didn't need his big brother hanging around and smoothing the way for him. He could manage a dance on his own if he managed being a dad.

"Hey," Violet said as she came up to them.

"Another champagne," Griffin told the bartender.

"How did you know?" Violet asked.

"Lucky guess," Griffin said.

Rebecca waved to Flora, who had taken a seat next to Alden near the entrance where she could watch everyone arrive. Flora waved back and smiled, and Griffin could see Rebecca's shoulders relax. It was sweet how she cared so much about Flora.

"I love your dress," Camille told Violet, bringing Griffin and Rebecca's attention back to their circle of friends. Violet's dress was black, and even though Griffin didn't know much about formal gowns, he could tell it was something special she'd ordered into her shop for herself. No one else had anything quite like her dress, which fit tight all the way down and then flared out at the bottom.

"I found some interesting hotel guests to dance with," Violet said. "There's an engineering convention going on so there are a whole bunch of single men." She grinned and cocked her head. "At least I hope they're single."

Griffin handed out glasses of champagne and offered a toast to Christmas Island. They clinked glasses and drank as people in party clothes swirled past them. The orchestra played "It's Beginning to Look a Lot Like

Christmas" and couples danced to the cheerful music.

Violet finished her drink and grabbed Camille's arm. "Let's go find those engineers and see if they want to dance."

When they left, Rebecca sipped her champagne slowly and looked at Griffin. "Does it bother you that there's an engineering convention at the hotel?"

"It would have a few years ago, even a year ago," he said. "I'll admit to feeling sorry for myself that I gave up college, but I've moved on."

Rebecca smiled. "I'm glad."

"I still miss my dad every day, and my mom, too, even though she seems happy living down in Texas with her sister. She wasn't originally from the island, so maybe she doesn't miss it like I would if I ever left again."

"Do you think you ever will?"

He shook his head. "No. My life is here. Maddox and I are building something we hope to pass down to the next generation. His son already has sea legs."

"If I'd grown up here, I doubt I'd ever leave," Rebecca said. She watched the dancers with an expression on her face that was half-happy and half-sad.

"Why don't you stay?" he asked.

"I can't."

"Why not? Is there something so important elsewhere that you can't stay here where you seem so happy?"

"You don't understand," she said.

"Of course I do. I had to make the tough choice to come home and stay here, and I'm glad I did. You have friends here now. People who care about you."

Rebecca looked up at him, her eyes and smile soft. Was he persuading her? Was it time to say what was in his heart?

"I care about you," he said.

She swallowed and put her hand to her neck, fingering the expensive necklace Flora had loaned her. "There's so much about me that you don't know."

"Then tell me what I need to know," he said. "This party goes until midnight and it's an open bar."

"We shouldn't stay out too late. We have to make sure we get a good night's rest so we can win the race tomorrow," Rebecca said. "I probably should slow down on the champagne."

"The race starts at ten so the off-island competitors have time to come over on the first morning ferry. Wish I could stack the deck by making the ferry run late, but that wouldn't be very sporting of me, and I'd have to persuade my part-time captain to take the long way from the mainland."

Rebecca laughed. "I think you're above those kinds of tricks."

Griffin waggled his eyebrows. "So you think. And luckily for me, I've got the best partner on the race, so my chances of getting the cash prize are solid without cheating."

"Assuming the race challenges do not involve leaping aboard a moving ferry while pulling a large suitcase," Rebecca said. "I'm not good at that."

"I'll never forget that night. Or this summer," Griffin said.

"Neither will I." Rebecca tilted her head up and Griffin couldn't resist. He touched his lips lightly to hers. She kissed him back, and he closed his eyes and enjoyed it. When she pulled away he opened his eyes and the colored lights seemed to swirl dizzily. He didn't care if people knew how he felt about Rebecca. Maybe they thought he was foolish falling for a summer visitor who would leave him lonely at the end of the season.

All he cared about was Rebecca.

"I should go find my friends," she said. "I promised I'd dance with them."

The words hit him like an icy shower. "I thought you'd dance with me."

The orchestra began a slow song. Rebecca glanced over at the musicians and then back at Griffin. "I do like this song," she said.

Griffin took her glass and set it next to his empty one on the table behind them. He reached for her hand and they walked to the dance floor together. Something about the moment felt like a transition. Were they moving toward a new phase in their relationship, or were they moving slowly toward an exit? Either way, he pushed back the worry and resolved to just enjoy dancing with Rebecca.

He passed his brother, who was dancing with someone he'd never seen before, almost certainly a hotel guest. Violet and Camille were also on the dance floor with strangers. It was odd; the tent contained everything he loved about Christmas Island, with the festive atmosphere and the people who were as familiar as his own heartbeat. But it also contained the fleeting elements of his island world. Hotel guests, summer visitors, the effervescent champagne with its bubbles that rose and disappeared just as this summer would end.

He held Rebecca a little tighter as they swayed with the music and she didn't stiffen or pull back. "I'll miss you," he whispered.

She didn't answer, but she nodded, and her borrowed earring bobbed and reflected the lights winking over them on the dance floor.

CHAPTER TWENTY-FOUR

ON SUNDAY MORNING the early mist turned into a steady rain. Rebecca planned to eat an early breakfast so she could get downtown and meet Griffin in plenty of time for the official race start. To her surprise, Alden was in the kitchen at the Winter Palace drumming his fingers on the counter while he waited for his toast to pop up. It seemed so…normal and domestic.

How well did she really know Alden? She had harbored a negative impression of him as a businessperson before she got to the island—based on the stories she'd heard around the company. She also knew that Jim Churchill had been worried about Alden's future role—if any—in Winter Industries when Flora passed on.

Looking at him waiting for the toaster, butter knife in hand, made her wonder if he'd gotten a fair shot in life. Maybe he was just…

waiting for his life to start? Dependent on the charity of an aunt he didn't know very well?

"You're up early," Rebecca said. "Can I pour you some orange juice?"

"Just coffee," he said.

Did he want her to make coffee? He didn't specifically ask, but Rebecca didn't mind starting a pot.

"I'm going home later today," he said.

"Will you watch the race?"

An annoyed look passed over his face. "Probably not. Everyone on this island lives or dies for that event and the cash prize, but it's not enough money to tempt me to make a fool of myself."

Rebecca forced a smile. "You're probably right about making a fool of myself. I agreed to be on a team, but looking at the rain, I'm not very enthusiastic right now."

"Griffin May's team?"

"Yes."

"Flora's 'real' nephew," he said, making air quotes.

Rebecca poured cold water into the brewer. "You're her real nephew, and I know she cares about you."

Alden crossed his arms over his chest and ignored the bagels that popped up from the toaster. "You know the thing about long family histories?"

She wanted to tell him she knew nothing about family history since she didn't have any herself, but she'd been an observer of plenty of others. "What about them?"

"For every winner, there's a loser," he said. "Every favorite has an equally disappointing opposite."

"Why are you telling me this?" she asked.

"I've seen how you've cozied up to Flora all summer. She even loaned you her expensive jewelry—you know that necklace alone is worth thousands, right?"

"I put them in a safe place when I got home because Flora was already in bed."

"Uh-huh," Alden commented.

When Camille had driven her up the road to the Winter Palace, Rebecca thought she saw a light on, but as they'd pulled into the driveway, the house was totally dark. Had Alden been waiting up? If so, why had he switched off the light when she arrived? The thought made her shiver and reminded her of those other nights she'd found him pawing through Flora's papers. What if he had found something at last and now he was leaving the island? He seemed somehow…pleased with himself.

"My dad wasn't the family favorite. That honor went to Flora."

"There's room for everyone in a family," Rebecca said.

"You'd think."

Alden smeared butter on his bagel, smashed it back together and left the kitchen. A rumble of thunder made Rebecca jump, but then she pulled herself together and focused on the issue at hand. She needed food, a rain jacket and her water-resistant backpack with a change of shoes and clothes. It was going to be a wild day, and even though Alden's words were unsettling, she knew exactly what she had to do—anything she could to help Griffin win. He deserved it.

The clouds parted and revealed a pink sunrise as Rebecca drove Flora's golf cart downtown. Griffin had asked her to park behind his hotel because he was afraid the rest of the downtown parking spots would be claimed by visitors and spectators.

"He wasn't kidding," Rebecca said aloud as she turned onto Holly Street. It was packed full and pedestrians obscured the street even with a cool drizzle still hanging in the air. She zipped behind the hotel and Griffin opened the back door before she even gathered up her backpack.

"Come in and stay dry," he said.

"Too late," Rebecca said, smiling. "Well, almost. I'm only a little soggy from the drive."

Griffin rubbed her arms and gave her a quick peck on the lips. "For good luck," he said.

"Do we need it?"

He laughed. "Everyone needs it. The planning committee hasn't revealed a thing, but they seem to take twisted pleasure in making each year more complicated than the last. Can you do a cartwheel? I never thought to ask. How about juggling?"

"Yes on the cartwheel, no on the juggling," Rebecca said.

He pointed to a red bicycle and a blue one waiting by the hotel's back door. "Our transportation for the race. No headlights, though, because if we're still out there when it gets dark, we're definitely giving up."

Rebecca's thoughts flashed back to their dark bike ride around the island and how she'd bravely switched off her light, trusting Griffin and her other friends. What a magical summer it had been.

She sat on a stool in the empty bar while Griffin poured coffee and then peeled the lid back on a plate of scrambled eggs, bacon and biscuits. "Hope you're hungry," he said. "I am. I haven't eaten since last night's party."

At the mention of the ball, Rebecca's heart rate quickened. It had been such a beautiful and perfect night, but she'd spent too much of it trying to keep Griffin at arm's length. And trying to resist telling him the truth, just as she'd told Flora. Maybe Flora was right. There would be time after the race, and Griffin deserved a partner he could believe in. A few more hours wouldn't matter, she hoped.

She dug in to her plate of food and Griffin did the same. Between bites she glanced out the front window and noted that it was brightening up.

"I think the rain's over, but the island trails are going to be muddy," Griffin said, following her gaze. "Which could make it very messy, depending on what's planned."

"I brought extra shoes," Rebecca said, patting her backpack on the empty seat next to her. "And a jacket, first-aid kit, water bottle and emergency cookies."

Griffin put a hand over hers. "I'm so glad I chose you."

Rebecca stilled. He'd chosen her. Aside from Jim Churchill choosing her for the special Flora assignment, there had been very few times in her life when someone had pointed in her direction and wanted her for what she had to offer. It was so sweet…but bittersweet. Griffin would be so disappointed when she revealed her lies and when…if…he ever found out that she'd known about his inheritance even as she danced with him, kissed him, played a special song for him on the piano.

She would seem like the fraud she was, and hurting him had never been part of the plan.

"So," she said, her voice cracking, "where is the official starting line?"

Griffin smiled and kept his hand over hers. "Rebecca, would you promise me something?"

She nodded, hoping it would be a promise she could keep.

"Whatever happens today, let's have fun. You make me happy just being with you, and I want this to be a day we both enjoy. Even if I make an utter fool of myself, I'm going to laugh about it, no matter how much I truly want to win that prize."

Rebecca let out a *whoosh* of breath. "I promise to have fun and laugh, even if I slide on my butt down a muddy hill or forget the island motto just when I need it."

"There's an island motto?" Griffin asked.

Rebecca laughed. "Kidding. They considered one in 1950, but the governing board couldn't agree on it. One of them called another member a bah-humbug and they tabled it forever."

"Who knew?" Griffin asked.

"The island history book," Rebecca said.

Griffin sighed. "Finish your breakfast, smarty-pants. And then we'll line up by the flagpole at the marina. We get our clue packets and then the chaos begins."

"I'm ready."

THIRTY MINUTES LATER, as Rebecca sized up the competing teams, she wasn't so sure she was ready. Some were older, some were younger, some appeared incredibly athletic and some had matching outfits right down to their socks, but they all had one thing in common. They looked like they were here to win. Twenty thousand dollars was a lot of money, more money than Rebecca would ever have imagined as she was working her way through college. However, her job at Winter Industries paid well, and she'd discovered the blessing of financial security the past several years. She saved every dollar she could, though, knowing that security wasn't as permanent as it sounded.

"There have to be fifty other teams," she whispered to Griffin.

He tightened his grip on her hand. "Exactly fifty teams are allowed every year. It makes for a serious competition."

To her surprise, Flora Winter stood at the podium to make a small speech, opening the race. The Bentley was double-parked on a street nearby. She felt a stab of guilt that she hadn't arranged Flora's transportation for the day, especially knowing that Flora didn't like Alden driving her car. There was a lull after Flora's speech while the prize committee called each team to come forward and pick up a sealed packet, so Rebecca made her way to Flora's side.

"I'm sorry," she said. "I didn't realize you'd need a ride this morning."

Flora patted her arm. "I drove myself."

"You did? I…" Rebecca stammered.

"I'm not as helpless as people think." Flora smiled. "I even got up to second gear. My nephew wanted to stay at the house, so I took matters into my own hands."

"I thought Alden was going home today," Rebecca said.

"He's leaving later."

"Okay," Rebecca said. "I just don't want to let you down."

"Don't let Griffin down," Flora said. "Now hurry over there and get ready to rip open that packet when the starting gun goes off. Every second counts if you two want to win the prize."

GRIFFIN HELD THE large brown envelope, one finger under the seal. He and Rebecca stood next to their bicycles, ready to hop on and go.

"My heart is racing," Rebecca said. "The tension is already killing me."

He laughed. The starting gun blasted, and he ripped open the envelope to reveal the first challenge. He held the card so they could both read it at the same time.

Halfway point ice cream stand. Show us your shake skills, but hurry because there are only five ice cream stations open at a time.

"We have to be in the first group," he said, but Rebecca was already shoving off on her bike. He liked her competitive spirit and the way she stood on the pedals to power up a fast start. Griffin caught up and they rode side by side as fast as they could.

"Know any shortcuts?" Rebecca asked, not taking her eyes off the road or reducing her speed.

"No, the lake road is the fastest. Some of the mainlanders might look at the map and try the route across the island, but they're going to get a big surprise when they discover it's all uphill to the halfway point."

Rebecca laughed and shifted into a higher gear. She'd come a long way from the Rebecca who'd been so out of practice on a bike that she'd worried about navigating the island roads in the dark. He just hoped she knew how to make a good milkshake.

"I just ran over a dead toad," she said. "Poor thing must have been out late last night."

She flashed a smile at Griffin. They'd shared so many moments in the summer— but did those moments add up to a relationship that would outlast the season? He wished it could. Wanted to tell her how he felt. And he planned to as soon as the race was over. No matter what she chose to do, she deserved to know he loved her.

Three miles later they were among the first five teams to arrive at the halfway point ice cream stand, and Griffin leaped off his bike to grab a number securing their spot. Using the instructions in their packet, Rebecca made a strawberry-vanilla-mint milkshake with the exact proportions specified. She blended it, poured it into a tall glass and added a dollop of whipped cream and a cherry.

"You've done this before?" he asked.

"Summer job back in high school."

Griffin held his breath as the judges tasted it, paused, nodded their approval and then handed him and Rebecca an envelope with their next race clue.

"We're leaving in first place," he said as they ran back to their bikes and paused long enough to note the location of the next challenge. Rebecca's cheeks were flushed, and she was so beautiful he was tempted to risk kissing her and using up part of their precious lead.

"Where?" she said, her tone implying she meant business. He found her even more attractive because of it, but he focused on the card.

"Winery ruins."

They pedaled onto the lake road with two other teams right behind them.

"What are we doing at the winery ruins?" Rebecca asked as she leaned forward and rode.

"I didn't read the whole card, but I think I saw the words *bare feet* and *crushing grapes*."

Rebecca laughed. "We said we were going to have fun."

Griffin couldn't remember the last time he'd been happier as he biked along the lakeshore by Rebecca's side. When they reached the winery, they had slipped to third place because the other teams had road bikes instead of mountain tires, but Griffin wasn't worried. They had plenty of time to make up a few minutes, and their mountain tires would pay off later if they ended up on unpaved island roads.

At the winery he and Rebecca grabbed a bench and stripped their shoes and socks with the other teams.

"This is madness," Rebecca said, laughing as he helped her into a wine barrel. He kept his hands around her waist just a moment longer than necessary, and she smiled at him. "Get in your barrel and start squishing," she said, laughing. They crushed grapes with their bare feet until the judges were satisfied with the liquid mess in the bottom of the barrels. Griffin hosed off Rebecca's feet and then his own, and they both slid their socks and shoes on their purple-stained feet.

"Island airport," Rebecca said, reading off the clue from the judges.

"This time I do know a shortcut if you're willing to go off-road a bit," Griffin said.

"Willing," Rebecca said. "I'll follow you."

He grinned. "I was hoping you'd say that."

They were still among the top three teams, and Griffin began to feel glimmers of confidence. He and his brother had fared pretty well in previous races, but Rebecca's determination was impressive. She raced as if her future depended on a win, even though Griffin suspected she didn't need the money. He was certain Flora paid Rebecca well, and her living expenses were covered. She also had a job to go to at the end of the summer. He was the one who needed the quick infusion of cash, and Rebecca was going to help him get it. She was doing this for him.

He was usually the person taking care of everyone else and sacrificing for them, and having Rebecca knock herself out to help him made him love her even more. He wished he had time to appreciate that thought.

On the way to the island airport, one of the other teams stayed on the lake road, another took a marked gravel road that led into the island's interior and Griffin led the way down a path through the woods that he knew by heart. It might be muddy, but it would be worth the risk.

Ten minutes later they emerged from the woods and rode straight onto the runway at the small airport. They were muddy, but Rebecca was right behind him.

"What are we doing?" she asked.

"You okay? That was a tough trail."

"I stayed with you," she said, laughing and putting a hand to her chest. "But I'm glad you couldn't see me struggling."

Griffin handed her the card. There were no other teams in sight, and he took a moment to enjoy watching Rebecca's bright, eager expression as she scanned the card. "Oh, man," she said. "This could take all day."

The assignment was to measure the distance between the lights marking the runway. They weren't allowed to use a tape measure, but the instructions stated that they were printed on a paper that was exactly eight inches wide and they could use the paper.

"I have an idea," Rebecca said, tapping one finger to her forehead. "There's a fast way to do this without using this little piece of paper." She turned and ran into the woods and then appeared a moment later with a long stick. "We make our own yardstick!"

Griffin grinned. "Let's be quick before the other teams get here and steal your idea."

Using the makeshift yardstick, they finished their calculations just as the other teams emerged onto the runway. Rebecca wrote the number on the race card and handed it to a judge waiting nearby. He nodded and handed them the next clue. They had a comfortable lead on the other teams, and Griffin couldn't resist leaning close and brushing a kiss over Rebecca's lips. Her eyes opened in surprise, but she smiled.

"We have a race to win," she said.

CHAPTER TWENTY-FIVE

THEY WERE AHEAD, but barely. Rebecca and Griffin had completed nine challenges that took them all over the island. There was only one left, and the race card didn't describe it. It simply directed them to the ballroom at the Great Island Hotel for a skill challenge.

"If it's dancing, I apologize in advance for losing us the race," Griffin said as they biked up the driveway of the historic hotel.

"It's got to be dancing," Rebecca said. She had a decent amount of rhythm from a decade of piano playing, and there was no doubt about the chemistry between her and Griffin. Would it be enough to keep their lead and put them across the finish line first?

They ran into the ballroom, and Rebecca had a vivid memory of dancing with Griffin. She'd known she was falling for him at the time, and the feeling had only grown since then. Even if she did leave the island soon—and she had to—how would she leave Griffin? He'd stolen her heart. She'd carefully guarded it her entire life, not knowing when she would move next, afraid to get close to people and fall in love with them. No one had tempted her to sacrifice everything and take the ultimate risk.

But Griffin had. And she doubted she would ever be the same.

The ballroom lights shone brightly overhead, and the orchestra stage was empty. Maybe it wasn't dancing? A judge handed her an envelope and she pulled out a piece of sheet music.

Piano music.

Her mouth dropped open and she looked up at Griffin, who was smiling and pointing behind her. She turned. There were three pianos lined up on the dance floor.

"I can't believe it," she said. "The task is to get help from the Great Hotel's piano player and play one verse of 'Jingle Bells' without making a mistake."

Griffin started laughing and couldn't stop. He doubled over, holding his stomach.

Rebecca smiled. No way was she blowing this chance. She turned and marched to the piano, pulled out the bench, settled the sheet of music on the stand and played a verse of the Christmas song perfectly.

The piano player, standing by ready to coach, put a hand over his mouth. "Okay," he said. "You've done that before."

"I can't believe my good luck that this was the final challenge," Rebecca said. She felt arms come around her from behind and a kiss pressed to her temple.

"I love you," Griffin whispered in her ear. "I—"

Her words were interrupted by another team sitting at the piano nearby and painfully working through a line of music with one finger.

"We have to go," she said. "We could win this."

She grabbed the red envelope the judge held out. It didn't contain a clue, but they needed to present it at the finish line to prove they'd passed the final test. Rebecca grabbed Griffin's hand and they ran through the hotel lobby and got on their bikes. The ride into town was exhilarating, and they both knew nothing could stand in the way of their win.

"What were you going to say back there?" Griffin yelled over the lake breeze as they pedaled into downtown, where a crowd had gathered at a platform decorated with Christmas trees and colorful lights.

Joy, hope and excitement bubbled through Rebecca and she couldn't hold it back. "I was going to say I love you, too."

She took only a second to enjoy his expression of pure happiness, before turning back to the racecourse. Side by side, they burst through the narrow green-and-red ribbon and the announcer declared them the winners. Rebecca braked and came to a stop next to Griffin near the platform. She saw Flora seated in a big red chair near the podium and waved to her. Flora waved for her and Griffin to ascend the platform, and Griffin hugged Rebecca and then took her hand and led her to the steps.

"This is the best day of my life," he said.

"Because we won?"

"Not only because we won."

The crowd cheered, and Rebecca handed the judge her red envelope. He held two green envelopes and nodded to Flora, who stood behind the podium and declared Rebecca Browne and Griffin May the official winners of the Holiday Hustle. Rebecca took her envelope, waved at the crowd and turned to Griffin, who held his envelope as if it was a precious object. She knew that, for him, it was. If he only knew he would inherit millions and probably even the Winter Palace, would he have tried so hard to win the race? She was glad they'd had that time together and an unforgettable adventure. Leaving would be even harder now that they'd both admitted what was in their hearts, but she had no choice.

Rebecca glanced up at the Winter Palace, on the bluff above town. It was so beautiful and such a lovely part of her—

She narrowed her eyes and used her hand as a sunshade. Was that smoke coming from the chimney? Why? The July sun was hot on her shoulders and she was overheated from biking and racing, but a cold chill washed over her.

"Did Alden say why he was staying home?" she asked Flora.

Flora looked surprised and then flicked a quick glance at her grand home. "He didn't care to come downtown for the fun," she said. "He had reading to do."

"By the fire?"

"Who needs a fire in July?" Flora asked.

"What's the matter?" Griffin said. The applause had died down and people had turned their attention to Holly Street to watch for the second-place team that would win a smaller prize.

"Something's not right," she said. "Flora, can you hurry? We need to get in your car and get to your house."

"What are you—" Flora began.

"Please," Rebecca said. "I'll…explain it in the car."

She didn't know what she was going to say because the thoughts were racing through her head and were too unformed to make sense.

Griffin stared at her a moment, but then he held out an arm for Flora. "I'll drive," he said.

They hustled to the vintage Bentley parked behind the podium and Flora got in the backseat while Rebecca and Griffin got in front.

"Wait," the judge said as he ran after them. "Aren't you going to stick around for the other teams to come in?"

Flora stuck her head out the window. "Too much excitement for an old lady," she said cheerfully.

Griffin put the car in gear and maneuvered as fast as possible through the street crowds.

"Tell me what's going on," he said, not taking his eyes off the road ahead.

"Alden's alone at the Winter Palace, and he's burning something," Rebecca said.

Flora leaned forward and stuck her head between Rebecca and Griffin. "What do you think he's burning?"

"I have a theory," Rebecca said. "A suspicion. I've caught him several late nights going through the papers in your library, obviously looking for something. I can't quite figure out what it would be that he thinks helps his case with you."

"His case?" Griffin asked.

"Helps him get more of my money," Flora said. "And my company."

"What would be there?" Rebecca asked, twisting in her seat. "Could there be any papers that demonstrate he owns more of Winter Industries than everyone thinks? Does he know you changed your will?"

"Wait a minute," Griffin said. He gave Rebecca an incredulous stare and then turned back to the road. "How do you know about this?"

Flora leaned back into her seat. "He might have found the papers from when my brother and I split the company decades ago and he called his part WinterSon Corporation.

Maybe Alden thinks he has some claim and that his father never got his due portion."

"Wait, what?" Griffin asked.

"In fact, there are papers, very old ones, that we had drawn up all those years ago," Flora said.

"Oh, no," Rebecca said. "He's burning something. Could he be destroying the proof that you had sole rights to Winter Industries?" Panic clawed at her throat. "This is awful. Your company could be in jeopardy." Griffin turned and stared at Rebecca. "Your inheritance," she said.

"It's Alden's inheritance," Griffin said. "Why's the guy going to hurt himself?"

Rebecca shook her head. "He wouldn't be hurting himself. He'd be hurting you." She turned and looked at Flora, expecting her to be shocked, upset, but she wasn't. The older woman was laughing.

"I know what he found. And he can burn every paper in that library if he wants to," Flora said.

"How can you say that?" Rebecca said. "So many people depend on you, your company. You know how I—"

"Do you remember our trip to the library

when we first got to the island?" Flora asked. "And then the post office?"

Rebecca rewound her memory to that day and Flora's errands she insisted on doing herself. "You made copies and sent them somewhere," she said, relief slowing her heart rate.

She nodded. "My lawyer. Alden probably burned the papers from a long time ago, before we had computers, that gave me the part of Winter Industries that I've made successful through my own hard work. I left copies in the library at the Winter Palace. But it doesn't matter. My company is safe, and so is Griffin and Maddox's inheritance."

Griffin turned an openmouthed look on Rebecca and ground the gears as he stopped the car in the driveway of the Winter Palace. "Someone tell me what is going on."

"You tell him," Flora said as she shoved open her car door. "I'm going to go in there and tell my nephew what a ninny he is. I almost regret making that recent change to my will to give him anything at all."

Flora sailed into the house and Griffin switched off the ignition and put both hands on the wheel as if it was a life preserver. There was no way for Rebecca to dance around the truth for one second longer, even though she knew what she was going to say would change his life completely. She faced Griffin and let out a long breath.

"Flora is leaving her entire personal fortune and island property to you and your brother," she said. "Millions."

GRIFFIN HELD ON to the classic car's wheel to prevent his entire world from spinning. He focused on the fancy hood ornament and tried to breathe.

"She thinks of you and Maddox as the grandsons she never had," Rebecca said, her voice soft. "She loves you."

"I still don't understand," he said. "How is it possible that Maddox and I are her heirs? We can't inherit a million dollars. We just… I never…"

"It's more than a million. And that's just her personal fortune. Her company will remain in the hands of a governing board. There are trustees."

Griffin turned and looked at Rebecca for the first time, and he felt as if he was talking to a stranger. Where was the sweet, piano-playing woman he'd fallen in love with? This Rebecca seemed more assured, more businesslike. They'd just shared an incredible day and won twenty thousand dollars together. He'd thought no day could possibly be better.

"How do you know all this?" he asked.

Rebecca sighed. "I'm not just a summer companion for Flora," Rebecca said. "I've worked for Winter Industries for five years as a financial analyst."

A cold weight settled in his chest. Nothing made sense.

"But why are you here?"

"Aren't you more interested in hearing about the money you'll be inheriting?" she asked.

He shook his head. "I don't give a damn about that money. I want to know how you're involved in all of this. I thought I knew you, and now I don't know anything."

Rebecca's face turned pink and her eyes glistened. "You do know me."

Griffin got out of the car. He felt suffocated in the confines of the Bentley and needed fresh island air to clear his head. He started walking down the long driveway that led away from the Winter Palace, but Rebecca called his name and he paused. It wouldn't do any good to walk away, but the pain in his chest when he heard her voice reminded him how much of his heart he'd invested in their relationship.

His feelings for her had been worth more than millions of dollars, but were her feelings for him just as real?

He turned and waited for Rebecca in the shadow of the grand home on the bluff. Could it possibly be his home in the future? He'd never even imagined such a thing. When Rebecca approached, her cheeks and eyelashes were wet with tears.

"You don't know everything about me, but everything I told you was true. I just left out the part about working for Winter Industries and being sent here by the CFO to watch over Flora. We heard she'd made a recent change to her will and we were afraid someone was trying to influence her."

"You thought Maddox and I were trying to swindle an old lady out of her fortune?" Fury stormed through him at the thought.

"No." Rebecca put a hand on his chest. "That wasn't the recent change. She decided to leave you her money quite some time ago. The recent change involved Alden. He shouldn't have gotten anything, but it appears she's softened toward him and left him a piece of the company, something he can't do much damage to, I hope."

"Do you really care what happens to her company?"

"Desperately," Rebecca said. Fresh tears fell over her cheeks. "Winter Industries paid for me to go to college, offered me a summer job every year and then sent me to grad school. They sponsor orphans from the Chicago area who wouldn't have a chance otherwise. That's why I agreed to come out here, even though I hated the idea of spying on a sweet old lady."

"I can't believe you got away with it," Griffin said. How had she fooled them all? The thought left a trail of bitterness.

Rebecca smiled. "I didn't. When I confessed all this to Flora a few nights ago, she told me she'd known all along. I should have known she would."

"Is that when she told you she was leaving a fortune to me and Maddox?" Griffin asked. How long had Rebecca known? Did it have anything to do with the way she treated him?

She hesitated and glanced up at the sky and then shook her head. "It was before that. I've known for a month, but I couldn't tell you."

He wanted to laugh because it was all so ridiculous and he couldn't begin to process the emotions conflicting inside him. "Why not?"

"Because Flora trusted me with the secret."

"While you were lying to her about why you were on the island," he said flatly.

Rebecca swallowed and looked at him sadly. "I wanted to do the right thing for my employer, but that got complicated. I care about Flora, so the least I could do was keep her secret. I didn't think there would be any harm since I was leaving at the end of the summer anyway."

Griffin crossed his arms over his chest, trying to hold himself together. He felt like a boat being tossed between waves and slipping its anchor.

"I never thought I'd care about the island, Flora and you," she said, her words ending on a whisper.

It took everything he had not to pull her into his arms and kiss her when she said that, but he had to remember that she'd kept a life-changing secret from him. How could he trust that her feelings were real?

"Griffin May," Flora called from the house. "If you're heading downtown, will you please take my nephew along in the Bentley? He's ready to catch the ferry right away."

His conversation with Rebecca was far from over…although, was there really anything left to say? Griffin looked up at Flora, nodded and got back in the car. It was second nature to do as she asked, even though everything was different now.

"Please bring the car back at your convenience later and we'll have a nice talk," Flora said.

Griffin waited for Alden to get in the backseat with his suitcase and then he drove away from the Winter Palace.

"Crazy old bat," Alden muttered. "She cheated my dad out of his half of the company and now she's handing me some scraps so she doesn't feel guilty about screwing her only living relative out of her money."

"It's her money," Griffin said neutrally. Did Alden know Flora was leaving it to him and Maddox? She wouldn't have asked him to drive Alden in that case, would she?

"She says she's leaving it to someone more deserving than me," Alden grumbled. "Probably that Rebecca woman she seems to love so much. Ridiculous."

Griffin almost smiled. Maybe it would be better if Flora did leave her millions to Rebecca. How the heck were he and Maddox ever going to manage a fortune?

He shook his head. Rebecca hadn't been

truthful with him all summer long, and it would be far better when she took her deceit and left the island. She didn't deserve Flora's money any more than he did, and he wasn't sure he deserved it at all. Aside from indulging Flora as if she was a slightly intimidating old aunt, had he and Maddox ever done anything to deserve such massive generosity?

He drove the rest of the way to the ferry dock in silence, parked in a secure spot behind his hotel and pocketed the keys. After Alden left for the ferry, Griffin put the green envelope with its ten thousand dollar check into the hotel safe and walked straight past his bar, where the Christmas in July party was already swinging.

He had to tell his brother, but first he needed to be alone.

CHAPTER TWENTY-SIX

"GIRLS' DAY OUT," Camille declared after she and Violet knocked on the door of the Winter Palace early Monday morning. "It's the Monday after Christmas in July weekend, and we all close our stores and take the day off."

"I can't take the day off," Rebecca said. "I have…work to do."

"Tell Flora she can come, too," Violet said. "She's a girl and our big plan is to sit by the water and eat a basket full of stuff we shouldn't and then hit one of the bars downtown that stays open for locals."

"No, thank you," Flora said from behind Rebecca. "But I insist you go along. You need some fun after all the drama yesterday."

"Drama?" Camille asked. "Only the good kind, right? And you're buying drinks since you're ten grand richer after winning the race."

Rebecca didn't feel richer than she had the day before. Ten thousand dollars did nothing to fill up the empty space where Griffin's love had started to carve out a nest in her heart.

"I don't know," she murmured.

"Nothing to know," Flora said. "Now go have fun with your friends before summer's over and you're back behind a desk. Can't put a price on summer days."

"Okay," Rebecca said. She didn't feel like having fun and she didn't feel as if she deserved it one bit. She'd lied to everyone except Camille about why she was here, and she had kept the secret of Griffin's inheritance even from her best friend.

Griffin had returned the car late yesterday evening, but he'd just left it in the driveway without ringing the bell or stopping in to say hello. Rebecca had seen him from her bedroom window. His brother followed a moment later in Griffin's truck, and the two paused for a moment, looking at the house, before they both got in Griffin's truck and drove away.

She could guess they'd both been thinking about their inheritance, assuming Griffin had told Maddox. But she wondered if Griffin was also thinking of her as he looked up at her window.

"I've got company coming, so I won't be lonely," Flora said.

Rebecca gave her a questioning glance and then she realized the company was almost certainly Griffin and his brother. After all, they had a lot to talk about. And it would be better if she was out of the way for that conversation. She was sure Griffin felt betrayed by her, angry at her deceit and overwhelmed by a massive windfall.

"If you'll be okay, I'll get out of your hair for a while," Rebecca said.

Flora smiled and patted Rebecca's cheek affectionately, and the simple gesture made Rebecca want to burst into tears. How ironic that both she and Griffin felt that Flora was the grandmother they never had, but he had the far greater claim to Flora's affection. That realization reminded Rebecca how alone she really was in the world and how much of an outsider she remained, even though she'd given her heart to Christmas Island.

There was only a little time left to savor, so she went up to her room, grabbed her purse and left with Camille and Violet in Camille's golf cart. As they descended the hill, they passed another golf cart coming along the road. It had to be heading for the Winter Palace, but there was only one man driving. As the golf carts drew nearer, Rebecca realized she knew the man driving the other cart very well.

It was her boss. Jim Churchill had come all the way to Christmas Island to see Flora. The thought struck sorrow in Rebecca's heart, and she almost asked Camille to turn around so she could go back to Flora's house and face her fate, whatever it would be. She knew she had failed in her task of being a secret liaison for the company. And she'd failed to communicate to Jim Churchill the one piece of really interesting information she'd uncovered—that the Maddox brothers would inherit Flora's personal wealth.

She was doomed to lose her job, the one place other than Christmas Island she'd ever loved and felt welcome. "Oh, my God," she breathed.

"What?" Camille asked. "Did you know that guy?"

"He's my boss at Winter Industries."

"Oh, man," Camille said.

"Wait," Violet said. "How's he your boss? You don't even work for that company."

Rebecca sighed. "I do."

Violet's eyebrows wrinkled. "I don't understand. I thought Camille helped you get this job so Flora would have a companion."

"She helped, but I was really sent here because Flora had changed her will recently and my boss was worried about her—and the future of the company, of course. I'm loyal to Winter Industries, so I agreed to do this." Rebecca swiped away tears. "But I never expected to fall in love with the island and the people."

"Has Flora found out?"

Rebecca smiled through her tears. "She figured it out immediately but let me keep up the ruse. We actually had a lot of fun together. When she bought me the dress at your shop, though, it was the final straw for me. I had to tell her."

"And did you?" Violet asked.

Rebecca nodded. "Before the Christmas Ball a few nights ago."

"That's a relief," Violet said. She leaned forward from the middle seat and put her arms around Rebecca. "As long as you told her before you wore that fabulous dress, you're not a rat fink. You just had conflicting loyalties."

Rebecca squeezed one of Violet's hands. "You're a true friend, but you still don't know the half of it."

"So tell me."

Rebecca shook her head. "It's not my story to tell, but I suspect you'll be hearing about it soon."

Camille cut her a confused look. "There's more?"

"So much more," Rebecca said. "Which is why I'll probably be leaving soon."

"But summer's not over," Camille protested. "You still have another month."

"I think it's best if I go a few days before everyone finds out. It's a real doozy."

Violet sat back and laughed. "If Flora recently changed her will and it has anything to do with this island, I hope she suddenly decided I'd be the best beneficiary in the world. I'd even change my name to Violet Winter if she wanted."

"And with your taste in clothing, you'd be an excellent rich lady," Camille said. "I think we need to put all this talk aside and have such a fun day that Rebecca won't even consider leaving Christmas Island early. I'm still trying to convince you to stay," she said with a smile for her best friend. "I would have thought Griffin might be a persuasive force, as well."

Rebecca bit down on both of her lips. It would be so nice to tell her friends what was in her heart—how she loved Griffin but had damaged their relationship irrevocably. They would sympathize and make her feel better, but she couldn't trade his secrets for their sympathy. She owed him silence as long as he and Maddox chose to keep their inheritance quiet.

"Your win yesterday was amazing," Violet said. "I can't believe you got piano playing as a challenge. If the categories weren't sealed in a safe since last January, I might think it was rigged, but the Holiday Hustle committee takes itself seriously. It was pure luck on your part."

Camille shrugged. "I heard you were winning at that point anyway."

"We were winning, but if the last challenge had been spinning dinner plates on poles or making a perfect souffle, we might never have taken home the cash prize."

"What will you do with your half of the money?" Camille asked.

Rebecca tried to shake off her worries and be a good friend for one more day. Camille and Violet deserved it. "Ideally, I'd spend it all on fudge from your shop," she said to Camille, "and clothes from Violet's boutique."

"That's it," Camille said. "You can't leave Christmas Island."

Rebecca looked at the lake scenery whipping past as Camille drove around the island, and she wished her friend could make those words come true. Thoughts of staying had crept into her heart dozens of times, but it was impossible now. Camille lived with seeing Maddox May nearly every day despite his betrayal of her years earlier, but Rebecca didn't think she could live with the chance of seeing Griffin every day when there was no way he could still love her.

FLORA KEPT HER seat when Griffin entered the library at the Winter Palace, but the gray-haired man next to her got up.

Griffin had told his brother everything late the night before, but the two of them were keeping it to themselves for plenty of reasons—one of them being that they couldn't believe it was true.

"This is Jim Churchill, a man I trust to run my company, even though he didn't trust my judgment about my will," Flora said, indicating the man in the white shirt and tie.

"Glad to finally meet you," Jim told Griffin as he extended his hand. "Flora has told me a lot about the May family over the years, and you run a solid ferry line. I admire that."

"Thanks," Griffin said. "Why didn't you trust her?" If Jim Churchill had some objection to his and his brother's inheritance, it was best if he found out right now. He wasn't callous or greedy enough to even consider fighting for money he didn't think he deserved, but he wanted all the cards laid out on the table. All summer he'd been missing things. Had he been blinded by his feelings for Rebecca? Too busy with the ferry line and hotel?

"I—" Jim began, but Flora interrupted him.

"He thought I was being taken advantage of," Flora said. "Because I'm such a sweet old lady."

"I would never take advantage of anyone," Griffin said. "That's not who I—"

Flora laughed. "Not you. I'm talking about my irresponsible nephew, Alden. I suppose I'd say worse things about him, but he's my only living relative—officially anyway. My real ties are on Christmas Island. Your family."

Jim Churchill sat down and Griffin considered it a sign that he could do the same. Everything seemed to be shifting under his feet, and he hoped sitting down would keep his world from spinning any faster.

"I secretly changed my will in the spring, but I should have known there are no real secrets as long as lawyers golf together," Flora said. "And people have imaginations."

"Is that when you...added...me and Maddox?" Griffin asked. Rebecca had said it hadn't been a recent decision, but he needed to hear the truth from Flora.

"Heavens, no," she said. "You and Maddox have been in there for ten years, ever since you were old enough to convince me you were a lot like your grandfather."

For the first time in over a day, Griffin felt his shoulders relax. He smiled. "Thank you. That's worth more to me than—"

"Millions?" Flora asked. She grinned and leaned forward to pat Griffin's knee. "You're probably right. But I'm leaving this house and my money to you anyway. When I changed my will, it was to give Alden a small role in running my company, basically a branch that he could probably mess up without hurting the main trunk of the company. I thought he deserved a chance because his own father, my dear brother, hadn't done a very good job of raising him."

"Why?" Griffin asked.

"Why was my brother too indulgent as a father?"

He shook his head. "Why are you leaving everything to me and Maddox?"

Flora laughed. "I'm not leaving you everything. Winter Industries is going public and will be run by a board of trustees to ensure its longevity and a future for all the people who work there."

Griffin's mind flashed to Rebecca, one of those people depending on the company.

"My personal fortune is mine alone to disperse," she said, her voice softening. "You should know I loved your grandfather."

Griffin nodded. "We all did."

"Truly loved him," Flora continued. "I thought we'd get married, but I went to Europe for a few summers and when I returned he'd married your grandmother instead. Maybe he thought he couldn't be happy with a girl who wasn't a true islander, just a summer visitor."

Griffin acknowledged he'd had the same worries about Rebecca and wondered how such a relationship could work...but wait... had Flora just confessed to a longstanding love of Grandpa May?

"When your sweet grandmother died so

young, I thought there would be a chance for me and William, but he remained devoted to her memory," Flora said. Her eyes glistened with tears, and Griffin imagined her as a young woman pining for a love she couldn't have. Pain slashed his heart, and his throat felt thick. "I watched his son grow up, and then his grandsons," she continued. "I always thought of you and Maddox as the grandsons I never had."

"I never knew," Griffin said, barely able to speak.

"That's okay," she said. "I was happy to love you from a distance."

Griffin put a hand over hers and let out a long breath. "One day earlier this summer I told Rebecca that I always thought of you as the grandmother I never had."

Flora smiled. "I know. Rebecca told me."

Somehow, the thought of Rebecca reporting his words to Flora confused him. Was it a betrayal? He hadn't asked her to keep it a secret, even though he now knew she was good at that.

"I see that look," Flora said. "And as the grandmother you never had, I would advise you to search your heart before you go doing anything stupid where she is concerned. I've seen you two together this summer, and it would be a shame if you're sitting in this library in fifty-five years talking about the love of your life who was never quite yours."

Griffin opened his mouth and then shut it again. He couldn't argue with Flora, but he had no idea what to say.

"If I may," Jim Churchill said, "I'd like to make our future relationship clear. As the heir to Flora's personal fortune, you may cross paths with me while I serve as the chair of the board of trustees running her company. So I have some documents that lay out that future relationship." He handed Griffin an envelope. "You'll find all the information you've probably been afraid to ask for in there, plus quite a few things you wouldn't think to ask. I know this is all sudden, and I want to assure you I'll be on hand to help."

"You can trust Jim," Flora said. "He's been with my company for thirty-five years, and the only time he ever deceived me was a few months ago when he suggested I needed a summer companion and helped me 'find' one." She made air quotes when she said the word *find*, and Griffin almost laughed.

"I have a lot to think about," Griffin said.

"Take those papers and review them with

your brother. You'll have a lot to talk about right away, even though I may live another twenty years."

"I hope you do live another twenty years," Griffin said.

Flora smiled. "You're just as sweet as your grandfather, but I want to enjoy the time I have left watching you and Maddox spend my money. So I'm giving you half of my estate right now."

Griffin felt the air leave his lungs. He couldn't speak or breathe.

"Don't look so shocked," Flora said. She put her hands on both of Griffin's arms and gave his elbows a little squeeze. "Pull yourself together and go to work building your business. That's the way you'll honor my gift, and I can't wait to see you get started."

Griffin kissed Flora's cheek, just as he had dozens of times in his life, but somehow it felt different now. He went outside, emotions still rushing through him like a raging river. As he walked into the cool, dark evening, he saw Rebecca getting out of a golf cart before it drove back down the driveway. She stopped and put a hand on her chest when she saw him.

"Surprised to see me?" he asked.

"I wasn't expecting to. I thought Flora's visitor was Jim Churchill."

"He's in there. We just had a talk." The envelope of papers in his hand explaining the terms of his inheritance felt like a barrier between him and Rebecca that could never be crossed.

"Of course, nothing we talked about would surprise you," Griffin added. "Since you seemed to know more about my business than I did."

She drew in a breath, but she didn't say anything.

"You were very good at keeping secrets."

Rebecca crossed her arms and turned to look at the moonlit lake. The breeze blew her hair out behind her, and Griffin had to fight the urge to remember how beautiful she'd been to him just one day earlier.

"I was," she said. "I had to."

"No, you didn't. You should have told me the truth."

"I couldn't. Flora told me about your inheritance in confidence. It wasn't my secret to tell," Rebecca said.

"I'm not talking about that."

Silence hung between them and Rebecca shivered in the night air. Griffin took off his jacket and put it over her shoulders. It was the same captain's jacket he'd worn the first night on the ferry when they'd met, and his simple act brought back the memory in sharp detail. If he'd known then why she was here, would he have let her into his heart? He swallowed back the thought. He'd give a jacket to anyone who was cold.

"I don't give a darn about you keeping the secret of Flora's money. But you were lying to me all summer about why you were here. What would you have done if you'd discovered that I was the one unduly influencing Flora to change her will?"

Rebecca pulled the jacket tight around herself. "You weren't."

"You didn't know that when you showed up on Christmas Island."

"I didn't know anything," Rebecca said. She straightened her spine and squared her shoulders. "Actually, I did know one thing. I was loyal to Winter Industries. I don't expect you to understand what it felt like to grow up as I did, never belonging anywhere or owning anything. You grew up on an island where every single person knew you and cared about you. Even enough to consider you family when you weren't."

Her words stung Griffin and he almost took a step backward.

"So I don't expect you to understand my blind loyalty to my company when I was asked to do something that might be necessary to safeguard that company's future." Her voice shook with emotion. "And when my loyalty was torn because I fell in love with Flora and this island and…you—" she stifled a sob "—I guess I don't expect you to know how hard that was for me."

She took off the jacket, handed it to him and then walked to the door, her back turned.

"I want to know what was real," Griffin said.

Rebecca paused with her hand on the ornate door of the home he would inherit.

"That night we kissed on the hotel's front porch was real. And our dance at the Christmas Ball. And running the race yesterday."

Had it only been yesterday? His entire world had changed in less than a day.

Rebecca turned and looked at him in the glow coming through the stained glass on the door. "And that night I played your favorite Christmas song. That was real."

CHAPTER TWENTY-SEVEN

AFTER DINNER REBECCA SAID good-night to Flora and then got in the golf cart, knowing she was making a mistake. She should have left on an earlier ferry. Instead, her pesky sense of loyalty had her putting on a cocktail dress—the sapphire-blue one—and showing up for her Tuesday night shift at the piano bar. She didn't know if Griffin and Maddox could find a replacement for the Friday and Saturday night crowd, but at least they'd have decent notice. Abandoning them tonight would be too soon, she reasoned.

Her heart told her she had other reasons, but she was trying to ignore it. Of course, she wasn't ready to leave Christmas Island. She loved the island, Flora, the Winter Palace, seeing her friend Camille almost every day, spending time with her new friend Violet... and then there was Griffin May. She would never be ready to walk away from him, but her bag was already packed on the chair beside her bed and she would get on the first ferry in the morning...after one more beautiful night at the piano mixing Christmas songs with love songs, evoking memories of happy times she'd spent all summer. She'd allow herself one more night.

She turned at the bottom of the hill and followed the lake road downtown. The early-evening light was soft and a breeze redolent with pine trees mixed with lake scents imprinted itself on her senses. Emotion swept over her and she felt a sob rising in her throat, but she took a deep breath and focused on getting through her shift without turning to mush.

If she was very lucky, Griffin wouldn't be in the bar. He'd been out late the night before—as she well knew since he'd basically told her he couldn't forgive her for lying to him all summer. When he'd put his jacket over her shoulders, she'd thought for a moment there could be a chance for them, but his words had dashed that.

Griffin and his brother took turns with the late-evening ferry runs, so it should be Griffin in the wheelhouse tonight and, perhaps, Maddox in the bar.

Camille and Violet were already at a table

near the piano when Rebecca strode into the bar with her piano music in a bag over her shoulder.

"Last hurrah," Violet said. She waited for Rebecca to get closer to the table and lowered her voice. "Camille told me you were leaving tomorrow, and I had to come and help her give you a send-off."

"That was nice of you," Rebecca said, feeling the lump of emotion in her throat again.

"We'll be here all night in case a certain member of a family that is officially dead to me wants to come in and give you a hard time," Camille said with a grin that bolstered Rebecca's courage and took her back to their fun college days. "I love history, but some of it we may be better off forgetting."

"Thanks," Rebecca said. Her friends knew Griffin was angry, but they didn't know about the inheritance. No one did. The news would leak out, probably sooner rather than later, but it wasn't Rebecca's place to share it. The May brothers would have to choose that for themselves.

"I'm glad I've never dated either one of the May brothers," Violet said. "In fact, my love life has been so drama-free it almost seems nonexistent."

"Maybe you should come back to Chicago with me," Rebecca said. "There are more men to choose from."

Violet laughed. "I'm never leaving Christmas Island. This is my home and I'm going to build my boutique empire here."

"Well, I hope your empire eventually expands to Chicago so I can have you pick out clothes for me. I'm not sure I want to go back to my boring work outfits."

"I'll put you on the mailing list," Violet said.

"Drink before you start playing?" Camille asked.

Rebecca shook her head. "You know I never drink and play."

"Even on your last night on an island you may never come back to?"

The thought of never coming back drained all the warmth from Rebecca's body. Would she never see the harbor, the houses on the bluff, the Great Island Hotel, the quaint downtown with its holiday decorations?

"I may make an exception," Rebecca said. "Later."

"We'll be waiting," Camille said. "And we'll order food when it's time for your break."

"A true friend," Rebecca said, her smile

lingering as she met her college roommate's glance. "I'll miss you."

Camille blinked fast. "You better go play something happy or this will be the least cheerful going-away party in island history."

"Dashing through the snow," Rebecca said, holding up one finger. "Coming right up."

She sat at the piano and opened with the fun holiday song, transitioned into "White Christmas" and then into a love song that had been overplayed on the radio when she was still in high school. With her fingers on the black-and-white keys and her eyes on the big book of piano favorites, she felt her calm sense of herself return. She'd always been the one person she could count on, and she needed to dig deep and remember that as she said farewell to her island friends.

The hard business of moving on had been the story of her life.

"Can you play 'I'll Be Home for Christmas'?" a voice asked as Rebecca finished a light classical piece. Rebecca glanced up at a middle-aged woman who stood next to the piano. "It's one of my favorites and since we're on Christmas Island, I thought it would be fun to hear it even in the middle of the summer."

Rebecca wanted to tell the woman she didn't know the song. Couldn't play it.

"Of course," she said. "Happy to."

She'd been happy the last time she'd played it as Griffin sat at a nearby table. He'd shared a personal story about how the song evoked his memories of home. Rebecca had never felt more at home anywhere—even Winter Industries—than she did on Christmas Island, but she couldn't stay. If Griffin asked her to…

But that was a pipe dream, she thought, even as her fingers keyed the familiar words to "I'll Be Home for Christmas."

She finished the piece, giving the woman a generous two verses and an extra refrain, and a tear splashed on her right hand.

Camille put a hand on Rebecca's shoulder. "Break time."

Rebecca nodded, followed her friend to the table and sat as Camille went to the bar.

"You play so beautifully," Violet said. "Did you go to music school?"

"No," Rebecca said. "I had some lessons, but I mostly just figured it out with a lot of perseverance." The same way she'd tackled everything else. It was a skill that kept her in good standing at Winter Industries, and the thought that she could go back there took some of the weight off her shoulders. She would be okay.

The bartender came over and put down three big glasses of wine. "Not like you to drink during your shift," Hadley said.

"Special occasion," Violet answered for her.

Hadley surveyed the group. "From your glum faces, I'm guessing someone has serious boyfriend trouble—been there myself—or this is a going-away party."

She waited, but no one answered. Finally, Hadley nodded slowly. "I'm going to miss you, Rebecca," she said softly before turning and walking back behind the bar.

"Maybe I should go now," Rebecca said. "The bar's not crowded tonight and I could get to bed early."

"Have something to eat first," Camille said. "We ordered each of the appetizers on the menu so we could all share in the fatty, salty goodness. It should be out any minute."

Rebecca clinked her wineglass to Camille's and Violet's in appreciation of their friendship and planning, and she spent the next half hour trying to enjoy her last night on the island and reminding herself to be positive. She had fulfilled her mission for Winter Industries, even though the information she uncovered wasn't what she expected. She had reconnected with Camille and made new friends. She'd challenged herself physically by biking, hiking and even winning an adventure race.

And she'd fallen in love and had the first true summer romance of her life. She would never forget Christmas Island and everything her time here had meant to her.

BERTIE KING WAITED at the dock before the first ferry run of the morning, and Griffin nodded at him politely, even though his nerves were stretched like mooring ropes in a storm.

"Outgoing mail for the mainland," Bertie said.

"Got it," Griffin said as he took the US Postal Service bin from the longtime postmaster.

"Not much of a crowd this morning," Bertie said. "Thank heaven for quiet Wednesdays on this island."

"Uh-huh," Griffin said. He couldn't concentrate on anything the older man was saying. Maddox had called him last night to report that Rebecca had shown up to play at the bar but her friends were there, too, and

Hadley suspected it was a final farewell because Rebecca had left a sealed envelope at the front desk addressed to the hotel management. He could guess it was a resignation. If it was personal, it would have been addressed to him.

She was leaving. The thought left an empty hole in his gut. When he'd found out that Rebecca had been holding back information all summer—even huge pieces of information that directly concerned him—he'd felt betrayed. He'd needed and wanted to keep her at arm's length while he processed the life-changing news involving Flora Winter.

Three days hadn't been enough time to process it all, but one thing was standing out. Flora Winter loved him like a grandson. She was leaving millions to him and his brother, which would mean a life of possibilities for them and for his nephew. It was incredible news that shook him down to his sturdy deck shoes.

But Rebecca had said she loved him as they pedaled to a victory on Sunday. And even in the midst of their argument on the windy cliff Monday night, she'd been brave enough to say it again. She'd defended her loyalty—divided though it was between Flora and Flora's company—and Griffin had run out of reasons to feel betrayed. All he had to do was figure out the way forward.

Griffin looked up to the Winter Palace. He and Maddox had devised a plan the night before, but he had no idea if Rebecca would agree to it. They were in far over their heads when it came to managing an estate and the business expansion that was now possible. They needed someone with business and financial sense. Otherwise, what on earth were they going to do with a sudden infusion of such unexpected wealth?

"You look like you lost your best friend," Bertie King said. "It's too nice a morning to look so serious."

Griffin forced a smile. "Sorry about that."

Bertie waved to him, and Griffin went through his morning checklist. The ferry would leave in ten minutes, but only a dozen passengers waited in the queue by the ticket office. After he welcomed the passengers aboard, he went up to the pilothouse, where he commanded a view of the ferry itself and the docks, and then he sounded the two-minute warning for departure.

A golf cart's white roof caught the morning sun as it drove along the lake road. He stopped and watched it approach. Even from a distance he recognized the driver, and his heart lurched in his chest when he saw a big red suitcase on the back of the cart.

Rebecca couldn't leave. Not when he loved her and wanted her to stay.

He hadn't made up his mind what to do or say the night before, but now he knew it as clearly as he knew the ferry route even during a storm.

She parked the golf cart, swung the huge suitcase off the back and started chugging toward the ferry. Other passengers were already seated on deck, and the ferry's motors thrummed in anticipation of leaving.

He sounded the one-minute warning. What was he going to do? He couldn't let her get on the ferry, didn't want to let her leave the island before he had a chance to tell her how he felt about her.

Rebecca started running, apparently thinking she was going to miss the ferry. Her suitcase lurched behind her and almost tipped over, and Griffin wanted to run down the stairs of the pilothouse and take the heavy bag himself.

People were waiting for the ferry to depart. Maybe they had important things to do on the mainland and needed to be on time. The ferry sometimes encountered weather or other obstacles and got off schedule, but never in his life had he idled the ferry and exited the pilothouse with every intention of delaying the morning run.

He paused on the steps to appreciate Rebecca's triumphant final swing onto the boat with her suitcase behind her. It was a more successful replay of the scene earlier in the summer, the night they'd first met. She glanced up at the pilothouse and their gazes met. Even though the rhythm of the dock and the harbor continued around them and he heard the big clock downtown strike the hour, Griffin felt time stop as he and Rebecca stared at each other.

The first move was his to make. She'd already made hers by boarding with her suitcase. He went back into the pilothouse, got on the public address system and announced a ten-minute delay in departure with his apologies for the inconvenience.

Griffin ran down the steps, never taking his eyes off Rebecca, who stood near the gangplank. She hadn't moved to a seat. Was she waiting for him?

He approached her, his throat thick with

emotion, and he said the only thing that came to his mind.

"You can't leave."

Rebecca's eyebrows rose and her cheeks flushed. "I have to leave."

He shook his head, took the handle of her suitcase and hoisted it onto his shoulder. He walked toward the gangplank and turned to look back.

"Are you coming?" he asked.

"Are you stealing my suitcase?" she asked, a small grin forming on her face.

"Yes."

"Because it's bad luck? It already sank once as you probably remember."

Griffin held out his free hand. "I think that incident was good luck."

Rebecca's smile widened. "You do?"

"It brought you to me."

She took his hand and followed him off the boat to the bench under the broad shade tree on the dock. Maddox came out the back door of the ticket office, waved at his brother and swung onto the ferry. A moment later Griffin heard the ferry's engines power up and he knew the passengers would be in good hands and only a few minutes late.

"Rebecca," he said, "I didn't know why you

came to Christmas Island two months ago, but I realize now it doesn't matter why you came as much as it matters why you stay."

"I can't stay," she said, her voice a cracked whisper. "I have to go back to work. People are counting on me."

"People are counting on you here, too," he said.

She shook her head. "Pretty soon I'll be just a summer memory."

Griffin put his arms around her and pulled her close, his cheek resting against her hair. "I don't want you to be just a memory, even though I would never forget you. My brother and I have a proposition for you. We want you to stay and help us manage our finances and our business."

"Is this because I smoked the finance category at trivia night?" she asked.

"Yes. And we trust you."

He felt her give a small shake of her head. "I thought you felt betrayed because I kept secrets from you."

He let out a breath and pulled back so he could see her face. "That was my first reaction, but I realized I was wrong. Flora and Jim set me straight, but I also figured it out on my own. You're the most trustworthy person

I know. Who better to manage Flora's huge gift than someone she entrusts with her secrets who helps run her company?"

Rebecca looked up the hill toward the Winter Palace and then back at him. "So you want me to stay and be your CFO?"

"Yes, but—"

She stood up. "Griffin, it's nice that you're offering me a job, but I already have one and—"

He jumped to his feet. "Rebecca, you don't have to take this job. That's not the reason I stopped the ferry. I love you, Rebecca, and I don't want to be on this island without you."

She blinked and put both hands over her mouth and then lowered them slowly. "I love you, too."

"This island has always been home to me, but it won't feel like home unless you're here, too," Griffin added. "Please stay and be mine."

Rebecca put her arms around him and rested her head against his chest. "No one has ever said words like that to me," she said. She pulled back and looked at his face. "But even if they had, this is the best offer I've ever gotten."

"Is that a yes?"

"On which part?" she asked with a smile. "Running your business or being yours?"

"Your love is all that matters to me," he said, holding her close and kissing her tenderly. "Although," he admitted after the kiss, "your brains are a nice part of the deal. Would you believe Maddox and I had an actual argument over how many zeroes there are in a million dollars?"

Rebecca laughed. "You know that song 'The Twelve Days of Christmas'? It's the number of geese a-laying."

Griffin smiled. "I'd love to hear you play that song, but you already know my favorite. You've given it a whole new meaning for me."

"Me, too." Rebecca kissed him. "And this year we'll both be home for Christmas."

* * * * *

HARLEQUIN SELECTS COLLECTION

19 FREE BOOKS IN ALL!

From Robyn Carr to RaeAnne Thayne to Linda Lael Miller and Sherryl Woods we promise (actually, GUARANTEE!) each author in the Harlequin Selects collection has seen their name on the *New York Times* or *USA TODAY* bestseller lists!

YES! Please send me the **Harlequin Selects Collection**. This collection begins with 3 FREE books and 2 FREE gifts in the first shipment. Along with my 3 free books, I'll also get 4 more books from the Harlequin Selects Collection, which I may either return and owe nothing or keep for the low price of $24.14 U.S./$28.82 CAN. each plus $2.99 U.S./$7.49 CAN. for shipping and handling per shipment*.If I decide to continue, I will get 6 or 7 more books (about once a month for 7 months) but will only need to pay for 4. That means 2 or 3 books in every shipment will be FREE! If I decide to keep the entire collection, I'll have paid for only 32 books because 19 were FREE! I understand that accepting the 3 free books and gifts places me under no obligation to buy anything. I can always return a shipment and cancel at any time. My free books and gifts are mine to keep no matter what I decide.

☐ 262 HCN 5576   ☐ 462 HCN 5576

Name (please print)

Address   Apt. #

City   State/Province   Zip/Postal Code

Mail to the Harlequin Reader Service:
IN U.S.A.: P.O. Box 1341, Buffalo, NY 14240-8531
IN CANADA: P.O. Box 603, Fort Erie, Ontario L2A 5X3

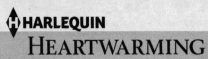

#395 A TEXAN'S CHRISTMAS BABY

Texas Rebels • by Linda Warren

Chase Rebel and Jody Carson wed secretly after high school—then life and bitter hurts forced them apart. Now they're back in Horseshoe, Texas, still married, but no longer sweethearts. Can past secrets leave room for second chances?

#396 A SECRET CHRISTMAS WISH

Wishing Well Springs • by Cathy McDavid

Cowboy Brent Hayes and single mom Maia MacKenzie are perfect for each other. Too bad they work together at the dating service Your Perfect Plus One and aren't allowed to date! Can Christmas and some wedding magic help them take a chance on love?

#397 HER HOLIDAY REUNION

Veterans' Road • by Cheryl Harper

Like her time in the air force, Mira Peters's marriage is over. When she requests signed divorce papers, her husband makes a final request, too. Will a Merry Christmas together in Key West change all of Mira's plans?

#398 TRUSTING THE RANCHER WITH CHRISTMAS

Three Springs, Texas • by Cari Lynn Webb

Veterinarian Paige Palmer learns the ropes of ranch life fast while helping widowed cowboy Evan Bishop. But making a perfect Christmas for his daughter isn't a request she can grant...unless some special holiday time can make a happily-ever-after for three.

Visit
ReaderService.com
Today!

As a valued member of the Harlequin Reader Service, you'll find these benefits and more at ReaderService.com:

- Try 2 free books from any series
- Access risk-free special offers
- View your account history & manage payments
- Browse the latest Bonus Bucks catalog

Don't miss out!

If you want to stay up-to-date on the latest at the Harlequin Reader Service and enjoy more content, make sure you've signed up for our monthly News & Notes email newsletter. Sign up online at ReaderService.com or by calling Customer Service at 1-800-873-8635.